T0208728

The Curse of La Croix

Vinquist's Tale, Volume One

AS TOLD BY DAN KINGSLAND
WRITTEN BY JASON KINGSLAND

iUniverse, Inc.
New York   Bloomington

The Curse of La Croix
Vinquist's Tale, Volume One

This is a work of fiction. All of the characters, names, incidents, organizations, and dialogue in this novel are either the products of the author's imagination or are used fictitiously.

iUniverse books may be ordered through booksellers or by contacting:

iUniverse
1663 Liberty Drive
Bloomington, IN 47403
www.iuniverse.com
1-800-Authors (1-800-288-4677)

ISBN: 978-1-4502-7034-2 (pbk)
ISBN: 978-1-4502-7035-9 (cloth)
ISBN: 978-1-4502-7036-6 (ebk)

Printed in the United States of America

iUniverse rev. date: 11/9/2010

Prologue

One of the greatest wizards ever to walk the earth was naked and chained to a wall, high in a castle he had never seen or visited. The chains that held him were black and covered in runes, written in a language long forgotten by most.

He tried to escape the chains, writhing this way and that, hoping against hope that an error had been made when imprisoning him, but to no avail. He only stopped when he heard soft laughter coming from a corner of the room, where a pair of burning eyes watched his laboring with evident glee.

"At long last, I have thee," came a voice as the laughter abated from somewhere in-between this world and the next. "Watch, old man, as I turn your world to ash."

His eyes were opened to horror after horror: friends he had known for many years were struck down; places he had visited turned to cinders; dark figures, so many that they covered the ground, devoured the countryside; a small cabin, set aflame by those same dark figures, belched black smoke as the screams of those within accompanied his own. Held tight, he was helpless to do anything about it, and then he saw one last image that did not match the terror of the rest.

He saw a young girl, very thin, with the look of one who spent most of her time either ill or indoors. She was sitting up in a bed, the covers drawn to her chest, and an older lady, her maid perhaps, was reading to her from a large book. The girl's eyes shone with delight and wonder. But his mind was not strong enough to hold on to the image, and he could feel himself spiraling away.

He came back to himself. Tears streamed down his face, and his body shook from all he had seen. The figure in the corner rose and slowly walked towards him. Its eyes burned brightly into his as it crossed the room, one clawed hand reaching out and touching his chest where his heart beat frantically within. He let out an ear-splitting scream as the claws dug into his flesh, worming their way towards his heart as the creature in front of him laughed.

In his last seconds of life, just before the end came for him, he awoke to find himself alone, with only the echoing sounds of his screams and the glowing embers of the dying fire to keep him company. The nightmare had taken him far and shown him many things. That he could handle, but what he could not deal with was the feeling of utter and complete helplessness that had gripped him so tightly. He reached to the small table next to his bed, not for water, but for wine. His shaking hands found the bottle and removed the cork, and he took a long drink, dark red liquid falling into his beard and onto his sheets. He rose, threw two logs on the fire to light the room and banish any lingering shadows, and then headed for the door.

He stepped outside into the cool night air to clear his head. He studied the stars and the crescent shape of the moon as he tried to shake off the fear and hopelessness that clung to him from the dream. He knew the power of dreams and visions, and this one had the touch of destiny. He resolved not to let these things come to pass idly. He closed his eyes and listened to the wind, knowing that it would reveal to him the next step in the journey. After several minutes, his eyes opened, and he knew that the first step would start with the young girl. Walking back into the cabin, he put on his traveling cloak, put all the supplies he would need within its myriad pockets and folds and grabbed his walking staff. As he walked out the front door, locking it behind him, he took one last look at the place he had called home for the last few years. He had been happy here, but he doubted he would ever see this place again.

"It begins, and it begins in La Croix," he said aloud to the night as he raised his hood, and thus he started the long walk that would take him thousands of leagues and many months to complete.

Chapter One

Ten years later...

Despite the darkening sky, the ever-loudening rumble of thunder and the crashing of waves against the docked ship, the travelers, having little experience in such things, had no way of knowing for certain how close the storm actually was. The shortening lapse of time between each flash of lightning and clap of thunder, however, gave notice that the squall was closing in on them. The group knew that if they were going to make it to town without getting soaked, or worse, they would have to move quickly. Roland, their leader, signaled for them to board the over-loaded carriages that they had contracted out at the port's livery.

Upon their arrival, they had been laughed at by the port workers when they inquired about hiring a driver for the trip inland. It would be impossible, said the dockhands, to find anyone willing to take them to La Croix. The troupe, at the time, had assumed that it was the impending storm that dissuaded the men from accompanying them to town, and so they brushed off any deeper warning that lay in the men's unwillingness to help. Undeterred and anxious to push onward, Roland set a brisk pace at the head of his company, hoping to watch the storm from inside, a mug of cold ale in hand, instead of outdoors, soaked to the bone, wishing he was relaxing in one of the cozy inns for which La Croix was so famous. The noblemen and their wives who had elected to make the journey with him pulled their cloaks tighter about their bodies and looked to the sky, praying silently for the storm to hold off a while longer.

They had come from far across the sea, having heard many stories over the years attesting to the beauty of the exotic town. They came from aristocratic families whose wealth and fortunes had increased with each generation. These men and women stood to be infinitely richer than their forefathers and, as a consequence, infinitely more bored. As is so often the case with those who have too much at their disposal, an overabundance of leisure had made them restless, and thus, as time went by, their desires turned to new kinds of commodities, things rarer and more coveted than the most precious of stones. Above all, they sought adventure.

So plans had been brought up over the span of several nights—for in their minds, such hasty planning would more than suffice—and a ship large enough for all who would take the journey, along with their horses, was procured. This ship, they hoped, would save them from a great flood of boredom and discontent. Supplies were secured, and they launched amid a chorus of cheers from their families as they set out in search of their adventure across the sea.

Now far from the rallying commencement of their journey, Roland stopped his horse in front of a guidepost marking the path and cursed under his breath as he felt the first raindrop hit him squarely on the nose. He could only shake his head in bewilderment as he stared at the sign covered in moss and lichen, which read, "La Croix—Two Leagues." The last part had been partially scratched out, so that he had to take a closer look in order to decipher it. Upon further examination, he noticed, too, that someone had etched into the sign a rough drawing of what appeared to be some strange animal. Tucking that information away in his mind for the time being, he waved his group onward as he pulled his hood over his head. The storm close on their heels, they made their way towards town.

"What in the world?" Roland asked no one in particular for the third time as he sat his horse at what should have been the main entrance to La Croix. Instead of grand, massive estates, they found homes half-destroyed by the elements; the occupants, it was clear, had fled long ago with no apparent intention of returning. While Roland and his men could imagine what these structures must have once looked like in their prime, nothing but hollow shells, mere skeletons of their former splendor, remained. The travelers, heartbroken and exhausted, made their way dourly towards the center of town in the dim hope that shelter could be found within.

Disappointment showed on their faces as they rode through the streets and saw the state of disrepair that seemed to increase as they approached what must have once been the town's main square. Building after building stood bare, their doors torn off and windows broken. A sun-faded banner that read, "Welcome to Beautiful La Croix!" was a sad reminder of what this place must have once been. As the travelers made their way through the maze of deserted streets, they saw no sign of life whatsoever. They were ready to give up and return to the relative safety of their ship, when, all of a sudden, they caught a glimpse of a light coming from the common room of one of the inns. Without thinking, they headed directly for it. Securing their mounts and carriages safely in the stables behind the building, they made their way through the now blinding rain towards the front door.

Inside the room, a fire crackled in the large pit that took up most of one stone wall. A kettle bubbled over the fire, emitting a wonderful smell that permeated the dining room and set their mouths watering.

"Come in, come in, young ones," a voice greeted them. "This is no night to be lingering in dark doorways, and Old Petri could sure use the company." Startled by the sound of a human voice in this deserted town, they strained their eyes in the speaker's direction.

The old man sat at a corner table, hidden in the shadows. A younger man, empty tankard still clutched in one hand, snored loudly at his side. A lute lay on the floor at his feet. Petri, as he had introduced himself, rose from the table and shuffled over to the fire, his old age showing in his labored gait. He opened the lid on the huge kettle that hung hissing over the fire and slowly stirred the contents within, filling the room with its smell once again. Putting the lid back on the pot, he looked back at the group, who now huddled just inside the doorway dripping water all over the floor.

"Oh, don't mind my friend there—he's never had a head for drinking, and I suspect he'll sleep for a while now. I am Petri, and that is my traveling companion, Jon. I'm surprised to have guests join us on a night like tonight in a place like this, but you're welcome to share our simple meal and our fire. This is no night to deny anyone such basic comforts." He moved behind the bar, set out bowls for the stew, and pulled from the cupboard several loaves of rich, dark bread, which he placed on platters beside the bowls.

"I'm sure you'll want to dry off before we eat," he said, motioning with his free hand towards the stairs leading to the upper level. "You should find towels enough for everyone, and our supper should be ready by the time you return." Before Roland could utter a word, Petri had abruptly turned back to his meal preparations, staving off any questions, at least for time being.

After they had dried off as best they could and come back downstairs, they found steaming bowls of a meaty stew set out for each of them, together with pieces of dark bread and mugs of ale, which Petri claimed to have found wasting away in the cellar. Their hunger and thirst reasserted themselves and, for the moment, supplanted their curiosity of what had happened to La Croix and its people. They sat down and dug in with a ferocity which made the old man laugh. The food was far from the finest any of them had ever had, but, hunger being the best seasoning of all, it was immensely satisfying and comforting, and none of them could remember enjoying any meal more. After they had finished, stomachs full and bodies finally dry, Petri removed the dishes and refilled their mugs, saving his own for last. They sat back down at their tables, facing the fire. After everyone was again seated, Petri threw two large logs on the fire, sending a shower of glowing embers and ashes flying from the fireplace and startling the guests who had just begun to settle down. He sat beside the fire just as thunder sounded, and lightning, as if on cue, illuminated the room. A thousand questions were mirrored in their eyes. Removing his long pipe from his jacket pocket, Petri struck a match on the stone wall and lowered the fleeting flame into the tobacco-filled hollow. After a long drag from the pipe's bit, he let the smoke trail from his wrinkly, pursed lips towards the ceiling, where it disappeared among the rafters. Then, just as they began to wonder if he had forgotten they were there, he spoke.

"A night such as tonight is only fit for eating and telling stories. I should know. That's how Jon and I make our living, after all. I'm a storyteller, and he's a minstrel of some small repute. We travel from town to town, making our way by plying our craft for folk such as yourselves and for folk not quite as noble as you as well. Any who have the ears for them are welcome to our tales because we lay no claim to them, only the love of sharing them. That is how we ended up here. We wanted to see the town we so often tell of and to see if the stories are true, and we chanced upon this inn in time to avoid the storm. So, if you have the patience to hear an old storyteller out, I will tell you what I know of the tale of this town. And if you listen closely, you will find how folklore becomes myth, myth becomes story, and story becomes legend."

And so he began the long tale of the fall of La Croix.

Chapter Two

La Croix has not always been in the state that you have chanced upon it. Indeed, it was once a center of beauty and elegance, a hidden-away jewel of the empire. While the king commanded most of the finest artisans, jewelers, blacksmiths, bakers and entertainers to attend him in the capitol city, the finest among the craftsmen not called to the king's court, who nonetheless had within them the desire to become truly rich, made their homes here. As a result of their residence, there was not a town outside the capitol that could equal its grandeur, and at the center of it all—the entertainment, the fashion, the dining and the architecture—sat the Duke of La Croix, Meirmont Rochelle.

Now, it would not be fair to say that the Duke did not love his town, or that he was an evil man in the traditional sense. In fact, his greatest crime came from loving all too much this town that had been left to him when his father passed away nearly twenty years before. The Duke could often be seen riding his bay stallion through the cobblestone streets and admiring the chalets and mansions of the many nobles who lived there. He would nod to minstrels and artists as they lounged about and gossiped with one another in courtyards dominated by huge fountains soaring towards the sky, while servants scurried to and fro to cater to their every whim. But he never lingered long on the outskirts; instead, he would hurry to the town's center where the heart of his interest lay.

The closer he came to the marketplace, the more excited the Duke would become, for he loved money more than anything, even more than his own family. The Duke loved to see the commerce in his fair city because a large portion of the merchants' profits were heavily taxed and eventually ended up in his own pocket. Even though he had far more riches than he could hope to spend in many lifetimes, his insatiable lust for money never abated. It was even whispered behind his back that his heart must have changed years ago when he assumed the mantle of Duke at the passing of his father. Whether the Duke never heard these rumblings or heard them and did not care what his underlings thought of him, he did not make known.

The first places he passed on his way into town were the massive forges of the blacksmith guild. On this street, instead of the sound of hawkers peddling their wares, hammers clanging on anvils echoed through the air. Here were produced the finest weapons and armor throughout the land. To carry a piece made of La Croix steel at one's side marked him as either a nobleman or some person of noted wealth. These were some of the finest smiths in the entire kingdom, and their prices matched their work. So it came that if one wanted his weapon to mark him as important, he would travel to La Croix and the Street of the Crucible to find it.

Directly across the street from the blacksmiths' area were the tidy, quiet places where the jewelers in La Croix plied their trade. These shops were in direct contrast to their noisy neighbors and seemed out of place, but Meirmont fiercely defended his decision to set them across from each other. He argued that the wealthy ladies, not wishing to spend time with their husbands and sons in the noisy, smelly smithies, would need a nearby place to pass the time. What better place than a jeweler's shop? And his decision had proven wise, as business in the shops, whose wares ranged from ivory combs and brushes to the rare gems that would cost a king's ransom, was booming.

The next shops were in direct contrast to the noise and activity that dominated the smiths' area. The Isle of the Rose, as it was known, was an island in the middle of the sea of commerce that filled the center of La Croix with the sweet smell of wild roses. It was populated by herbalists, apothecaries and fortune tellers, who offered either readings into the soul or charms that could grant wishes. The Duke seldom went into such places, as they gave him a strange feeling of unwelcomeness every time he stepped across the threshold into one of the shops. However, as long as they paid their taxes the same as everyone else, he found no good reason to shut them down. Besides, he often mused to himself, if the people couldn't find some sort of hope or solace for their intangible needs here, they might actually turn to him for help or guidance—something he did not desire in the least.

He next made his way to the main market square, a huge area where peddlers of all sorts of wares had set up shops and stalls next to one another, vying for the business of the townsfolk. Behind them all, lining the streets, were the famed inns of La Croix. Here, it was said, the singing, food and other entertainment found within were second only to those found in the King's own castle. The inns produced the Duke's main source of income, and since the town enjoyed a temperate climate year round due to its proximity to the sea, they were always packed to the brim. Many had waiting lists several months long of nobles who wished nothing more than to be able to boast that they had spent their holiday in the grand town of La Croix.

The air in the marketplace was always filled with excitement and the enticing smells of freshly baked bread, spiced meats and salted fish of all varieties. An array of fruits and vegetables could be found on every corner. People jostled and bumped into one another, beginning at sunrise, to try to find the best bargains on the most exotic items before retiring to one of the inns to find respite before another evening of excitement. There was never a dull moment, and no visitor ever left with a complaint that the experience was not what they had expected, despite the fact that their pockets were always emptier upon departure than they were upon arrival. The rich were driven through town in elegant carriages by bored drivers who looked as though they would rather be doing anything else than trying to navigate excited and wealthy patrons through large crowds day after day. The Duke always passed through the central area of the marketplace, which was dominated by a large statue of Thomas de la Rochelle, who was the town's first Duke, and who, more than two-hundred years earlier, had established La Croix as the pinnacle of commerce in the kingdom. The statue stood as a constant reminder that his line would ever remain, continuing the legacy he had so painstakingly created for himself.

Many times the question has come up: "If his name was Rochelle, then why is the town called La Croix?" A legitimate question, indeed. It so happened that Thomas, a man whose terribly astute business sense was only matched by his prowess when dealing with the fairer sex, had fallen in love with the daughter of Henri de la Croix, a baron of a nearby province. Thomas decided he would prove his love to the baroness once and for all by naming his town after her, thereby showing that she was far more important to him than any material thing. Alas, the gamble did not pay off for our good man Rochelle, for she met and fell in love with his younger brother. Heartbroken, he settled for marrying her younger sister, who, it must be said, did not dip so deeply into the gene pool as her older sibling. At least this way, he consoled himself, he would always be close to the woman he truly loved. So began another tradition for the men who governed La Croix: marrying for convenience and sacrificing the love of another for their love of finance.

And in this way the Duke passed many of his days: traveling with members of his household guard at his side and overseeing the workings of his busy town. Some days he would ride through the countryside on his horse just to clear his head and monitor those working the fields. Other days he spent holed up in his massive mansion where he attended to affairs of the state and heard petitions from new merchants who wished to set up shop in his town. Often these requests were met with approval, as more business meant more money for the Duke. Some whispered that the Duke would even spend hours of the day closeted away within his home counting his money.

His own family received little of his attention, though they had long ceased to notice or care, for this was the way it had always been, and families have a way of getting used to their own peculiar order of life. His wife, Selene Rochelle, was a beautiful woman who had enough good spirit in her to balance out the bad qualities of the Duke. Her very presence was sufficient to keep him and those around him happy. An accomplished rider, the Duchess often left the comfort of her palatial home to ride about the countryside and visit the workers in the fields and the fishermen who were returning with their catch. On one particular day, she was enjoying one of these rides on what had promised to be a pleasant, sunny morning, when, without warning, a rainstorm came upon her. In one tragic instant, her horse slipped. She was thrown from the saddle and lay motionless in the wet sand, her neck broken. An elderly fisherman and his son, having just rushed ashore in order to avoid the sudden storm, were witnesses to the terrible accident. They hurried to her side but were too late. Later that day, after the storm had passed, the two fishermen drew near to the palace. Their worn-down buggy, pulled by an aging ox, seemed out of place as it creaked down the neatly-manicured path to the palace gate. There stood the Duke, along with a group of servants and noblemen. The news of the Duchess's fatal fall had reached them well before the arrival of the makeshift hearse. No words were exchanged between the Duke and the fishermen. He failed to even acknowledge them as he collected his wife's lifeless body into his arms and began to walk back down the path, away from the palace. Many whispered that the last good part of the Duke died that dark day.

The Duke had fathered three children by his wife during his rule of La Croix. Brendan, the oldest and heir to the family fortune, seemed the spitting image of his father. Short and portly at the age of thirty, he had taken after his father in the notion of not doing anything for himself when there were others to do it for him. The servants complained among themselves that he had never done an honest day's work in his life. He was a man given over to black moods if he did not get his way. Much of the mansion's staff learned to avoid that situation. Brendan, however, did excel in matters of finance and state. He was growing into just the heir his father wanted him to be.

Cass, the Duke's second son, was the complete opposite of his older brother. At twenty-five, he had inherited his mother's lean form, blond hair, good looks and exquisite singing voice. His way with the servants put everyone around him at ease, and he could often be seen helping around the estate with some menial task that his brother and father would have readily turned their noses up at and many times did. Popular opinion was that Cass would be far better suited to assume the mantle of Duke instead of his brother, but these thoughts were never voiced aloud, for fear of the terrible wrath it would bring upon them. And Cass, ever the free spirit of the household, desired no position of authority over others.

His only wish was to travel the land as so many of the minstrels he had heard in his father's sitting room did. His voice was said to be unmatched in all the kingdom. Indeed, he could have easily set out to make it on his own if he had not been confined to living in his brother's shadow and under his father's yoke. While he dreamed of saving enough money to set out on his own and see the wonders of the wide world while paying his way with song, it seemed an unattainable aspiration. For a while, he often sang in the common rooms of the inns in town, with his father keeping the money he earned for himself, saying it was Cass's only way of paying him back for the countless years of generosity he had heaped upon his son. As months turned to years and stories of the great bard of La Croix circulated the land, the greatest voice of a generation wasted his talent earning his father more coin, all the while dreaming of something better.

Month after month, year after year, the town of La Croix, under the shrewd guidance of Duke Rochelle, continued to prosper. Its wharfs saw more and more vessels coming into port laden with exotic goods that would fetch a grand price in one of the finer shops in the merchants' guild. The list of nobles waiting for a chance to visit grew longer as innkeepers frantically tried to find more rooms to accommodate their guests and expand their pockets. Everything had settled into a pattern that greatly pleased the Duke. The merchants continued to make more money, and the Duke reached deeper and deeper into their pockets with new taxes every year to line his own. Only the lower class, the ones who did all of the backbreaking work, lamented that life in La Croix was not as it should be.

Most of the town's workforce lived either in the smallest rooms in their masters' houses, supporting families as best they could on their meager wages, or in hovels scattered about the great fields surrounding the town. The Duke never allowed the servants to set up a small gathering of homes, for if a fire were to break out, it might destroy them and end up killing most of the help at the same time. That would cost time and money, as he would have to go through the inconvenience of finding new workers. Thus, they were scattered throughout the town. Many dreamed of making new lives and leaving, but their spirits were heavy, and most never imagined that they could truly make anything good happen for themselves. They, too, lived life according to a pattern and toiled endlessly for thankless masters with little hope of change.

Consequently, events in La Croix progressed in the same manner day after day and week after week. The Duke and his household were the only ones who seemed comfortable with the stream of life in their bustling town. Not all of the Duke's household were content with life in La Croix, however, for the unhappiest soul to be found for many leagues was the Duke's only daughter, Sophie.

Chapter Three

Anne, Sophie's maid, whose kind heart had endured many tireless years of service to the Duke's family, was used to opening the door to the girl's bedroom to bring her breakfast and to seeing the frail young woman still abed. But despite her feeble body, the young girl's indomitable spirit prevailed, and she would rise at the maid's entrance and bid her a pleasant "Good morning, Anne! Have you brought me my favorite today?" For that kindness, the maid loved the girl with all her heart and prayed fervently for her to find a way to escape her current life.

Sophie de la Rochelle, who would have been a young noblewoman without peer had circumstances played themselves out differently, had been confined to the grounds of the Duke's vast estate since the age of two. On a rare family outing, which the Duke had arranged solely for the purpose of showing off his new baby girl, the child suddenly began to shake and convulse violently. All her poor mother could do was hold on to her and weep while she waited for the quaking to abate. When it finally did, the family rushed home and took turns watching over her, in case the fits returned.

The Duke, grieving that his only daughter should suffer thus, sent throughout the land for the best doctors, priests and even magicians to come and examine his daughter in order to heal her sickness. Each one who examined the girl offered up some different way of treating her infirmity, none of which worked. Not long after each of the prescribed treatments was given, she would inevitably relapse into another of her fits, and the doctor would be run out of town by the Duke, claiming the entire lot of physicians as charlatans. Sophie's mother took to spending less and less time with the child out of grief, while the Duke's sorrow intensified and turned to anger.

The worst examination came from a court magician from one of the faraway islands to the north. Having gotten word of the Duke's massive fortune and his daughter's predicament, he traversed near impassable seas to do what no other could do: heal the child with only his touch. The magician, garbed in robes of midnight blue velvet adorned with signs of the sun and moon, entered the room and immediately touched the child on the head with his staff, the length of which was wrapped in strands from a wild orchid that was known only to grow on his island. This seemed to calm the child for a moment, and the entire family marveled that she had finally been healed. Then a seizure more violent than any before wracked her small body for what seemed an eternity. The magician declared with arrogant finality that the child was possessed and would be better left to the wolves than kept with the family. He belatedly realized it was the wrong thing to say when, a very short time later, he found himself trussed behind his horse and dragged out of town.

Thus ended the steady stream of physicians looking for some way to heal the young girl. The Duke made it well known that he was not about to leave his own flesh and blood to the wolves, but neither was he going to let her wander around town where she wouldn't last five minutes. Instead, he ordered that she never be allowed to leave the estate until he deemed her cured. While the rest of the household grumbled that surely this was no way for the child to grow up, the Duke's will was immovable in the matter. And so, in the spring of her second year, Sophie began her imprisonment in the Manse du la Rochelle. Not long after that, Sophie's mother suffered her fatal riding accident, and the care of the sick young girl was given over to the maidservants under the Duke's employment.

It became apparent that the seizures would not abate completely as she grew up, as many had hoped they would. They did, however, occur far less frequently. Sadly, the Duke, by that time, had turned his attention back to his golden town and barely took any notice at all of her existence. Whole months passed when Sophie didn't see her father. She endured in her large room, where she spent much of her time reading and looking out her window at the sea, dreaming of a life that one day might be her own.

While Sophie was by no means a strong or hale child, it was obvious to all who cared to notice that she possessed a kind and intelligent nature. She was taught to read at an early age, and from that point spent most of her days reading any books she could get her hands on. She studied histories, learned languages and memorized geography, all in the hope that one day she might be able to travel to the places she had read about. Her favorite books, however, were the fairy tales, because they grabbed her attention and stretched her imagination to great lengths. Within those books, full of brave knights saving fair maidens from horrible dragons, she found the life she truly wanted to live. These characters became her friends and family, and she spent many hours walking through their worlds, rejoicing with them in their triumphs and mourning their losses as if they were her own. Brendan often teased her that she cared too much for these fantasy worlds that weren't real. She quietly mused that, to her brother and father, she wasn't real either, but merely a fantasy they could interact with if they so chose.

Her favorite characters were the young maidens with their long hair and beauty that could steal men's hearts with one glance. She often looked in the mirror at the pale, skinny girl with limp hair and imagined some knight riding off to do battle with a terrible beast to win her favor. But those musings eventually came to an end, and she would be left staring at a girl in the mirror for whom, according to Brendan, nobody would be willing to fight. The truly remarkable feature about Sophie was her sea-blue eyes, which could convey the full spectrum of human emotion with just one look. She often wondered if she would one day have a chance to look upon anything beyond her tiny little world with eyes that hungered for so much more.

Her one true friend was her brother Cass. He often came to her room, day and night, and read her stories from her favorite books or sang the songs that told the same tales, enhanced by his beautiful voice. They would laugh and talk with one another long into the night, as they had much in common. Both seemed destined to a life that was not their own to lead and dreamed of escaping this place in order to see what the world might offer two souls such as theirs.

The saddest night of Sophie's life came when Cass told her he was leaving. It was only a couple of days after her eighteenth birthday, and he and their father had gotten into a terrible fight because Cass did not want to work at the inns in La Croix like the Duke expected; instead, he planned to make a name for himself elsewhere. He had endured working for the Duke long enough, he at last decided, and would no longer allow his own dreams to slip away. So on the same night that he bid goodbye to his beloved sister, he left the city under cover of darkness with a group of hired players. Before he departed, as Sophie's tears soaked into the shoulder of his cloak, Cass held her close and told her that he loved her and promised to one day return as the most famous minstrel in the land. He also promised, as he was leaving her door for the last time, that he would take her with him when he returned. She accepted his word with a brave face and prayed that day would come soon.

The morning of her twentieth birthday found her sitting in her window seat finishing another fairy tale and dreaming about the life she so desperately wanted. She was excited, for this birthday was to be different from any that had come before. She and Anne had conspired for weeks to spirit her out of the estate so that she could see the town for herself. As she bundled up in the gray cloak that Anne had snuck into her room with her usual breakfast of tea and porridge, Sophie wondered if she might meet the handsome prince of her dreams, who would take her away from this place forever.

Dreams, when one wants them badly enough, have a funny way of coming true, though hardly ever do they unfold the way we imagine they will.

Chapter Four

None of the Duke's guards stationed at the main gate took any notice of the lone traveler in black, hunched with fatigue and covered in road dust, who passed between them on his way into town, perhaps because there was such a throng of people seeking admittance into the famed city this day. Though none of the townspeople knew it at the time, just as the sun came up over the trees and made La Croix appear for a few moments as if it truly were some pure, mythical city pulled out of legend, the winds of change had blown their way. After this day, none who lived or visited there would ever be the same.

The traveler stopped just as he entered the city's gates to lean on his long staff and take stock of the town he had so long been meaning to visit. Although somewhat stooped from a long trek, he was still a tall man, measuring well over six feet. He didn't carry himself with the usual self-preserving, tired shuffle of a true beggar. More so, he held himself like some king of long ago, noble in bearing and movement. His long hair, pulled back in a ponytail, seemed to shift color in the sun's rays from black to silver and every shade in between. His long beard of the same hue came down to the chest of his oft-patched black cloak. His eyes bore witness that he was no common beggar or wanderer. Ageless and calculating, they betrayed that the soul behind them went far deeper than his frail body suggested. As he turned his eyes to the already bustling market, he sighed and prepared himself to play the role he had adopted for so very long now.

Most of La Croix's residents, accustomed to seeing only other aristocrats such as themselves, took the presence of a beggar in their town as a personal affront. None would spare him even a second glance as he stumbled up and down the main square in the market district, asking for a few coins so he might buy himself a hot meal and perhaps a place to rest for the night. The braver ones shoved him away when he came near. If any had taken note of the look of anger that crossed his face in these moments, nothing like the cowering look beggars usually adopt, they might have reacted differently. But, as we have already established, the people of La Croix were not used to seeing one such as him moving among them.

As the morning wore on, finding no aid in the market square, the drifter was eventually lured to an area of delicious smells, both savory and sweet. Here, amongst the shops of butchers, fish merchants, bakers and makers of rare, exotic dishes, the hungry man hoped to at least find some measure of kindness. He wasn't surprised, however, to find his reception much the same as it had been in the other parts of town. After some time, he considered simply leaving and casting his lot with the next town. But he reminded himself that he had come here with a purpose, and he did not take such obligations lightly. Pondering all of this, he was taken completely by surprise when a middle-aged woman came rushing out of the baker's shop carrying a basket brimming with freshly baked loaves for the market. She didn't get two steps out of the door before she crashed headlong into him.

Bette, anticipating what her master would do to her when he heard she had somehow managed to drop almost every loaf of bread he had given her to take to his stall in the market, immediately turned to the man and launched into a stream of curses that would have made even the hardiest sailor blush. She stopped short, however, when the full gaze of his black eyes came to rest on her, and gasped.

"I know you," she stammered as she backed slowly away from the man who was simultaneously dusting himself off and gathering up the fallen bread. "You came through Renwold many years ago when I was just a young girl first apprenticed to the town baker," she said, wide-eyed and gaining back a small bit of her composure. "I haven't forgotten what transpired soon after you left. Are you here on similar business?" she questioned, realizing before she had even finished her sentence that he must be, as this didn't seem like a coincidence. He smiled a benign smile, leaned towards her and whispered something in her ear. Backing away, he put a finger to his lips, a polite request that she not draw any attention to his presence.

The man she knew from so long ago had begun to move away, back towards the center of town, when Bette hailed him to wait for just a moment. She ran up to him and placed the only loaf of bread that hadn't fallen on the ground in his hands. She felt the deed appropriate and wished she had more to offer, but she knew that very soon she would probably leave here and no longer cared what her employer would say. The old man merely smiled and said, "Thank you, dear Bette, for the single act of kindness I have encountered in this unkind place. Your charity shall not be forgotten, and I am in your debt, gentle lady." With this, he started walking away, but a slight premonition stopped him in his tracks. Turning back to her, he said, "I may have need of you once more before I leave here, and when that time comes, you will know in your heart what to do. Thank you, dear madam. I bid you a long and happy life." Saying this, he hurried off down the street towards a commotion that had begun near a flower merchant's stall in the town square where a group of people had gathered around a young woman lying on the ground.

Bette watched his retreating back and purposeful steps until the only sign of him was his silver hair, towering above the rest of the crowd. It wasn't until several minutes later that she realized she hadn't even told him her name.

Chapter Five

The second Sophie was free of her family's vast estate, she knew she had entered a world far different from the one she was used to. Being confined in her room had poorly prepared her for this overwhelming assault on her senses. As she rode in the back of a covered carriage driven by her co-conspirator, Anne, she reveled in the fact that she would finally be able to see things for herself—things that she had previously only read about.

Anne was terribly cautious, for she knew her punishment for sneaking the Duke's daughter out of the estate would be severe should they be discovered, and she was also terribly weary. Sophie had kept her up until the late hours of the night asking question after question about what she would see and experience in town. "What color are the streets? How many people are there? Do the ladies all wear beautiful dresses and the gentleman all look very dashing and carry bright swords at their sides? Is the market truly as exotic as everyone says? How far do my father's lands reach?" Finally, Sophie had grown tired, and Anne had convinced her that she needed sleep if she was going to have the energy to make the trip. Now, as Anne thought about the fragile girl riding in the back of the coach, she hoped trouble didn't take the time to find them today.

The townspeople they passed took little notice of anything unusual. Here was just another of the Duke's servants running an errand, picking up supplies for his massive estate. The few who did happen to see a startling pair of blue eyes peeking out from a gap in the curtains passed it off as just a trick of the sun's rays and went on about their business. Sophie looked on from her hidden perch. She couldn't believe the astonishing designs of the homes and gardens they passed, together with the garish colors of the buildings themselves, which paled in comparison to the plants and flowers decorating their fronts.

She took great delight in everything and had to restrain herself several times from shrieking and pointing out birds and other animals that she had so often read about in her books. Bright cardinals, jays and finches of all colors darted from branch to branch in the trees as they passed, and far above Sophie spotted a beautiful hawk effortlessly riding the currents as it looked for prey below. She stared for minutes on end at the sight of a shepherd guiding his entire herd of sheep into town to be fleeced. The wooly creatures would have probably held her attention a while longer if she and Anne had not had to stop short because of some sort of large commotion in the middle of the road leading to the market square.

Sophie listened intently, hidden away as Anne called out to a man nearby, asking what the hold-up was. He came over and leaned in close to give his response. "A beggar was seen here in the marketplace just a short while ago causing all sorts of trouble," he whispered to Anne as if she were his accomplice in some grand scheme. "Disturbing all of the common folk just trying to go about their business. I can't rightly imagine how someone like him got through the gates. Their superior is asking the guards right now how they were lax enough to let a creature like that slip by them. We are organizing a party to ferret him out from wherever he's gone and make sure he knows how unwelcome he is here." Then with the air of a crusader setting out on a task of imminent importance, he moved off to join a steadily growing number of men gathered at the statue of Thomas Rochelle in the middle of the square.

All of this piqued Sophie's curiosity, and questions flooded her mind. She didn't quite understand why the townspeople would hate a beggar so much. He probably only desired the base comforts of humanity, just like anyone else. She would have thought more on the subject, but her musings were interrupted by the sound of Anne muttering that they would probably be stuck for a while, as traffic on the road had backed up both in front of and behind them. Suddenly, Sophie realized this was her chance to embark on an adventure of her own while they waited for the road to clear. She silently slipped out of the back and was gone long before Anne realized she had let the girl escape.

Upon her entrance into the market district, Sophie could only stare in awe as entertainers of all sorts stood at every crossroads and street corner and in front of the many shops, encouraging people to spend their money. She saw that several men seemed to have cleared out a grassy area and were performing an impromptu play for a crowd of about twenty people. It appeared to be something about some wolves and children, but she dare not go too close, for fear of someone recognizing her. She backed away slowly, barely avoiding bumping into a heavily tattooed, bare-chested man, busy tossing knives back and forth to what could pass as his twin, both of them singing at the top of their lungs all the while.

Everywhere she looked, she saw hawkers shouting for the people to come to their shop or inn, clamoring myriad reasons for why their establishment was more worthy than the rest. Samples of roasted fish, meat pies and pastries were shoved into the eager hands of those passing by. The square was a bustling hive of activity. All of it seemed good natured, and Sophie, marveling at the life that suffused this place, tried to take in all of the sights and sounds coming from every direction. It was then that she spotted the group of men converging at the base of a nearby fountain and decided she had better move on, lest they start to ask questions for which she had no good answers.

Carefully keeping her hood up, Sophie quickly moved away from the gathering and towards the center of the marketplace. She wanted to see the town in its entirety, not through a crack in the back of a carriage. Reveling in the feel of the warm cobblestones beneath her feet as she headed towards the sound of hammers ringing on anvils, she wandered onto the street of the blacksmiths, wanting to see where the weapons were made that so many came to La Croix to purchase.

She was awed by the size of the men hammering out the iron to be made into swords and daggers. All had massive arms and wore leather aprons that protected them from the heat and stray sparks. Workshops were open to the street, allowing a breeze to blow in from the sea. Business seemed to be brisk, and Sophie noticed that most of the smiths had assistants to tend to the wares and to customers while they concentrated on making the weapons. As she came to the last stand on the street, she felt the hot sun begin to take its toll upon her body, both physically and mentally.

Geren sat serenely in his stand at the end of the Street of the Crucible, watching the faces of the rich and powerful as they went about their day. He had been here for a while now, posing as a blacksmith and making a decent profit from it. Although life in La Croix had begun to lose its luster, he could not help but chuckle at the thought of what these people would say if they knew, truly knew, who he was.

Being the youngest son of the King of the Elves came with both its advantages and disadvantages. He was free from the stuffy court life and posturing of politics that his older brother had to deal with. Despite a paltry age difference of fifty years, his life was quite different from his brother's. His father had trained him from when he was very young to observe everything he saw and report it at the end of every day. He had shown a great hunting prowess from very early on, and, when he came of age, his father began sending him out into the world to keep his eye on any situation he deemed interesting and to report back when he knew the time was right.

Why his father had sent him to this town he did not know, but he also didn't know of any time when his father had erred in these matters. So Geren obeyed and sustained his life as a blacksmith in La Croix, all the while waiting for something interesting to happen. But on this day, unlike so many before, he could feel something in the air. He couldn't quite put his finger on it, but things were somehow different, and he knew that this was the sort of day when anything could happen.

He heard the commotion from the market square and could make out the forms of men gathering at the fountain, his keen eyes picking out individual features that others would not. He heard them saying something about a vagabond wandering the streets and how they were going to track him down, and he decided that this was a matter he would like to investigate. Turning back towards the street, he moved to gather up the bows set out on display in front of his shop when the form of a girl staring at his goods stopped him short.

"I'm sorry. I didn't see you. I don't mean to be rude, and I hope you have not been standing there long," he said, watching her eyes as they looked out at him from under her hood.

Before she could respond to him, she stumbled once and caught herself on the edge of the table where his bows lay. She wearily passed the back of her hand across her eyes, and he could see she was having trouble reconciling her senses with her surroundings.

"Are you alright, milady?" he asked as he instinctively reached out to touch her shoulder, looking more directly at her face to discern for himself if she was, indeed, all right. "Stay here," he said. "I'll be right back." Then he moved away before she could respond.

He was back in moments, a cup in one hand and a wet rag in the other. He handed the cup to her and said, "Drink this." She took it from him and immediately relieved her parched throat with water that tasted as pure as anything she had ever had. He handed her the cloth in exchange for the cup, and she wiped her brow and face with it, immediately feeling rejuvenated, the sun's effects staved off for the time being.

"Thank you for your kindness. I must have underestimated how hot it is out here today. But I must be moving along. Thank you, again. I feel much better, now," she said, taking in his exotic appearance as she spoke and thinking that he must be from somewhere far away from here, as he looked nothing like any of the other people she had encountered that day.

"Well then, if you say you are well to go, I caution you to beware of the sun's power, milady. It can be especially brutal at this time of the day.

My name is Geren, and if you have any more need of me, you have but to ask it and it will be yours." He couldn't say exactly why he said this last bit, except that it felt right, and in his heart he knew that if this young lady asked anything of him, he would do all in his power to help her.

As she smiled at him and turned to walk away, he turned his back to her to put the cup and rag back in his shop. Then he heard her voice from behind him say, "Oh, and Geren, you have very nice bows. Much nicer than any of the others on the street."

"Why, thank you, milady," he replied distractedly as he arranged things inside his shop.

"Yes, they are very nice, but that is a very beautiful sword."

And before the impact of what she had just said hit him, he mumbled a "Thanks, again" and went to put the cup back on its shelf. His hand stopped in mid-air, though, and he dropped it on the floor. When he turned back to catch the one he had so long sought, his voice caught in his throat, for she was gone.

It had been almost seventy-five years ago now, he thought, as his eyes scanned the crowd for the girl's form. He slapped his thigh in frustration as he caught no sign of her. As an afterthought, he looked down at the sword she had mentioned. Its blue steel blade reflected the afternoon sunlight, and the platinum wire on the hilt shone brilliantly. It was his finest work—it and its twin. He had begun to despair of anyone ever coming to take it off of his hands.

Early on, Geren had shown a talent for crafting things. He had the ability to take a lump of rock, or wood or steel and reveal its truest form. Making weapons had always been his favorite thing. He loved taking what most people would only see as a piece of wood and bringing out its natural form in the shape of a fine bow. His swords and daggers were revered for their simple beauty and elegance.

The wizard, Vinquist, a very old friend of his family, had approached him one day in his workshop deep in the heart of Avereen. He asked if Geren would take a commission for him and, when Geren gave assent, proceeded to describe in detail two swords he would have him forge. They would be similar in make and design, with one crucial difference. Whereas one would be large, a broadsword, the other would be slightly smaller and thin. In short, the wizard wanted him to make one sword for a man and the other for a woman.

It took Geren nearly six months of working from daylight to dusk and long into the night to complete his masterpieces. On the eve when he at last put the final touches on the hilt of the smaller sword, he walked out of his workshop. Standing there, leaning against a tree and smoking his pipe, was Vinquist.

"I have never made any blades to equal these and do not think that I ever could again. I have put much of my heart into them, and I give them freely to you. No amount of money could ever do them justice, and so they shall have to be a gift, from a friend to a friend," Geren said.

A small tear rolled down the wizard's cheek as he examined the twin blades before him, whose equals he had never seen. He thanked Geren, who promptly asked him for whom he had wanted the blades made. Vinquist smiled in return and told him the larger blade was to go to the Vashon family, to be passed from father to son and generation to generation, and when the time was right and the need was great, this sword would play a large part in the shaping of the world. His answer as to whom the smaller sword went to surprised Geren, and he could only stand there and blink as Vinquist took it out of its scabbard, laid it on the ground in front of him and began gathering his power to cast a spell on it.

When he was finished, the blade flashed a brilliant white light then returned to its former state. Vinquist looked at Geren and said, "In truth, I do not know for whom the sword is meant, only that I have a need of a twin pair of blades. All the rest is hidden from me. I do have one more favor to ask of you, Young Prince. I would have you carry this sword with you always, and … " He paused and held up his hands, forestalling the incredulous response he could see jumping to Geren's lips; " … and when the one it is meant for finds it, you will know," he finished. "For the spell I have cast on this sword makes it invisible to all but you, me and the one meant to carry it. When you happen to run across someone who can see the sword, my advice is to give it to them." Vinquist led the Prince away to celebrate his finishing of the blades, and as they talked and drank long into the night under the protection of the trees of Avereen, Geren wondered how long he would have to carry this sword with him.

Consequently, it took Geren a few moments to fully register the impact of what the girl had actually said, and he glanced about, furiously searching for her hooded form. To have found the sword's owner after so long and then to have lost her was simply not an option. He hastily belted the sword to his own waist and ran out of his shop, praying that she had not managed to elude him in the busy afternoon market.

As Sophie moved away from the smiths' shops, the scent in the air changed from one of burning metal to sweet flowers. Signs in front of the shops lining this street proclaimed that every kind of flower could be found here, and judging by the aroma permeating the area, Sophie didn't doubt it. A trellis covered with ivy and dotted with flowers of white, purple and blue provided shade, transforming the lane into a fragrant tunnel. Roses, tulips, lilies, daisies, as well as every other kind of flower Sophie had ever read about in books now presented themselves to her in abundance, providing wonderful smells to go with what before had only been pictures in her mind. She soon found her favorites were the deep red roses that seemed to be the most popular purchase on the street. There were several stalls devoted to them alone, and she found their smell intoxicating.

She leaned closer to a particularly striking arrangement, inhaled deeply and sneezed abruptly, causing her hood to fall and revealing her face to the passing crowd. She knew, however, that ordinary allergies were the least of her problems, for she was overcome by a terrible yet familiar sensation. Her knees became weak, and she began to stumble about. Trying to steady herself, she grabbed hold of a nearby table, the top of which was lined with extravagant bouquets and vases, but it all came crashing to the ground. She managed to pull herself back up and stood trembling as a small crowd of merchants and shoppers began to form around her. One of the kinder men attempted to assist the distressed stranger, but as he reached out his hand, her body started convulsing and contorting uncontrollably, and she unwittingly knocked the would-be gentleman off of his feet. Another person in the crowd, perceiving Sophie to have assaulted the fallen man, shouted, "Stop her!" Half conscious of what was happening around her, Sophie tried to plead with the crowd, but she could only grunt and moan through her clinched jaw. Her pale eyes began to roll back into her head, and it wasn't long before the inevitable cries of "Witch!" and "Run her out of town!" could be heard piercing the air in the normally serene Isle of the Rose.

She wanted to escape into the shadows, but her body was almost completely paralyzed. All of a sudden, the first rock thrown by a townsperson hit her on the brow. Reeling from the unexpected blow, she found herself suddenly surrounded by a mass of people yelling at her. Names, rocks and more than one piece of food were hurled through the air in her direction. A wave of panic coursed through her veins as she realized she was caught in a situation that had quickly gone from bad to worse. Sophie silently started praying for deliverance as her slight body shook and she started to faint, knocking over another table filled with roses in the process and fashioning a fragrant and thorny bed for herself in the middle of the street. "She's possessed!" one merchant cried out. "We have to burn her before her spirit frees itself and takes over all of us." That was their battle cry as they all began pelting her with rocks, fruit and anything at hand, leaving her to cover her face and wonder if anyone could save her from this horrible end. Just as the darkness began to creep in around the edges of her vision, she saw a gap open and part the gathered mob.

The noise seemed to quiet somewhat, and Sophie's small form began to lose its battle with consciousness. She had fought as long and as hard as she could to stand, but her legs gave out, and she fell back, not onto the hot cobblestone of the market square, but into the arms of a large man in a tattered black cloak. As she looked up, she saw a face filled with kindness framed in a large black beard. His silver ponytail had come undone and now formed a protective netting for both of their faces. He smiled at her and said, "Don't worry, dear child. I will set all things right."

None of those gathered took any note of the young blacksmith, who stopped just at the edge of the crowd, his eyes going wide as he recognized first the girl he was looking for and then the man who was tending to her. Realizing the situation was in far better hands than his, he turned on his heels without a word and headed back to the Street of the Crucible to pack up his shop. It appeared the day had finally come for him to leave La Croix behind. His father would definitely want a report on these events as quickly as possible. He had to fight the urge to charge back and rescue the girl, so that he could give her what was rightfully hers, but he knew that fate had brought all of them together and that now was not the time for her to have the sword. He would make haste to tell his father of these events, and then he would return. For now, she was well taken care of, but if he was not mistaken, his sword and possibly his help would be sorely needed very soon.

Chapter Six

As the sound of the man's retreating footsteps became less audible, drowned out by the sound of the marketplace, Bette felt truly conflicted. She had spent so much time struggling to build a stable life for herself in La Croix. Now, after one chance meeting, the foundations of that life had been irrevocably shaken. She knew that after today she would never be able to return to the normalcy that had ruled her everyday life these many years, and she also knew that the town she had come to call home would not remain as it was for much longer. Not knowing what else to do with herself, she set down her basket of bread and wandered into the market.

She had seen him before, of course. He wasn't the sort of person one easily forgot. Years ago, when she was only a young girl still following her mother's every footstep, he had come to their town. Bette had been frightened at that time by this large stranger who seemed to radiate power and authority, though she wondered why one of such apparent rank would travel about in the guise of a beggar. He looked the same this very day, Bette marveled, as he had some forty years earlier. His hair color had not changed. He still wore the same tattered robe that had been patched so many times that its original color was hard to discern. He had wandered about the streets of her town, seeking some sign of goodwill from its citizens, and it was in an alley much like the one she had met him in this very afternoon that she had seen him approach and speak with her mother.

Bette's mother didn't seem shocked when the man first approached and gave them a grandfatherly smile. She simply offered him a fresh meat pie from the bunch in her basket, apologizing all the while that she did not have more to offer one such as himself. Smiling, he extended his hand to take her offering and said, "This is a far greater gesture than I have found so far in your town. You have a beautiful daughter, Millicent. She reminds me very much of a certain young woman I remember tagging along after her mother many years ago, far away, in a town much like this one. Your family has always been kind to me, and I thank you for that. However, if I were you, I would not linger in this place. After today, I do not think it will be hospitable enough to raise such a beautiful young daughter."

And saying thus, he thanked them again for their offering and bade them farewell, for his business in the town was not quite finished. As he began to shuffle away, resuming the beggar's walk he had discarded while conversing with them, he turned and took the young Bette by the hand. Looking deep into her eyes, he said, "A beautiful daughter, indeed. I wouldn't be surprised if our paths crossed again one day, my dear. I thank you now, though you may not remember it, for the woman you will one day become."

That being said, he turned from them and vanished into the crowd, leaving Bette with a very confused feeling, much like the one she was feeling at present. As she watched him walk away, she heard her mother's voice say to her, "Come, Bette. We have work to do." Remembering these things from her childhood and knowing in her heart what she now had to do, she prayed to her mother's spirit to lend her strength, and she walked across the market to the place where she had just seen her friend, Isaac, busily unloading a wagon that belonged to the butcher for whom he worked.

Forestalling any greeting he had to give her, she walked right up to him and leaned in close to whisper, so that she wouldn't be overheard by the other men and women nearby. His eyes grew wide as Bette described what she intended to do, and when she was finished, she leaned back and said, "Well, what do you say, Isaac? Are you with me?"

He looked at her for a moment to ensure that she was serious and then took a long look around the town that had been his home ever since he was a young boy. Realizing that for as long as he could remember he and his family had toiled thanklessly for masters who didn't care a whit for them, he looked back to her with a smile that lit up his face.

"Yes, Bette, I think I am with you," he replied.

She smiled, relieved to have at least one ally on whom she could count. She asked him if he was certain where to be and when to be there and turned to walk away, her business not yet done in the market that afternoon. She stopped short when she heard his voice calling after her, reaching her ears above the din of the marketplace.

"This is crazy, I hope you know!" he called after her, laughter in his voice.

She turned back to him, hands on her hips, and said, "I know. That's why I think it just might work." Then she walked away, leaving him shaking his head as he returned to loading his wagon.

All that day, Isaac moved about the market, pausing here and there to speak to those in the working community he regarded as friends. He asked them the same question he himself had been posed, and each time they would get that faraway look in their eyes that people get when they aren't sure whether they're awake or dreaming. Then they would all smile and nod "Yes," realizing that whatever the cost, this dream was worth risking everything many times over, the dream that their parents and grandparents had wished for so badly when they first came to La Croix: the dream of freedom. This was the chance to take hold of their lives and live them as they saw fit, beholden to no one and nothing.

All that day, the ostensibly important people of La Croix went about their daily lives, while the true backbone of the town loaded wagons and prepared to join Bette's grand plot that would change their lives for the better.

Chapter Seven

Captain Dupree, head of the Duke's personal guard, was enjoying an afternoon spent in the warm sun on the porch of one of the many taverns lining the streets of the market proper. He had left the Duke's estate earlier that morning saying he was going into town to get the provisions he would need to outfit several new recruits. His lieutenant had given him a sidelong glance, sensing that his captain really only wanted the afternoon away from the mansion. However, he knew better than to question the word of his superior and so quietly agreed to watch over things until Dupree returned.

Being in charge did have its benefits, the captain reflected as he sipped a cold mug of ale and savored the warm afternoon breeze blowing in off the harbor. But even though he was enjoying his time away from the tedium of guarding the Duke and his family, he decided that sooner or later his presence would be missed . He paid his tab and was starting to leave when a commotion near one of the florist's stalls caught his attention. Knowing full well that the city guard was more than capable of taking care of whatever problems came their way, he ignored the disturbance and headed for home. However, some inkling, a gut feeling that something wasn't right, stopped him in his tracks. Before he knew what he was doing, he found himself covering the distance across the square. When he arrived, moments before the city watch, he couldn't believe his eyes.

A girl, the spitting image of the Duke's daughter, Sophie, huddled in the arms of an old beggar while the surrounding crowd pelted them with any items available. It took his astonished mind only a couple of moments to realize that this was indeed the Duke's daughter and that something needed to be done about the situation quickly or else he and every other member of the guard would be lucky to lose only their jobs. For while they all relished the security of working for the Duke, he was not known to be a kind or forgiving man. Dupree then saw the arrival of the city guard, led by its particularly large and nasty lieutenant, Gaston. He felt relieved that the situation would soon be in hand and ran off to inform the Duke of what had happened. Of course, the Captain also realized that, if he were the one to bear the news, he could paint a good picture of himself and his role in the affair, lest another account reach his employer's ears to tell a different tale.

Gaston was bored. He had been appointed head of the city watch by the Duke because he was extraordinarily effective at getting order restored when the need arose. His brutal knack for getting answers on the rare occasion when the Duke wanted someone questioned shocked and amazed his subordinates and appealed to the Duke's own distorted sense of values, so he had risen quickly to his current position. But having been in this station for over two years now, he didn't take the same joy he once had in his daily work. Perhaps, he mused, he would soon take his leave and find work in one of the less reputable towns where there would be more sport than jailing drunk aristocrats for the night to sober them up, only to release them the next morning.

The town's jail was conveniently located in a large building near the beginning of the gambling and drinking section of the town. It had a small room at the entrance for the guards and constables to gather and pass the time playing dice and drinking while off duty. Iron doors lined a tight hallway. Beyond the doors lay cells inhabited by drunks and anyone else found breaking the law. There were enough rooms for fifteen or more prisoners, but they all stood empty, as no one had dared to cause trouble ever since Gaston had made examples of the last few who had broken the law. At the end of the hall was a door leading down to a single cell where the Lieutenant kept his instruments of questioning. The day was quiet as a few guards played dice, and Gaston silently prayed for something exciting to happen.

Suddenly one of his boys threw open the door and hurried in to deliver the news that a beggar had been seen causing trouble in the market square and was even now attacking some innocent girl in front of all of the townspeople. Gaston smiled wickedly as he grabbed his order-restoring cudgel, pointed to several of his men and told them to accompany him as quickly as possible.

The crowd was getting out of control as mob mentality took hold and removed all rationality and reason from the minds of those gathered around the old beggar and the young lady. Gaston realized that he would have to take control of the situation quickly or else he would have a genuine riot on his hands. He dispatched his men to different sections of the crowd and ordered them to move the people back. "And for God's sake, get them to stop throwing things so we can get close to those two!" he barked as he dodged a head of cabbage, and his men scrambled to obey his orders. Hefting his cudgel, ready to use it should anyone not move out of his way, Gaston waded through the fray towards the center of the mess.

The presence of the guards slowly shocked the people back to their senses. They stopped heaving objects at the beggar and the young girl and moved back so that the constables could investigate the disturbance. When it appeared that order had been restored, Gaston calmly observed the two figures huddled on the ground, apparently oblivious to everything going on around them. As his men came up to report what they had discovered, he was surprised to learn that the mob had formed when the girl, a suspected witch, appeared in the market and frightened the people. The beggar had been seen earlier skulking about town and had reappeared moments after the crowd descended upon the girl. No one seemed to know how, or if, the two were connected. But Gaston, tapping his cudgel against the palm of his hand as he stepped towards the two figures, intended to find out.

As he approached the girl and the beggar, Gaston noticed the crowd parting for two mounted men who were forcing their way through the throng. Surprise registered , and he raised one brow, as he recognized the Duke and Captain Dupree, who were now heading towards the two figures. As he calmly stepped forward, he wondered how much more interesting things would get before all was said and done.

Chapter Eight

The sounds of the mob quieted to a distant buzz in Sophie's mind as she felt her entire existence shrink to the space between herself and the stranger who held her in his arms. A calm washed over her, while his body absorbed the blows that were meant for her. She cautiously opened her eyes and looked up at him.

As he held the girl, her body slowed its shaking until the mighty tremors wracking her small frame were reduced to intermittent shivers. She had endured much pain in her short life. He could sense that from just looking at her, but in order to heal her ailment, he had to know the entirety of her story. He looked her in the eyes and said, "Child, I am going to help you, but you must trust me and open yourself up to me. I have the power to make you well, but first you must accept my aid." As his dark eyes locked onto Sophie's brilliant blue ones, she slowly nodded her head with all of the energy left in her exhausted body and whispered into his ear, "I just want to be free." In so saying, her body succumbed to its exhaustion, and her eyes closed.

"One way or another, though perhaps not in the way that you think, dear one, you will be," he said. "I promise." With those words, he touched her forehead with the sapphire-inlaid signet ring upon his right forefinger. The ring started to glow and was soon brighter than even the hot afternoon sun. Time stood still, and, in what seemed only an instant to the others, he saw the story of the lonely daughter of La Croix.

He saw her first memories of her parents and siblings. Early on, they had loved her dearly, but as she began to get sick, they visited her less and less. He also saw the fragmented thoughts of her mother's smiling face appearing over her crib, disappearing one day never to return again, replaced by that of her maid, Anne. Even more infrequently were the visits from her stern and harsh father who regarded her as the greatest disappointment of his life.

He watched as Sophie began to mature into a young girl whose greatest gift was her imagination. He saw how she loved the books that became her life and the characters within them who became her only friends during the darkest times. He also witnessed the overwhelming kindness with which she treated all those she came in contact with, never showing any signs of the pain and tragedy that filled her days.

Finally, he watched as the young woman he held in his arms, weary of captivity, dreamed of gaining an entire lifetime's worth of experiences in one stolen day of freedom. It was at this moment that he foresaw a glimmer of the girl's future. His heart began to warm, for he knew the events unfolding here today were setting something into motion of greater importance, but before he could move further along this path to destiny, he knew he had to cure her ailment.

Throughout her memories, he experienced all of the seizures and attacks she had lived through. They broke up her life's story, like she were somehow bobbing up and down in a river of icy cold water, and they denied her even one moment of true peace from the fear of constant physical affliction. Nevertheless, he discovered that her sickness was not life-threatening, and when he opened his eyes, he began to gather power unto himself, slowly letting his magic wash over the girl as he began the unseen battle against her illness.

Sophie felt changes in her body as his healing magic started working. Perhaps she was dying, she thought. But as the moment stretched on, she knew that was not the case. Life returned to her exhausted lungs and limbs, so that at last she could catch her breath. When she recovered enough to open her eyes, it was to a world far different than the one she had closed them to only moments ago.

The first thing she noticed was that colors were much brighter, truer to her eyes, and she wondered why she had been denied this sense of beauty all her life. Sounds also rang more musically in her ears, and she heard everything with a clarity long denied her. She could still smell the crumpled roses she had fallen on, mixed with the open-road scent of the old man's cloak. He was smiling at her, having walked through the darkness in her heart and emerged into the light with her in tow.

Sophie felt renewed and realized that these smells and sounds would normally launch her into another fit. None came, however, and she took a deep, deep breath. Her lungs finally worked as they should, and the blood coursed through her veins without hindrance. She smiled back at the man sitting next to her, tears of joy coursing down her cheeks, and then threw her arms around him. "Thank you," she whispered. "Thank you so much." To this, he replied, "I told you that I would set things right, and I am a man of my word. I'm happy that you have found new life here this day and urge you to live it and be free."

Soon they could both sense the crowd growing rowdy again and could see several of the city guardsmen coming directly towards them. "Listen to me carefully, child," he said, holding her at arm's length. "You have no future here, except the one you have known, locked in your father's house. They will not believe you are cured and will only imprison you again, only this time they will be watching you more closely to make sure you do not escape once more. Leave La Croix and never return. Find happiness elsewhere and forge your own destiny. This is no longer your home. Leave and never look back."

As he spoke, she sensed the truth of his words and knew he was right. Eager to begin her new life, Sophie stood up on legs that were now strong and began searching for a way out of the market square, but she felt despair as she looked at the mob surrounding them.

"I will create a distraction so you can escape, but fly from here and do not look back until you are in safety's arms." He recognized the concern on her face as she began to shake her head in dismay. Putting a hand to her cheek, he gently said, "Do not worry for me, dear Sophie; this is not the end of my tale. I promise you, we will meet again."

The old man turned abruptly, grabbed the closest guard by the collar and threw him into a large group of people. The strength he displayed was far greater than a simple beggar should possess. The crowd gasped, and the approaching guards hurried their steps and clutched their cudgels tight in hand as they drew near.

Looking one last time into her eyes, he said, "Run, Sophie, as far and fast as you can. I will find you." With one last, desperate hug, Sophie turned and, feeling in her body a strength like never before, fled both the mob and her life as the Duke's unwanted daughter.

The last thing he saw, as the blow he knew was coming from the guard's club connected with the back of his head, was Sophie's form retreating down a side street. He was thinking how fate truly did work in mysterious ways as the guard's club finally fell and everything else was lost in darkness.

Chapter Nine

Sophie marveled at how her body had been healed. Her legs, which before would not have taken her several steps before they tired, now pumped a steady pace against the cobbled streets as she considered her many paths of escape. Her lungs drew precious air into her body without constantly threatening to fail her, and her heart beat stronger than it ever had. For the first time in many years, she felt alive. Even though she was not yet free, her spirits soared as they never had before.

As she ducked into a darkened doorway in the back of one of the city's many taverns, Sophie took the first chance to pause since her escape and considered the remarkable events that had led to her flight. Who was this man who had so unexpectedly helped her and made her body whole? He must be powerful indeed to heal years of affliction in a matter of moments, succeeding where so many others had failed. She would have to wait until they met again to have her questions answered, though, for she heard the sounds of her pursuers at the foot of the alley, signaling that they had once again picked up her trail.

She didn't know how long she had been running and hiding, but her renewed body was finally beginning to reach the limits of its strength. She also realized that while she had grown up a stone's throw from the main part of town, she had no real knowledge of how to navigate its twisted maze of streets. Without a plan or another miracle readily available, she began to worry. Hunger pangs gnawed at her belly, and she grabbed a loaf of bread that she noticed on the ground. She brushed it off and ate it as she moved through the streets.

Having momentarily lost sight of her pursuers, she decided to take full advantage of her respite and formulate a plan of escape. Not knowing how long it would be until she could eat again, she decided to save some of the bread for later. She headed down the main street that she knew must surely lead out of town, but when she arrived at the gate, she found it guarded by two armed watchmen. She was trying to think of some distraction that would allow her to sneak past the guards when the shout of two of her pursuers shocked her into action. She stopped short as her father's carriage, driven by Anne, pulled behind her, directly between her and the men chasing her. "Run, dear one, as fast and far as your legs will carry you!" Anne shouted, a tear in her eye as she silently acknowledged that she may never see her beloved Sophie again.

She turned down another side street hoping they would hesitate before following her into a place so deserted. Her lungs burned with the intensity of her flight, and a stitch throbbed in her side, but she dared not slow, knowing that they would be upon her in a moment if she did. She paused for one heartbeat at the end of the lane and asked herself, should she turn right or left? Suddenly, a door opened, and two hands grabbed her and pulled her into an abandoned building.

The two men seeking the girl emerged at the head of the alley, but all they saw were two men who had pulled their carts, heaped tall with foodstuffs and firewood, abreast in the middle of the lane, making it impossible for the men to pass.

"You there!" the pursuers barked at the first man in their path. "Have you seen a girl run by this way? She should have passed through here just moments ago."

"No sir, ain't seen nothin' like that today. Sure do wish some pretty young thing would come my way, though. My friend Isaac here ain't too easy on the eyes. Ain't real excitin' company neither, being deaf and dumb and all."

The guard turned to the second man, and with a much louder voice, shouted, "Have you seen a woman run this way?" Isaac only looked confused as he turned to his friend to decipher for him what the man had just said. Using two fingers, Paul made the motion for running then drew the curvy outline of a woman's figure in the air. Isaac grinned and made some rather vulgar motions of his own. "No, you idiot!" Paul yelled. "We're not running after some women! Have you seen a woman running?"

Isaac shook his head from side to side and started to move his cart across the alleyway, but the officials halted them again. "Where exactly are you going with these goods at this time of the day, anyway?"

Paul turned to the man and said, "Well, actually, these are for the Duke's estate. We don't ask questions—just do as we're told. Now if you would be so kind as to give me your names, sirs, so that when the Duke wants to know why his supplies wasn't where they's 'posed to be at the time they's 'posed to be there, that I may direct him to you fine gentlemen. I'm sure he'll understand. His Grace is a very forgiving man."

The two guards blanched at the mentioning of the Duke, and their fear of drawing his wrath was evident as they spun on their heels and ran from the alley, retreating in the direction from which they had come.

"Deaf and dumb?" Isaac asked his friend in a clear voice. "You couldn't think of anything else for me to be but deaf and dumb?"

"Quit complaining. I didn't see you thinking too fast on your feet back there. Anyway, it got them to leave us alone, didn't it? Come on, let's get this stuff moving. The Lady Bette will be disappointed if we don't live up to our end of the bargain. I, for one, can't wait to leave this place far behind."

With that said, the two men maneuvered their wagons around and headed down the alleyway in the direction Sophie had gone only moments before. They could be overheard the entire way, Isaac arguing that he, a fairly intelligent man, didn't possess any of the characteristics of someone who was deaf or dumb. Paul finally gave up and, throwing his hands in the air, said, "Fine, next time we come upon some of the Duke's officials, you do the talking, and I'll be your idiot friend, ok?"

Isaac merely smiled and began to whistle a smart tune as they disappeared around the corner.

Chapter Ten

The old man awoke with a shock as a bucket of cold water was thrown into his face, rousing him from the unconscious state put upon him by the guardsman's cudgel. As his swollen right eye slowly opened to take in the scene before him, he belatedly noted the lack of cooperation from the left one. They must have gotten in a few blows while they were placing him in this cell, he thought as his lungs pressed out against aching ribs, a couple of which he suspected might be broken. He hung from shackles set just high enough for him to stand on his toes and take some of the weight off of his arms. His cloak and staff had been taken from him and thrown into a far corner. He was stripped down to only his breeches and could already see a small collection of bruises starting to take shape on his naked torso. As he took stock of his injuries and looked around his cell, he mused that his trip to La Croix had not at all gone the way he had expected.

His mind was broken from its reverie as a large guard grabbed his face and lifted it from his chest, bringing them eye to eye. "Old man, did you ever make a mistake coming here," the guard growled, their faces mere inches apart.

"My only mistake," he replied, "was in not coming years ago." He could sense the guard was the dangerous type, having dealt with men like him all over the world—not overly smart, but making up for the lack of brains with brawn and a large enough cruel streak to bully their way through life. The guard's men, of which there appeared to be three scattered about the room, seemed to know the measure of their leader's temper, and they made no move to separate him from his prisoner.

"My name is Gaston, and I am Lieutenant of the Guard. If you want to survive this night, I would suggest you cooperate and give straight answers to all my questions, or I won't be as nice as I have been." As he said this, he dropped the old man's face and took a couple of steps back. He crossed his arms over his chest and let the effects of his words sink in before he began his interrogation.

"We'll start with the simple ones: what is your name, and what are you doing in my town?"

The old man, his mind and body slowly regaining their strength, lifted his head and turned to the guards, meeting their gazes in turn through his one good eye. Each of them flinched as he did so. Finally, his eye met those of his inquisitor, and he spat on the floor at Gaston's feet, saying, "You will have nothing from me but one chance to set me free. If you do not accept it but choose instead to follow the course you have already started, then I do not foresee any of you surviving the night. My name is my own, and I would never stoop to give it to one such as you."

He could see Gaston's eyes grow wide with rage as he spoke and was not surprised at the fist that caught him in the stomach, knocking the breath out of him. Gaston stepped back, letting him absorb the full aftereffects of the blow. Noting the collection of interrogation tools on racks about the room, the old man could see that they considered him no ordinary prisoner and intended to have their answers, no matter what the cost. He only hoped that Sophie had evaded capture long enough to find aid in escaping, but he couldn't afford to think about her at this moment. This night's proceedings were going to require considerable effort on his part, and he knew that he must stay focused on his immediate surroundings.

Gaston suddenly lunged forward, grabbed the back of the prisoner's hair and gave him a sharp backhand slap across the face, opening yet another cut above the cheek.

"No one has ever spoken to me like that and lived, old man. Lucky for you, the Duke wants to ask you some questions himself, so I can't beat you to death before he gets here. Otherwise, you and I would be spending a very long and painful evening together. Mark me, though," Gaston growled. "Let your tongue loosen itself like that again, and I'm not sure if I will be able to show the same restraint." He paced the room, impatient for the Duke to arrive so he could start getting some answers from his prisoner. The two younger guards glanced nervously at one another, silently hoping that the Duke would arrive before they had to step in and attempt to stop Gaston from killing the man. They dreaded having to face down their much larger and meaner Lieutenant, despite the fact that they both disliked the man and wished that one day he would finally get what was coming to him. After long moments of uncomfortable silence, during which Gaston had sat on the lone stool in the room cradling his riding crop while he stared at the prisoner, they at last heard movement in the outer hallway. When the doors swung open, the nervous guards sighed with relief.

Torchlight from the hallway outside flooded the dim room, and one lone man entered. The Duke had arrived. As he looked first at the prisoner, then at his guardsmen, the Duke's contempt for the whole situation became apparent. It was clear to all that he would very much like to resolve the situation quickly, so he could go back to his warm, downy bed. Taking in the old man's state with one glance, he turned towards his Lieutenant and said, "I assume, Gaston, you have already obtained the answers I requested. My daughter is still missing, and I intend to find her before night's end."

"Your daughter?" the man spat from where he hung suspended in chains from the grime- covered wall. "To you, the girl is a nuisance who should have died in childbirth. There is no profit to be had for you in her life, and so you ignore her existence, thinking that if you avoid her for long enough, she will simply disappear, problem solved. You are no more a father to her than I am to these chains that hold me to this wall for the time being. The girl is better off alone and free in the world than held a prisoner in your large, loveless mansion, Meirmont."

His words stunned everyone in the room into silence. That this man had spoken so to Gaston earlier was trespass enough, but to now speak the same way to the Duke made him either crazy or eager to die. Before the Duke could get to him, however, Gaston had closed the gap across the room and struck him with his riding crop, raising a huge welt and a trickle of blood down his already-bruised chest. The Duke calmly held the man's gaze, as showers of pain wracked the man's body. "I would like your name," he said. "I think you will give it freely now that you see what my Gaston is capable of. I have much to discuss this night, and the sooner I get my answers, the sooner this will all be over for you." Having said this, the Duke turned and sat down on the stool that one of the guards had pulled over for him. "By the way," he added, "I don't know how you came by the knowledge of my first name, but for the duration of our evening together, you may address me as 'Your Grace.'"

The old man lifted his head and, with an intensity and an authority that took all in the room aback, replied, "Before all is said and done here, Meirmont, you will wish that I had never come to see your pathetic town." .

"You pompous fool! Have you no comprehension of the term 'Your Grace'?"

"I have dined in the golden halls of a hundred castles that would make your paltry little town seem like the lowliest common room of any inn across the land. I have taken oaths of fealty from princes the world over, just before I crowned them King. I have seen wonders and experienced more joy and sorrow on this earth than a small man like yourself can ever begin to imagine.

I have sung the song of farewell at funeral pyres for men who were far more worthy to walk this earth than one such as you, yet who died because some power-hungry man wanted just a little more than he already had. So, out of respect for those who have truly deserved the title of 'Your Grace,' I believe I shall retain that honor for those who have earned it.

"As for my name, I have held many over the years. Some have been forgotten with the passing of time. My true name has not been known or spoken in this world for centuries. I will, however, give you one of the names that you might be familiar with. For the remainder of our time together, when you address me, you may call me Vinquist."

Chapter Eleven

Silence and awe filled the room after the man's announcement of his name. It seemed not even the howl of the wind outside could penetrate the deafening quiet that hung in the air. The Duke and his guards took turns looking at one another, first with glances of disbelief and then, in the case of the Duke, flashes of anger. Gaston appeared to be the only one in the room not affected by the announcement. Perplexed by the queer reaction of the others, he shrugged his shoulders and, breaking the silence, said, "I don't understand." He looked at the other men in the room and waited for one of them to shed some light on his confusion. "I've heard the name before—everyone has—but it is just a name out of some fairy tale we all heard as children. A good story, to be sure, but a story nonetheless. This man before me is flesh and bone, which I think I have proven," he added boastfully. "I believe in what my eyes can see and my hands can touch, and I refuse to believe that this pathetic, bleeding old man before me is some creature come out of myth to punish us for our wrongdoings."

"Do you think me some great fool?" the Duke spat at the prisoner, emboldened by Gaston's confidence and incredulity. "I am no mere child to be so easily galled at the mention of a name. A creature of myth, my Lieutenant has named you. One of the old legends come to walk among us. Vinquist the Great: the man who was supposed to have been born over a thousand years ago and who possessed such power that no other could equal him. I think not," he laughed. "More likely you are some fool beggar who happened to hear the tales told by men deep in their cups on your journey to my fair town. So here you are, a broken old man claiming to be the greatest wizard ever to walk the earth yet hanging helplessly from the wall of my jail—you who dared to come into my town like some wild beast and abduct my daughter.

My patience is wearing thin, so I will ask you one last time: where is my daughter?"

The last words from the Duke were immediately followed by a backhand slap that, while not nearly as powerful as Gaston's, still managed to open up a cut above Vinquist's eye. Blood ran down his face, mingled with sweat, and stung his eyes, painting a gruesome visage of his face.

"A beast you call me, Duke of La Croix. I think you are the deranged one here, not I. Call me what you will. I have given you my name, and it is your choice to believe me or not. But I will give you one last chance to release me and save your town, which I know you care about even more than your daughter. Let me leave here now. Forget the search for your daughter and no further harm will come to you and your town."

Suddenly, one of the two guards stationed in the room cleared his throat and spoke up, "Are you the same Vinquist from the village of Renwold, some forty years ago?"

The Duke's ire was raised anew by the man speaking out of turn, but still the question struck him as funny somehow. Could it be that this simpleton actually believed the lunatic's claims? The Duke made a mental note to himself that as soon as this troublesome business with his daughter was resolved, he would personally see to the hiring of some new guards. More men like Gaston, he thought—men who didn't do too much thinking on their own and who did what they were told when they were told, not superstitious fools such as these before him, so easily entranced by the mention of a name.

"Ah yes, I have heard the tale of the legendary wolves of Renwold," interrupted the Duke. "It being a town not far removed from my own duchy, I received scattered reports of strange occurrences surrounding the arrival of a man in black. I discarded them as the superstitious ramblings of a townsfolk bent on keeping honest tradesmen from making a decent living. Imagine it—a drifter, a stranger who had no stake in the matter, arriving and causing that big of a stir. The rumors said he not only freed a band of twelve slave children from their master's caravan , but that he also turned them into wolves that came back and killed the slave trader and his entire crew that night while they slept under the light of the full moon. Ever since, good merchants like the slave trader, from whom I, myself, have purchased some of my workforce, won't set foot near the crossroads of Harmon-Gleese where it happened. The trade in our poor neighboring village has been all but shut down. I think that it was nothing more than common thievery by a group of highway brigands who made up some outrageous tale at the next inn they came to."

The Duke's tone had slowly begun to rise as he told the tale, and the last words were shouted at the guard who had spoken out of turn. However, the young man did not look properly chastened at being so addressed by the

Duke. He instead turned to his companion, who looked at the Duke and said, "Beg your pardon, sir, but we had kin in Renwold, and the story we heard from them is very much the way you told it. Wolves can still be heard at night near the crossroads, and some say that a pack of children can be seen running through the surrounding woods in the daytime, though few have been brave enough to enter the woods to see for themselves. All who risk venturing into the forest are never heard from again. Part of what you say is true, though. It was as if, after that night, the town had been poisoned and turned from a fair place of commerce into a ghost town. After the incident, all of our kinsfolk left there to seek a better life."

And with that, the lowly guard looked at the man chained to the wall and asked him, "Are you truly he? We saw with our own eyes the state of Renwold, and I have personally spent a night near the crossroads sleepless for the howling. I saw glowing eyes lurking in the woods near the road. We are but simple men and understand that events beyond our reach are unfolding here, so I beseech you, sir, if you are who you claim to be, let us leave this place."

The guard had boldly stepped up until he was merely a foot away from the man on the wall and found his gaze met squarely and without fear by their prisoner.

"You have heard what occurred in Renwold and know the lengths to which I am prepared to go. Leave this town tonight and never return, for it has no future. Ride to the city of Carne. There, you will seek out a man named Alain Jacoby and tell him that Reginald sends his best and to be prepared for a visit from an old friend."

"Bah!" the Duke exclaimed, interrupting the dialogue between the two men. "I've heard enough. I don't know who you think you are, but you can't crawl into my town like some ragged beast …"

"That's twice," the man called Vinquist said as he glanced levelly at the Duke, who never paused in his tirade.

"… and abduct my daughter right in the middle of my own market square. Now you have the audacity to give my guards orders of treason while you are strung up in my jail cell. You are nothing but a foul beast, and I will see to it that I have the truth of you before I remand you over to the custody of my very eager Lieutenant."

Saying this, he glanced at Gaston, who stood to one side of the room sweating and tapping the riding crop gently against the palm of his hand. He had the look of a caged animal who longs for release to expend its pent-up energy.

"However, there is still the pressing matter of my daughter's return, so we will leave you to think matters over for a while. Perhaps then we can begin our questioning again," the Duke crooned in the tone of a man who expected everything to go his way. "By the way, there must have been some clue as to this man's identity in his possessions. What did you find in his belongings when you searched them earlier?" he demanded of the guards.

The two men looked at each other for the right answer, for the possessions found in the man's cloak were very interesting and might have indeed provided some clues to his identity. Hidden deep in the folds of the cloak were a blood-soaked handkerchief, a lock of hair, a small obsidian bowl and, last of all, a petrified claw, six inches in length and razor sharp, that belonged to no creature either man had ever encountered. Just as they were both about to answer the Duke and turn over their findings, the older of the two was surprised to hear his own voice come from his mouth.

"We didn't find anything on his person. Just an old cloak and staff. That's all that he had with him, nothing to tell us who, or what, he is." As the words the guard had no control over poured from his mouth like some sort of rehearsed mantra, he looked at the prisoner and saw the old man staring at him from intense, black eyes and felt his voice in his mind providing him with the words necessary to sway the Duke and Gaston from looking in his cloak.

He also heard the man's voice telling him to do as he was bid and leave this town tonight. "Ride to Carne," it said. "I have need of your services this night and may have need of you again. Tell Alain the exact message I gave you and follow any orders he gives you as if they were my own. This evening will not be the last you see of me, I promise you."

As the guard felt the voice withdraw from his mind, Vinquist turned to the Duke and addressed him for what would be the last time. "A beast you have called me, Meirmont. Three times you charged me with that title. Even after I gave you chance after chance to save yourself and your precious town, you persisted. Thus, you have named your curse. Once called is a mistake, second marks you a fool, but three times marks your demise. This town is cursed forever after this night by my hand, and you shall soon witness the doom that you have brought upon yourselves. But you, dear Duke of La Croix, will I charge with a different fate. Since you love your town so much and have made it the whole of your existence, I will let you keep it forever. No matter how long you live, you shall remain the broken Duke of this town and shall endure here for all of your days. That is your curse: life unending in what is soon to become a shadow of the town you love so much. This is the fate that you have set down for yourself, and I leave you to live with it."

Gaston grabbed him by his face and looked at him with eyes filled with a great need to do violence. "We shall talk later, old man, for our time together is just beginning," he said, and then he sat a bucket of water on the floor at

Vinquist's feet, just out of reach. "You can stare at the water and think about how thirsty you are while you wait for our return. And I warn you, your tone had better change before then, or things will turn very ugly for you."

Saying this, he grabbed Vinquist's head and sharply smacked the back of it against the wall, rendering him unconscious, or so Gaston thought. He told the guards to leave the cloak and staff where they were and hurried to follow the hastily departing form of the Duke as he exited the room. They were soon followed by the two guards who, without any spoken word to those in the jail, walked straight past the staring forms of the Duke and the Gaston and out the front door, eager to be away from that place as quickly as possible. The Duke reached into a cabinet and poured himself a glass of brandy while they sat down to wait.

Had they bothered to check the cell moments later, they would have been greeted by the wizard's head raising up as the shackles silently slid from his wrists.

Chapter Twelve

"Why won't you let me finish this tonight?" Gaston asked, the disappointment etched plain in his voice as he hurled his empty glass into the fireplace. "If you let me try again, I know I can get the answers you need."

"If we let you at him again, he will have lost the ability to speak before you even begin asking him questions," said Captain Dupree, who up until that point had chosen to keep silent and quietly observe the night's events unfold. "It's answers we need, Gaston, not a bloodbath, no matter how much it galls you not to do this your way. Let him rest a bit. The main objective here is to find the Duke's daughter before daybreak, not for you to have your fun at the expense of some helpless old man."

The animosity between the two men was palpable. The Duke realized that if he did not intervene soon, they would happily tear each other to pieces in front of his eyes, and there was still business to attend to this night. He needed them both too much for the task at hand. There would be plenty of time later for the squaring of debts between them. The day's events had reaffirmed his belief that most of the people in his employ were incompetent. If they could not keep a sickly young girl under control, then they couldn't be trusted to do anything, and once this whole mess was over, he would see to the re-staffing of his town.

"I don't know how you do things sitting in the comfort of the Duke's gracious lodgings," Gaston retorted, "but down here in the streets we get answers any way we can. The last time I looked, we were in my jail conducting an investigation, not in the Duke's privy chamber. If you can hold your tongue—and the contents of your stomach—long enough, you might actually learn something, boy." Balling his hands into fists, he took a step towards Dupree.

"Enough!" the Duke shouted with enough authority to freeze both men where they stood. "I've had enough of your petty bickering for one night. This isn't about you two; it's about finding my daughter before this night ends. And unless one of you can magically make her appear before me on this very spot, that old man in there is the only real hope we have. I know it will take a while for Gaston's handiwork to wear off, but I want you to get some answers for me before he breaks. He'll face justice in the morning, but tonight he has the information we need. Gaston, I will be sorely disappointed if, when I return, you have not accomplished this simple task."

A smug smile crept onto Dupree's face as his nemesis was admonished by the Duke, but he was not quick enough to erase it before Meirmont turned in his direction.

"My faithful Captain, need I remind you that you have failed me worst of all this night, seeing as how my daughter is still missing. As head of my household guard, I hold you chiefly responsible for this grievous oversight. I want you out there looking for her, not in here picking fights with my inquisitor, and if she is not found by daybreak, my good man, I will see to it that Gaston has some questions to ask you."

The color blanched from Dupree's face as he looked from his Duke to Gaston, who now wore the most wicked grin that he had ever seen. Turning quickly, he saluted the Duke smartly and opened the door to leave and begin his search anew. All three men took pause to notice that a storm of tremendous ferocity seemed to be building outside and realized it wouldn't be long before they had to contend with the elements in their search for Sophie.

"What else can go wrong tonight? It isn't even the season for storms, and we have what looks to be a huge one on our front doorstep," the Duke muttered to no one in particular. Turning to the nighttime jail guard who had been roused from his slumber by the men's raised voices, he said, "Go and check on our prisoner and make sure he is still alive. Hopefully, he will be able to talk to us a little more tonight."

The guard, grateful for any chance to be out of the room where the Duke and Gaston waited, hastily grabbed a torch and headed down the hallway to the steps leading below. When he reached the bottom, he paused. This part of the jail seemed darker than he had ever encountered it. All of the light had bled from the hallway, and the only sounds he could hear were his own rapid breathing and the thunder from the approaching storm.

Standing before the door at the end of the hall, he reached out his trembling hand and inserted the key in the lock. He cursed himself for a fool—after all, what harm could one old man, chained and beaten nearly to death, do to him. "I'll just have a quick look to make sure he's still breathing and be off," he said to himself, turning the key with a sweaty palm. As he opened the door, he found that the room was even darker than the hallway.

Looking around, he waited for his eyes to adjust and tried to place where the prisoner should be. He waved the torch before him. He had not taken two steps when he saw a pair of eyes staring at him, not from where the chains were, but rather three feet in front of him.

Extending his trembling hand, his body froze in fear. The old man, dressed in his recovered robe, stared directly into his eyes. The guard felt a trickle of warmth snake its way down his leg as his bladder emptied itself, his mind paralyzed by the sight in front of him.

"You checked on me and found me well asleep. It will be some time before your good Duke can resume his questioning." The voice in his mind shocked him from his trance, and he began to nod his head dumbly as the man's gaze never wavered.

"You will report to the Duke what I have said, and then I think it wise if you left this place for the rest of the evening. Join the search for the Duke's daughter in the town. There is nothing more you can do here tonight."

The guard, needing no more permission to leave, turned and quickly slammed the door behind him, not even bothering to lock it. Taking the steps to the main part of the jail two at a time, he willed himself to calm down before he reached the room where the Duke and Gaston awaited his return.

When he entered, the Duke said, "Well, is he awake yet?"

"No sir. I checked, and he's still asleep. It will be some time before you can resume your questioning. I'll go and join the search for your daughter, as there is nothing more I can do here."

Before the Duke had any time to object, the guard left the room and headed out into the teeth of what was quickly shaping up to be a particularly nasty storm. The Duke turned to Gaston and said, "I'm leaving to check on the progress of my daughter's search. I'll return in the morning, though. That should give our friend downstairs ample time to recuperate. But I warn you, Gaston, do not harm him before I return, or the consequences shall be severe."

He pulled the hood of his cloak up as he left the jail, hoping to find things much as he had left them upon his return, not knowing how wrong he truly was.

Chapter Thirteen

As the guard's fading footsteps grew less audible in his cell, Vinquist began to assess his body to see just how much damage he had sustained. A brief check revealed nothing he couldn't overcome in time. For the time being, though, he would have to deal with the pain. What he had to do this night would take a considerable amount of effort. Having fought many battles, he was no stranger to pain, and tonight's would serve as only a minor hindrance.

He ran his hands, which had taken on a slightly white glow, over his face as if he were washing it in the cool water of a mountain stream. As he took them away, he felt satisfied that the cuts and bruises had faded away and that his lip had returned to its normal size. He knew a couple of ribs were broken, but those would take more time and effort to mend than he had at the moment, so he resolved to heal those when he got the chance and set about constructing the demise of La Croix.

He paused as he always did before committing to a course of action that involved the lives of so many. He asked himself if what he was doing was truly the last recourse left him by the people of this town. After a moment's reflection, he resigned himself to the task at hand and reminded himself that those here had sealed their own fate, as had all those in so many towns that he had visited over the years—towns like Renwold. Their punishments were all different, of course, each town owing its demise to different catalysts, but the end results were always the same. But this time something nagged at the back of his mind. More than once during his brief time in La Croix, he had felt the tickle of premonition and knew these events would reach far beyond the walls of this town.

Mind steeled for the effort tonight's magic would cost, he knelt on the ground in the middle of the room, drawing his power to him. He removed the items he would need from the folds of his cloak and carefully set them out on the floor before him, all the while humming an incantation. The room charged with growing intensity at the invocation of great power, and the storm gathered nearer as he continued his spell. Great peals of thunder and lightning strikes echoed ever closer. He took no notice of these things as he laid out a small bowl in front of him. Into it, he placed the lock of hair he had taken from the Duke's daughter during their last, desperate embrace. Next, he removed the handkerchief he had used to wipe the blood from her forehead and held it over the bowl. As his chanting increased, the dried blood on the cloth became liquid and dripped into the vessel, raising hisses of steam as each drop fell.

Next, Vinquist let three drops of his own blood fall into the bowl, adding some of his own essence to make the spell complete and to remind himself that, whatever came of tonight, he was forever tied to the fate of this town and its people. Finally, as the storm outside reached a crescendo, he pulled a claw from his cloak and held it in front of his face, contemplating what would come from such a small thing, and said:

"I require protection such as only you can provide. Forgive me, but the need is great, and only one such as yourself can fulfill all that is required here. The choice is hers as to how long you will be needed."

And saying so, he dropped the claw into the bowl where the entire contents ignited in a blue flame. He threw his arms into the air, releasing his magic into the bowl to complete the spell. A blinding flash of light filled the room, as if the very essence of the mounting storm outside had spilled over into it, casting the scene in shadows of green and purple against the stained walls of the cell. Then everything faded back to the safe, neutral colors they had been prior to the spell's casting. Vinquist slumped to the floor, exhausted, and waited for the sound that he knew would come to him out of the darkness.

A few hours later, an inhuman growl came to the wizard's ears through the cacophony of the raging storm. Any other person who heard the noise would have dismissed it as a peal of thunder and nothing more, but the old man knew what was coming to him that night. He thought of Gaston upstairs anxiously awaiting the next chance to question him and how the man's night was about to unexpectedly change for the worse. A very wicked grin spread across his face as he leveled himself to his feet.

Chapter Fourteen

It had been several hours since the Duke and his captain had left Gaston at the jail with the precise instructions that he was not, under any circumstances, to "question" their prisoner until they returned. They were weak—all of them—Gaston thought to himself, as he paced once again over the floor of the jail's common room. He knew they would only get answers from the old man by force, so after a few moments of indulging himself with visions of the adulations the Duke would bestow upon him when he returned and found that he, Gaston the simple, had unlocked the key to finding his daughter, he steeled himself to redouble his efforts with the man downstairs.

He downed another swig of his brandy then hastened towards the stairwell. Suddenly, the door to the jail blew open, revealing a ghastly scene of the storm assailing the town outside. All of the torches in the room were blown out by the gust of wind that rushed through the jail. Gaston hurried over to shut the door and made sure that it was well-latched this time. He marveled at his good fortune—that he was left behind in the warm, dry jail while all those other poor souls were out there, mucking about half-drowned, and that they were aimlessly looking for the Duke's daughter when he was about to solve that riddle singlehandedly and make fools of them all.

Bumping into a table on his way to relight one of the lamps, he cursed the darkness and only wished to find some light so he wouldn't fall and break his neck before he made his way downstairs. As he reached the lamp hanging on the wall and prepared to light it, senses sharpened by years of surviving life in the seedier parts of towns keyed him to the fact that he was not alone and that whoever was there was standing directly across from him, somewhere on the other side of the room. The maelstrom outside, coupled with the darkness of the room, prevented him from gaining a more precise sense of where his company stood.

Gaston felt the other's presence and realized that whoever, or whatever, it was must have been much bigger than he. His heart skipped a beat at the thought of being attacked in the pitch black by an unseen assailant. He was reaching for the cudgel that hanged handily on his belt when he heard a low growl emanate from the corner, building in intensity until the very planks of the wall vibrated under his hand.

Raising his arm in preparation for the blow was as far as he got, as a blur of movement too fast for any human reached him, and he was thrown across the room as easily as if he had been made of paper. Before he could regain his senses and defend himself, his assailant was upon him, a suffocating mass of teeth, claws, fur and wind. The first rush was over before he knew it, and he slowly stood to guard against the next attack, blood dripping from a dozen wounds covering his entire body. His fighter's instincts told him that he was no match for this thing and that he should try to get to the door, if for nothing else than to let in some of the light from outside so that he could see his attacker and better defend himself.

Dragging his left leg, which had been badly broken when he was thrown against the wall, he started edging towards the door, feeling about him with the cudgel. He had moved a few feet and started to hope for an escape when he felt a presence form beside him as if it had appeared from the darkness itself. A sharp claw, nearly eight inches in length, traced down his cheek as it said in a voice that was somehow human yet horribly not, "Gaston."

A tear slid down his face as the claw was joined by four others and a massive fist grabbed the hand holding his club as if it were no more than a baby's holding a rattle. The pressure on his arm was excruciating as the thing pulled him clear off the ground, and he saw his own terror-filled eyes reflected in those of his assailant. Still fighting for his life, he kicked vainly at the area where the creature's body must have been and met only air as the eyes before him flashed dangerously, just moments before he was tossed across the room once again.

With the last of his terror-born strength, Gaston began dragging his broken, bleeding body in the direction of his original destination, the stairs leading to the cell below. He hoped to possibly distract this thing with the old man while he escaped. As he reached the top of the staircase, however, his head was grabbed between two massive paws, and he was flung screaming at the top of his lungs, headlong down the steps. The last thing he saw before consciousness finally fled him was a huge shadow disappearing at the doorway above and the old man's face, which looked down at him, the prisoner no longer chained and dressed in his cloak once again.

"Well, well, my good man—how our fortunes can change in such a short amount of time. I trust my friend was not too overeager to offer you tutelage in the arts of pain and fear. It seemed a lesson you must learn, and there really is no time like the present, is there, Gaston?"

Gaston could do nothing but whimper meekly before darkness closed in on the edges of his vision.

Nearly an hour later, a thick fog blanketed the town, making vision impossible, and the search for the Duke's daughter was given up for the night. A figure emerged from the entrance to the jail and made its way unseen and unheard in the direction of the city's eastern gate, the one that led towards the woods nearly three leagues away. It was joined by another figure, this one cloaked in black and towering over the first. Not a word was spoken between the two as they made their way silently through the deserted streets. Turning down a side street in the baking district, the smaller of the two figures halted and knocked on a door that was barely distinguishable from the wall in which it was set and nearly invisible to one who was not looking for it. The knock was answered, and the door slid open, just wide enough to allow one other figure, smaller than either of the other two and cloaked in gray, to exit into the alleyway. Nothing passed between the three as they all fell into step together and proceeded in the direction of the gate.

If any had been around to bear witness, they would have been truly surprised to see the passage of the three, followed moments later by many more people who were moving less secretly, for they had no fear of discovery this night.

Early the next morning, as he returned for his usual watch, the old jailer was surprised to find the door already open and the common room destroyed. Broken furniture littered the room, and there were trails of blood in several places. Gaston's cudgel, or rather its splintered remains, lay near the entrance to the stairway. He hesitated to go back down, the memories of last night fresh in his mind, but curiosity won out, and he cautiously headed down the steps.

Nothing could have prepared him for the sight that greeted him when he moved down the hall and entered the room. That the old man was gone wasn't the surprising thing. He hadn't expected to find him here this morning anyway. What he hadn't expected, however, was to find the head jailor, Gaston, chained by the same manacles he had slid onto the old man's wrists not twenty-four hours before. Gaston was unconscious, beaten and bloodied almost beyond recognition. Pinned to his chest was a note written in a refined, regal hand, which would have been admirable had the note not been written in the jailer's blood. It read: "Your unmaking is of your own doing. Seek that which is lost at your own peril and only by the light of the full moon. The girl is finally free, as are so many others. Leave them their peace or pay the price. You have been forewarned." The note was signed with only a "V."

The old guard didn't touch anything as he bolted from the jail as fast as he could in the direction of the Duke's manor. As he sped through the town, he heard the grumbling of the merchants who had awakened to find that all of their help had disappeared during the long night.

Chapter Fifteen

Early the next morning, as the sun began illuminating the damage the tempest had wreaked upon the town the night before, the Duke was jolted from a restless slumber by an insistent banging on his door. After leaving the jail, secure in his belief that Gaston would deliver the required results, he endured a terribly uncomfortable carriage ride through the storm back to his mansion. Sleep was elusive, though, as the sounds outside kept him awake. Restless, he listened to the sounds of the storm and imagined that the sky had opened up and eagerly devoured his beautiful town. A few more glasses of his favorite brandy, however, finally tipped the scales in his battle against consciousness. But even this small victory was of little consolation, for he was assailed the whole night through with nightmares, in which his daughter stood with the old beggar, the two of them laughing at him in his folly as they together wrought the storm that consumed his steading.

Try as he might, he could not ignore the sound. Whoever kept knocking at his door was either insistent or reckless, not caring a whit for the consequences of waking his Grace, especially after the terrible night he had spent dealing with the events surrounding his daughter's disappearance. Resigning himself to a day of dealing with the storm's effects, he grunted and heaved himself out of bed, noting with great annoyance that someone had let the fire in the hearth go out, which had allowed an unseasonable chill to seep through the walls. His mood darkening, he threw on his robe and stormed over to the door to admit his visitor and perhaps find a suitable outlet for his building rage.

Throwing open the door, he expected to see the maid with his usual breakfast of poached pheasant eggs, fresh bread, plum jelly and tea but was greeted by the sight of his bedraggled captain of the guard instead.

"I hope for your sake, Captain Dupree, that you have a truly important reason for rousing me from my sleep at this ungodly hour. If not, your morning shall be cut very short indeed. And where in seven hells is Adeline with my breakfast?"

Dupree stared hard at the Duke before going on one knee, acknowledging the audacity of his brazen intrusion. But his news could not wait. He was shocked at the sight of the man standing in the doorway before him. The Duke, who usually looked so neatly put together and groomed, now looked as one who had spent a very long night battling his worst nightmares. A streak of gray had appeared in the hair at his forehead, and his skin had taken on a faint, grayish tinge. The circles under his eyes were so dark that he appeared to have anointed himself with pitch. The captain also noticed that the Duke seemed to be clutching a single gold coin in his left hand as if he feared it might be taken from him at any moment. He knew he should not comment on the Duke's appearance, however—there being far larger things at stake here than his liege's lack of sleep—so he launched into his rehearsed litany.

"Pardon Your Grace, but you need to come to the jail right away. It can't be explained—it's just something you'll have to see for yourself. Will you please come with us as quickly as possible?"

The Duke could see there was no rest to be had, as Dupree and his companion stationed themselves outside his door. He hadn't noticed the old jailer standing behind his good captain until the man moved nervously from his hiding place behind the larger man, all the while wringing his hands and avoiding the Duke's gaze.

"I can't wait to finish this business concerning the old man and my daughter, who I trust is safely asleep in her bed this very moment, Captain. As soon as we get to the jail, gather some workers and build a scaffolding in the shadow of the statue in the town square so I can have him hanged and get this whole mess over with. I have a town to oversee, and the repairs after last night's storm are bound to take time and money. Those I have, sir, but what I am in short supply of this morning is patience, so if you'll wait here while I change, I'll see what it is that you have to show me."

The captain and the old jailer merely stared at one another as the door slammed shut in their faces. They shrugged their shoulders, resigned to wait until the Duke came out of his apartment to escort him to the jail and show him their discovery. They were surprised, then, when the Duke reappeared only moments later and, with a scrunched up his face, said, "Oh, and Captain, you might want to consider taking a bath as soon as possible—you both reek!" With that last barb, the door slammed shut in their faces, and the Duke took his time preparing for his final visit with the prisoner.

The first thought that struck Meirmont as he and the two men made their way through his cavernous mansion was how empty and quiet everything seemed. Normally, servants would be scurrying about, even at this early hour, carrying out the routine chores required to keep such a large household in running order, but they didn't encounter anyone on their way to the stables. Also conspicuously absent were the delicious smells that normally emanated from the kitchen. The Duke loved his food and had spared no expense in bringing in some of the best cooks in the entire kingdom to cater to his exotic tastes. However, as they passed by, not a soul moved, and the ovens, which were constantly tended, had gone cold sometime in the night. The feeling of things terribly amiss started taking hold in the Duke's belly, and he wondered what other surprises awaited him this day.

Exiting through a side door that led directly to the stables, they had a clear view of the road at the front of the estate as they hurried over to where the Duke's horse stood saddled. Meirmont stopped short when he noticed that a large group of businessmen and women had gathered themselves at the gate and seemed to be yelling something about their lost workers. As they caught sight of him exiting his home, their pitch intensified, and the tiny feeling of dread that had started in the pit of his stomach worked its way up and wrapped itself like a constrictor around his heart.

"What is going on, Captain? What aren't you telling me?"

"Begging your pardon again, sir, but you need to see what happened at the jail first—then things might become a little clearer." The captain was clearly reluctant to say any more before they made it to their destination, so the Duke just shook his head and led the men towards the center of town. As an afterthought, he also wondered what had become of his daughter while he slept—if perhaps she had been washed away with the storm as had apparently half of the town.

The damage was tremendous. Windows were busted out all over, and debris cluttered the streets, washed there from the shops and vendors' stalls nearby. Meirmont's heart sank even further as he tallied up the enormous cost it would take to return his town to its former glory. All thoughts of money fled him, however, as soon as they turned a corner and saw the open door of the jail waiting for them at the end of the street.

They handed the reins of their horses to one of the guards, all of whom seemed afraid of entering the jail and were content to stand watch outside while they waited for their captain to arrive. The Duke merely glanced at the men stationed there and followed his captain and the jailer inside. Nothing he had imagined could have prepared him for the sight that greeted his eyes. The broken windows were stained red with what appeared to be blood, casting the scene within with a macabre light.

It looked as if a battle between a hundred men had been fought within these walls, so complete was the destruction. Furniture that had only a few hours ago been neatly arranged lay splintered and tossed about. A smell of fear hung in the air, mingled with an animal musk that the Duke doubted would ever leave the place. "What on earth happened here?" he mumbled as he moved about seeking some sign that would explain what had occurred after his departure. Finishing his inspection, he looked up to see his captain staring at him, waiting for him to say something. The only words that came out of his mouth, however, were "Where is Gaston, and where is my prisoner?" The Captain mutely raised his hand and pointed towards the stairwell leading down to the room where the old man had been kept the night before.

Meirmont grabbed one of the torches from a sconce on the wall, lit it and made his way down the steps. He sincerely hoped to find the answers to all of his questions below but all the while feared what he would find could only raise more questions. As he reached the bottom, the hair on his arms and on the back of his neck rose up, reacting to the lingering feel of the strong magic done there the night before. No guards were stationed, and no torches burned on this lower level of the prison, restricting his field of vision to the small area lit by the single torch he carried. As he turned the corner and finally entered the room, he could feel the sense of dread squeeze just a little bit tighter around his heart as he extended the torch and was greeted by a scream of terror from the wall where the old man had been chained the evening before.

The Captain and jailer had elected to stay at the top of the steps while the Duke went down to conduct his investigation. They had already been down and had no desire to revisit the scene. It was already etched in their minds forever. When they heard the scream, they turned and looked at one another wondering what they should do next, but they had only to wait a few moments for the Duke to scamper up the long staircase clutching the note left on Gaston's chest in his hand. Neither man said anything as the Duke replaced his torch in the wall and turned in their direction.

"I don't know what happened here, Captain, but for God's sake, get him down from there. After you do that, gather fifteen of your best men and come to my house. First, he spirits my daughter away and then my workers? Ha! This is my town, and I say what goes here."

Turning away and heading towards the door, expecting his orders to be carried out without question, the Duke turned back at the last second and said, "One other thing, Captain. Find my son before you come. You're going hunting."

Chapter Sixteen

Several hours later, as the sun began to lose its daily battle with the darkness and the moon arced its way victorious over the sky, the Captain stood with the Duke's elder son and twenty of his hand-picked men staring at something that, by all natural means, should not have existed. As the night-time chill began to take effect in the clearing of the woods where they had stopped, a deep mist began to gather, slowly obscuring the line between the clearly visible and mere fragments of the imagination. The men had been arguing among themselves for several minutes, and while they came to agree that the citadel did, in fact, exist and was now directly in front of them at the end of the cart path, none of them were sure of what to do about it. Brendan swore in exasperation as he slapped his gloves against his thigh and questioned his father's sanity in picking him for this particular task.

He had been rudely awakened in his bedchamber earlier that afternoon by the Captain, who declared that the Duke had commanded him to lead a hunting party to where his sister and the prisoner were thought to have disappeared, along with the entire working staff of his father's town no less. Cursing both the Captain and his father for ruining such a good, drunken sleep, he roused himself from his bed and made the journey down to the drawing room. There he found his father restlessly pacing, eagerly awaiting his arrival. They had spent the next hour discussing the events of the previous day, and after arguing that there must be a more capable hunter to lead these men, Brendan realized his father's will was immovable and relented. He hoped only to get the whole ordeal over with as soon as possible, so he could finally get some sleep.

Now he stood amongst his men, who were awaiting orders, and wished there was someone who could tell him what to do next. The garrison had been long abandoned, reclaimed by the earth from which it had sprung up so long ago. No one had reported seeing it, much less visiting it, in some time, yet here it was, looking not only whole but quite occupied. Lights could be seen burning in the upper windows of the keep, and every now and then a shadow would quickly pass before one of them, indicating that the keep was either lived in or haunted.

"Maybe both," he mused to himself as he finally began directing his men to spread out and space themselves along the eight-foot briar fence surrounding the castle. "Funny," he thought as he pulled his sword, which was really nothing more than a decoration piece, "I don't recall there being a hedge of wild rose bushes out here."

Whatever his beleaguered eyes might say, he had been sent out to retrieve his sister. Whether she be dead or alive at this point had no real bearing on him. His duty was to the man who financed his extravagant lifestyle and whom he addressed as "father" in the vain hopes that the term of endearment would win him a very large inheritance once the old man passed away. They proceeded upon the wall of thorns, and each man was slowly cut off from the one next to him by the thickening mist. After only a few steps towards the keep, no one could tell his place in relation to the rest of the group, and the full moon's reflections in the fog had them soon believing that a creature made up of mist and moonlight had detached itself from the castle wall and disappeared in their direction.

Cursing his father for sending him out on a night like tonight, Brendan gripped his sword even tighter and crept through the one opening afforded them in the barrier of foliage where the castle gate once would have been. He had taken a couple of steps through, when a grunt, followed by a wet smack, sounded thirty feet to his right. Realizing he was alone in the sea of fog and that he couldn't even make out the forms of his men in the dark, he did what any other reasonable man would do in his situation: he panicked.

In a shaky voice, he quietly called out in both directions, hoping for a signal that all was well, but he received only muffled cries and an occasional low-pitched growl in response. Suddenly, the night erupted in sound as all the men sensed that they had stepped within the reach of danger's claws and had no hope of escaping unscathed. Swords rang free of scabbards, and arrows were fitted to bow strings seeking the foe that moved so easily and silently through their midst. Beginning with the men on the outer edges of the group, each began to disappear as their unseen attacker moved with inhuman quickness and stealth, picking them off one by one.

Several of the men panicked and fled back in the direction they had come, not stopping until they had reached the safety of the town's walls. Others began swinging their swords at any movement they detected in the unnatural mist that encircled them. Those with bows took aim in the direction of every noise they heard. At the sound of the arrow's thump, they would let out a premature cry of "I got it!," only to be followed by human cries of pain from the unsuspecting companions who'd fallen to the ground with neatly-fletched shafts protruding from their bodies.

Brendan began to retreat back into the relative safety of the woods they had come from—had it been only minutes before? Time had lost all meaning in their maze of mist and pain, and he could only hope that he would somehow make it out alive. He knew his chances of surviving were better than those of the others. The Captain of the guard was only ten feet to his left, and he, of all those here, would be able to get him out safely. Crouching and slowly making his way back, he called into the mist, "Captain Dupree, are you there? We need to retreat! Captain?"

The only answering sound was the Captain's voice, raised several octaves, in a squeal of panic as several smart thuds sounded from his general direction. When the noise finally ended and only the stillness answered his query, Brendan feared the worst and began to scamper a bit more quickly towards the woods. He stopped short when he heard a snap behind him and watched in amazement as the Captain's bow came sailing over his head, only to land in a broken heap of polished wood and string two feet in front of him. Turning back to the area from which the bow had come, he had to duck in astonishment as the Captain himself sailed out of the mist, landing bloodied and unconscious on top of his bow. His eyes barely had time to widen in sheer terror at the sight in front of him before he was thrown to the ground and pinned under what felt like a massive paw in the middle of his back.

Dazed from the blow, Brendan didn't fully realize what was happening until he had been lifted from the ground like a doll and found himself eye to eye with whatever had attacked him and his men. The fact that he was held at arm's length and that his feet dangled nearly a foot off of the ground gave testament to the size and strength of his foe. Realizing it could easily kill him if it so pleased, Brendan knew that his only chance at survival was to talk his way out of the situation—granted, of course, that the beast could comprehend him. Reluctantly, he forced himself to look straight ahead into the glowing pair of eyes, the only thing visible except for an occasional glimpse of reddish-black hair and long teeth beneath the cowl of a large, hooded robe.

"Leave this place, Prince of La Croix, before it is too late. Leave and do not return here," rumbled the beast, only inches from his face, in a voice Brendan never would have attributed to such a creature. It spoke in a baritone, to be sure, but its voice also had a musical quality to it that did not match its speaker.

"I will leave once I have retrieved my sister and safely delivered her to my father with whom she belongs. I don't know who or what you are, or what you have done with Sophie, but these are my father's lands, and his law, not yours, governs here." Brendan's indignation at being handled in such a way won out over his better judgment, and the petty lordling he truly was began to show.

"Your sister? What do you care for her? To you she was only another one of your playthings, someone to torment. When you were younger, you brought your friends into her room and goaded her into one of her attacks. You never loved her. She is far better off now, away from your family. Abandon this quest, if you value your meager life."

"I love my dear sister more than life itself and only wish to see her and my father's workers back home safely where they belong." Brendan hoped that the feigned sincerity in his voice could fool the creature into believing his intentions were good.

"Lies are not becoming and will only make me angry. You are finished here. Take what's left of your men and scamper home. You will not get what you came for. I have been gentle today. Should others decide to seek us out, they will not receive the same consideration. You have been forewarned."

With that, the creature tossed Brendan aside, where he landed facedown next to the groaning Captain. By the time he turned back to get a better look at his attacker, all that remained was the mist. Having gathered the few survivors of their search party, he began the long haul home. He carried with him the beast's admonition to stay far away from the old citadel and wondered how his father would react.

Chapter Seventeen

Meirmont Rochelle, Duke of La Croix and by all accounts one of the richest men of the kingdom, was exhausted. Of course, he was angry, no doubt, but underlying his sense of wrongs done to him and his own was a weariness that went deeper than bone, one that seemed to reach down to his very soul and leech the lifeblood from his veins. Only coursing streams of utter apathy and an undercurrent of greed kept him going through the daily motions of life. It had come as a great surprise to everyone present that, instead of berating his son for failing to return his daughter and workers, he had simply rubbed his aching temples and announced that he was retiring to bed.

Even the Duke couldn't explain why he hadn't exploded in a sudden rush of fury. As much as he would have enjoyed such a tirade, especially one directed at his disappointing weasel of a son, he couldn't seem to muster the energy to do anything but go upstairs to his room, sit at his cherry wood desk and continue to count and re-count the piles of money he had stacked there earlier in the day. He sighed when he sat down and saw, next to his money, the large pile of documented complaints that his merchants had eagerly heaped on his already overburdened plate. Missives detailing lost income, expenses that would have to be recouped and workers that would have to be replaced were stacked nearly as high as his head. Furthermore, the complaints detailed, many of the wealthy tourists had left, griping that La Croix was nothing like they had been led to believe. The Duke's reputation was as good as ruined. He gave the pile of papers a disapproving glance and swept them off of the desk with a single swing of his shaking arm.

Money would solve his problems and bring his town back to its former glory, he convinced himself. It had never failed him in the past. Nothing should keep him from bringing in more workers to undo the last thirty-six hours. He cursed the minute that the old man had entered his life and sent every vestige of normalcy that he had clung to for so long straight to hell.

But he didn't just want to rebuild his town, hire new workers and return things to the way they had always been. The part of him that was the same old Meirmont desired revenge on those who had done this to him, and so he set out to demonstrate, before all of those who had proven themselves incapable of handling the situation, the extent of his power and resolve. They were all the same, he thought, living off of his largesse and goodwill, only to throw his generosity back in his face when it no longer served them. His workers, Captain of the Guard, even his own children—none of them truly appreciated what a great man he had been to them and had failed him time and time again.

"But how to capture this beast?" he pondered aloud. "It has already proven a challenge for Dupree. It has incapacitated Gaston, who at this moment lies sobbing in a darkened room, screaming at anyone who approaches him. I guess I'll have to find people better suited for the job—men whose talents go outside of those normally allowed by law. But where to find hardy souls such as these?"

Steeling himself for what lay ahead, he grabbed quill, ink and paper and began furiously scribbling notices of his reward and a brief, if not too descriptive, job outline for which he was seeking men. The next day, he left town before the break of dawn and traveled to the nearby harbor, giving several of the papers to the captains of each of the ships anchored there. He instructed them to distribute the notices wherever they next made land. He then began a circuit of the nearby towns, imploring anyone who would listen to his plight to pass the word along to any they thought might be of service. He was determined that, when he was done, there wouldn't be a soul in the entire kingdom who was unaware of the great beast of La Croix, and he smiled at the thought of the fame and recognition it would surely bring him.

Chapter Eighteen

Several months later, two of the most dangerous men in the world stood hesitating in front of a closed oak door as they decided whether they wanted to enter now or wait for a better time later in the day. The larger man, well over seven feet tall and at least four-hundred pounds, cringed as a vase exploded against the other side of the door, followed by a long string of curses.

"Sounds like he's in one of his moods today," the smaller of the two men commented dryly without bothering to look up at his companion's face. Craning his neck all the time just to talk proved bothersome, so he stared straight ahead, dreading what await them on the other side of the door.

"Mmm ... vocabulary's improving, though," said his partner, whose voice sounded like it had issued from the pit of a deep, dark hole and could shake the very mortar from the castle walls. Vigan Marsh, titan of the empire and the most widely feared and recognized man this side of the ocean, didn't do much talking. He usually just kept his mouth shut and let his axe do the talking for him. It was so much more eloquent than his words anyway.

No one knew for certain where he came from, and not many had the courage to ask. About six years ago, a young man with long, braided hair and beard, both fire-red, had shown up in one of the border conflicts and struck fear into the hearts of all those he faced on the battlefield. None could stand against him. At the end of a day's fighting, he was often surrounded by a circle of the dead or dying. The most disconcerting thing about him, though, was the way he just roared with laughter the whole time he fought. As his reputation spread, he had caught the eye of a prince—the man who was, at present, issuing curses from behind the door. The Prince hired Marsh and sent him on a mission to persuade one of his landowners to pay his taxes. When Marsh returned to the castle carrying the man's head in a bag, along with the deed to all his lands, the Prince was so pleased that he offered to retain Marsh's services indefinitely. Over the next few years, Marsh traveled throughout the kingdom for the Prince and used his unique negotiation tactics, as the Prince liked to call them, in order to increase his liege's land and fortune.

Kragen, Marsh's companion, was known by most people as "The Hunter" and moved with a predatory grace. He was completely aware of his surroundings at all times. Not small compared to any but the giant man next to him, he stood well over six feet tall and kept his black hair cropped close to his head so that he would leave fewer traces in the field when tracking. His pointy face ended in a short goatee. He had the appearance of a weasel or mongoose, with flinty gray eyes that took in every detail of his surroundings.

He always wore the same outfit: body-hugging leathers that moved with him when hunting or tracking. He had several sets of different colors and wore each as the occasion suited him, choosing whatever blended with his surroundings. Today his leathers were gray, matching the bleak castle walls as well as his mood. Kragen opened the door and went in without bothering to knock. The Prince needed no other guards than Marsh and Kragen, for the mere sight of these two walking the halls, Marsh with his battle-axe, complimented by a couple of long daggers strapped to his waist for good measure, and Kragen with his brace of throwing knives, slim rapier and two custom-made crossbows, proved enough deterrence for any wishing harm to the nobleman under their stead.

As they entered, Kragen's lightning fast reflexes barely saved him from the blow of another expensive vase that crashed into the door directly where his head had been moments before. Marsh suppressed a snicker as they entered the room and faced the wrath of their lord, Prince Duvaliet.

It was wise, when one first made the acquaintance of the Prince, not to break into fits of laughter, no matter how tempting the thought may be. Although small in stature, standing slightly over five feet, the Prince, the older of two sons born to the Duke of Leyburn, housed one of the most brilliant and power-hungry minds in the kingdom.

"Hello, Duvaliet. Is everything alright? Morning going okay?" Kragen inquired as he brushed shards of plaster and glass from the shoulder of his shirt.

"How's it going? How do you think it's going, huntsman? The gall. The impudence. I simply cannot imagine what was going through his mind. Has the old man finally gone completely insane?" Having someone to vent to seemed to momentarily curb his ire, and he sat down to further study the maps he had spread open on top of his large desk. Rich hues of gold and green detailed the lands across the great eastern sea and the best sailing routes from here to there. He tossed the message he had been reading to Kragen to examine while he studied his maps, pausing every few moments to make a few marks on a sheet of parchment.

Kragen grabbed the missive from where it had landed at his feet and started to read. It was a message, a very angry one, from Duvaliet's father, the Duke. It stated, in no short terms and without the usual niceties, that in light of the Prince's recent actions, his father had denounced his claim to the Duchy. All lands, titles and power that would have been relinquished to Duvaliet upon his father's death were forfeited. The old man had named his younger son, David, heir to his holdings and advised Duvaliet that if he didn't stop crushing other lives simply to entertain himself the King would soon take an interest in the situation and teach him a little (his father had underlined the word "little" in the letter) lesson in respect.

"Did you notice how many times he mentions the incident at Bitterknot? As if that were the straw that broke the camel's back." Kragen had moved and was idly sitting on a divan near the desk to have a better look at the maps his liege (though if the money were cut off, perhaps liege no longer) had been poring over most of the day.

"And you know that wasn't our fault. Things wouldn't have gotten out of hand had he not suddenly decided to develop a conscience and ruin everything," the Prince shot back, barely sparing a glance as he studied a detailed map of a town called La Croix.

He didn't have to say who "he" was; they knew the man in question. The man who had previously traveled as their companion had finally shown his true colors in Bitterknot, which led to the incident the Prince's father spoke of in the letter. Kragen's hand went, by habit, to the scar running down his left cheek that was just now starting to fade in color from the angry red of roses in summer to the softer pink of the last rays of sun in the evening. Even the mighty Marsh, who had kept quiet during the entire exchange, cleared his throat and raised his sleeve to look at the long, jagged cut running up his sword arm. He was the only man to ever mark either of them in combat, and he had gotten away. Both had sworn their revenge and wouldn't rest until satisfaction was theirs.

They were broken from their reverie by the harsh sound of the Prince's laughter drifting from behind his massive oak desk. Both men looked first at each other and then to him to see what was suddenly so funny about their situation.

"But don't you see, boys? This doesn't really spell the end of anything. All I have to do in response is send Mr. Marsh here to visit my brother after we return from our expedition. That should remove any obstacles between me and what is rightfully mine. If the old man gives us any more problems after that, I may send Vigan to visit him as well. I may even go so far one day as to send him to visit the King, but first I'll need more men and more money. No, that day is yet far away. But for now, pack your bags and gather the men. We're going on a trip."

"And where exactly do we have more pressing business than this?" Kragen asked with an askance look that said, "I grow tired of these games, little man. This had better be good."

"Why, to the fabled town of La Croix, my dear friends. Rumor has reached my ear of a magical beast that plagues the townspeople. None have been able to capture it. I thought that might be of interest to you, Kragen. The impossible quarry—isn't that what you're always searching for? The creature that even you will not be able to capture? For that alone, you should be willing to make the trip—and also because I have recently received word that a very dear friend of ours, one Alaric Vashon, was recently sighted gaining passage on a ship headed for that very town," Duvaliet said flatly, any hints of his previous jovial demeanor having vanished into the stale air of his study.

Without another word, Kragen threw the papers in his lap on the ground and headed towards the door, Marsh not two steps behind him.

"Where do you two think you're going?" Duvaliet inquired as they opened the door and stepped into the drab hallway of the keep.

"To gather the men like you said. We're going hunting."

Chapter Nineteen

The traveler stooped low over the bent neck of his large black stallion, beaten down not only by the rain that had begun to fall near midday and showed no signs of letting up, but also by the sorrows that choked the joy from his heart. Both rider and horse were exhausted from long days and nights of travel, and the temptation of a dry place to rest for the evening and a hot meal seemed too good to resist. Neither were at hand, however, and the man could not shake the sense of impending danger. The weathered sign before him pointed towards what he could only hope would be a respite from this soggy mire that had soaked him and his steed to the bone. Two words intermittently appeared when lit by the lightning that split the sky: La Croix.

"Well, boy, what do you think? Are my senses betraying me after so long on the road? Do I look for danger where it's not? A hot meal and dry bed do sound good, don't they?"

His horse, named Sunstriker for the white lightning bolt that ran between his eyes and down to his nose, simply pawed huge ruts in the earth. He flicked his head to relieve himself of some of the water that had gathered around his ears and turned to look at his companion.

Alaric Vashon, known as a man without peer in combat, with or without a blade, was afraid for one of the first times in his life. The events at Bitterknot had shaken loose the foundations of his spirit, and he wondered if he could ever be whole after everything he had lost in that little town across the sea. Right now, he was just running—running from something or towards something, which he didn't pretend to know, but as long as he was running and focusing all of his energy on that simple task, he didn't have too much time to dwell on the past—except in his dreams, of course. There, his mind had full rein to roam as it would, and it often took him to its darkest recesses to revel in his failures and underachievement.

He had traversed an entire ocean, and his path had led him to this crossroads. He had heard of La Croix during his travels, but the persistent splatter of raindrops drowned out his mental search for knowledge of the place. Right now, any place would have to be better than standing here in the rain. After all, he could always move on if things didn't feel right, so he flicked the horse's reins and said, "Alright, boy, tonight you'll have dry hay and a warm stable to sleep in, I promise."

As they headed down the path towards the town, he could not shake the feeling that all was not as it should be. A faint prickling of the senses had put him on highest alert, despite the fact that the night was their own, no other travelers being foolish enough to chance this weather. If others were out, in any case, they would have scarce been bold enough to confront a big man in black carrying a very big sword and riding an enormous horse. So, without any delays, they passed a broken gate at the southern entrance and headed into the heart of La Croix.

What Vashon saw upon their arrival did little to assuage his fears as he slowed his horse to a walk in order to better take in their full surroundings, marking vantage points and possible escape routes should their stay here turn ugly. What once would have been a very beautiful town seemed to have fallen in upon itself in recent time. Great residences lining the main road stood abandoned. Doors and windows were broken in, and yards that he imagined once held grand gardens and fountains now showed only overgrown weeds and rubble where the benches and fountains would have stood in more prosperous times. Keeping one hand on his sword hilt, Vashon guided his horse towards the center of the town. A few scattered lights indicated the only signs of life he had seen since passing through the gate.

Even Sunstriker seemed to pick up on the wrongness of the place and pinned his ears at any noise that issued from the darkness. As they continued to survey the wreckage, an old man with wild hair and a gray beard stuck through with twigs and dirt suddenly ran out into the road in front of them, bidding them enjoy their stay and be sure to enjoy the commerce in the market. Cackling madly, he turned and, muttering something about a beast and the fools that continued to hunt it, was swallowed by the darkness.

Skirting the area that once housed the marketplace, Vashon passed a long wagon train that had set up camp in the empty market square. On one wagon, he saw a huge iron cage, obviously meant to hold something very large, its metal form rising into the night. The other wagons were painted garishly, and several had fires burning in front of them, surrounded by some of the strangest figures he had ever seen. Having traveled far himself, he knew this to be some sort of circus, probably here hoping to catch the purported beast and add it to their attractions as they traversed the countryside. Most of the circus people he encountered were charlatans and fakes, but he had seen much in his travels and knew that some of them possessed a kind of magic of their own and were not to be crossed idly. One of the carts advertised a "Beast Repellent: None but the foolish enter the woods of La Croix without it!" Shaking his head, he moved towards the hustle and bustle of the inns.

Having been through many towns, he knew how to quickly judge the character of a place, as his first glance had so often saved his life. What he saw of the people in this place did nothing to quiet his fears, and for a moment he considered turning around and leaving. He knew that, whatever he found here, trouble would most likely follow. But human comforts won out in the end, and he decided to find a place to stay the night and leave early in the morning, hopefully without drawing undue attention to himself.

Passing buildings that looked all the same, he at last came to a place that seemed as promising as any. Tilting his head back, exposing his sun-weathered face covered in two months growth of black beard, he looked up at the sign. It depicted a vendor holding a bag of gold in one hand and shaking hands with another merchant—also holding a bag of gold—with the other. The sign read, "The Inn of the Lucky Merchant," which brought a small smile to Vashon's lips, as he seriously doubted that any luck, save the bad kind, could be found here.

As he dismounted, a grimy middle-aged man appeared in the stable yard to take his horse. "Treat him well and maybe he won't bite. Give him your best feed and make sure he is rubbed down and dry for the night. He's had a long road behind him." He flipped a piece of silver which the man deftly caught. The man muttered that he would not rest until the horse was seen to. Trusting his companion was well-taken care of, Vashon turned and pulled open the door to the inn, hoping no trouble would find him this night and that he could simply enjoy a meal in peace, but those hopes were all but dashed when he stepped into the room and saw the rugged men gathered within.

Chapter Twenty

The overpowering smell of smoke, mixed with the odor of too much spilled ale, set a fitting scene for an inn holding court to the types of characters before Vashon's studied eyes. He entered the room and settled on a table he thought to be out of the way of the main thoroughfare. Catching the attention of the barkeep, he indicated with a slight nod of his head that he wanted some service. He then dropped his eyes to stare at the pitted and stained wood of his table, all the while marking the various other inhabitants in his peripheral vision.

Where he imagined the wealthy had once gathered to share drinks and regale one another now sat some of the roughest looking characters Vashon had ever seen gathered in one place. Having dealt with men such as these his entire life, he wasn't immediately scared, but he also knew to take caution around them, for while none among them would be his match in a fair fight, men such as these tended to conveniently forget the niceties of civilized combat. Many were dressed roughly in leathers and worn travel clothes. "Highwaymen and mercenaries," he thought, as he noticed with chagrin that almost every man in the room was openly armed. "It could be that a few of them actually know how to use their weapons."

His thoughts were interrupted by the approach of the barkeep. He looked up to see a large man with a gold earring in his left ear busily wiping his hands on a filthy apron. The thought that the man would look less out of place as a mate on some pirate's vessel than he did manning an inn in what was one of the richest cities in the realm brought a smile to his face. But the smile fled as quickly as it had come when he realized that the normal laws of the land seemed to not apply here and that the man, in fact, probably had served on a pirate's ship at one point in his life.

"Can I help you, friend?" the man inquired in a tone that implied he neither wanted to help Vashon nor considered him a friend.

"I would like a room for the night and lodging for my horse as well. We'll be moving on in the morning, so a quiet room out of the way would be much appreciated."

"The room I have, though how much peace and quiet comes with it you'll have to take up with this lot." He nodded at the closest table of ruffians. "These aren't the kindest negotiators around. Your horse is in good enough hands, so long as he doesn't try to take a nip out of my man. I've seen him use a harsh hand with any horse not smart enough to obey him."

"Of the two, it isn't the horse I would be worried about if I were you. I've known my ride longer than you have known your man, I'd wager, and he can easily take care of himself." Vashon tilted his head back and met the barkeep's glare with one of his own and wasn't surprised when the bartender took the opportunity to look away first.

"Ahem," the barkeep cleared his throat after he had looked back at his customer. "I'll have the room prepared. Top of the steps, then three doors down on the right. I'll have one of the servants bring some food and ale over as soon as I can, assuming you have the coin to pay for all of the trouble?"

"I have the coin," Vashon said as he flipped a gold piece at the barkeep, whose quick hand snatched it, midair.

"A word of advice, friend: if you have gold around here, you don't talk about it, and you definitely don't want to be throwin' it around. Most folk in here would just as gladly cut your throat and take your gold as they would sit down and dine with you, so I'd be just a little more cautious 'round here from now on if I were you. I don't know what you heard about La Croix before tonight, but things've changed in the last few months."

"Thanks for the advice. I'm not looking for trouble, though—just a warm meal and a bed."

"That doesn't mean trouble won't come looking for you," the barkeep said as he shrugged his shoulders and turned to stomp off and yell at a serving girl who had just dropped a tray of ale at the other end of the room.

Left alone, Vashon unassumingly observed the other occupants of the room. The main contingent was gathered at a table near the bar around a large man with a long black ponytail and a patch over his right eye. If trouble was coming, it would start with him.

At a table apart from the rest, six of the rangiest men held their heads together and whispered furiously amongst themselves. Once in a while, one of them would turn from his companions and stare directly at Vashon but would quickly turn away when they found his gaze returning theirs.

He was distracted by the large plate of stew and mug of ale laid on the table before him by the same serving girl who had dropped the tray a few moments earlier. A purplish bruise was spreading fast across her cheek, punishment for her clumsiness, but she still managed to give him a weak smile as he passed a silver into her hand and thanked her for the food. The girl's eyes went wide as she stared at the coin in her palm, worth more than she would make in six months in this place.

His eyes drifted over the first warm meal he had eaten in days, and the savory aroma of the food snaked its way into his nostrils. Even as hungry as he was, Vashon couldn't help but notice an old man in a very tattered cloak laying with his head down at the table directly across from his own. The man had a spilled mug in front of him, and a buzz of heavy snoring came from his direction. Vashon smiled as he envied the other's drunken sleep. Unaware of the danger and cruelty all around him, he had simply done what he could to deal with the situation—gone to sleep and hoped all would be well when he awoke.

Vashon began shoveling food into his mouth, each bite more delicious than the last, when the large man with the eye patch detached himself from his circle of lackeys and sat down at the vacant seat directly in front of him. He continued to spoon his meal into his mouth, albeit more slowly, and shifted glances between the men in the corner and the man now sitting three feet away from him idly scratching on the table with a dagger.

"Ain't seen you 'round here 'fore, stranger. These're dangerous times. Y'oughtn't be travelin' through this place without protection. We'd be 'bliged to offer our services—for a small price, 'course."

"Look, mister—"

"Call me Kerrick, ol' chum. Kerrick One-Eye. No doubt you've heard the name. See, the thing is, there's only two things people got to do in this town: hide from the beast or hunt the beast. Now, if you're of the hidin' persuasion, you can pay a nominal fee, and we'd be more'n happy to accommodate you. If you're looking to hunt the beast, I'm 'fraid you'll need the proper license for that—again for a nominal fee. Lucky for you, you've come to the right place. Ol' One-Eye runs a sort of one-stop operation here, you see?"

"I'm sorry, but I'm not here for the beast, Mr. Eye," said Vashon coolly. "In fact, this is the first I've heard of the creature. I was just traveling through and decided to stop for a hot meal and a night's sleep. I promise I'll be gone in the morning and that'll be the end of our acquaintance. You can have your beast. I just want to finish my dinner in peace."

Vashon turned his eyes back to his cooling dinner but not before catching the bright eyes of the now-awake old man at the table across from him. As he picked up his utensils, a flicker of recognition crossed his mind, and he puzzled about where and when he had seen the old man before tonight.

"That's a pretty sword you got there," returned Kerrick, pointing at the sheathed blade with his dagger. "Very pretty indeed. Been some time since I've seen steel of that mark 'round these parts. You must be an important man, am I right? Now I don't claim to know much about important men, but I suspect 'em to be, in all likelihood, good a speculatin' and makin' propositions. You know anything about propositions, important man? 'Cause I gots a proposition for you. What would you say if I decided all you owned now belonged to me?"

"I would say my possessions are my own, earned by me, and they go with me when I leave here. I would also say there is nothing I own worth you and your men dying for. Now, how about I buy you a bottle of their best and go about my business tonight, instead of in the morning. I'm too tired, and it's much too late to die. I'd happily kill you all in the morning, but I'd rather avoid all that mess since I don't really know you. The choice is yours how we proceed, but I beg you make it quickly because my dinner's getting cold."

Pausing, Kerrick weighed his options and, after a few seconds, laughed loudly and smacked Vashon across the back. "Alright, friend—a bottle of their best, you go your way and we'll call it settled. But if our paths cross again …"

"They won't; I assure you I have no business here. Now, if I could just finish my dinner in peace. Tell the barkeep to put your drinks on my tab. He knows I'm good for it."

Kerrick got up and slowly sauntered his way back to his table. Vashon watched him go the entire way and saw him tell the barkeep to bring a bottle of his best and "put it on the big guy with the sword's tab." The man brought out a dusty bottle and set it in the middle of the table. Vashon noted that, although the men had begun a very heated discussion, none of them seemed very interested in drinking anymore. He resolved to leave his meal half-finished and vacate the premises before any more trouble found him this night, but as he began to leave, he noticed that a few of the men he had counted were missing from the other table.

One by one, the remaining men got up to leave. One left out the front door, two exited up the stairs and the rest slowly stood and began moving in different directions to different parts of the bar. As if upon cue, the bartender arrived and stood directly in his line of vision, just in time for him not to see which direction the very last of Kerrick's men took as he left the place.

"Anything else, friend?" the barkeep asked with a slight tremor in his voice that completely gave away any false sense of ease he was trying to impart upon his guest.

"No, my business inside is done." He tossed the bartender another silver and picked up the remainder of his dinner and ale and placed them on the table in front of the old man, whose eyes hadn't left him the entire time.

"Here you go, sir. I hope you can enjoy this a little more than I have. I have business elsewhere this night. Good luck to you." As he turned to walk out the front door, loosening his sword in his scabbard in a motion as regular to him as drawing breath, the old man's hand, surprisingly strong, caught him by the forearm.

"Not to worry; all things will be set aright," he said, and with a wink the old man set to devouring the rest of the food in front of him.

Vashon left the inn with the man's words resounding in his head. It was as if he had heard them somewhere before but couldn't place it. Then, not ten feet out the door, a flood of recognition stopped him dead in his tracks. He smiled and turned around to go back when, all of a sudden, a man with a wicked grin and a dagger in his hand dropped to the ground directly in front of him.

Cursing quietly and drawing his sword, Vashon realized where the sixth and last man had gone.

Chapter Twenty-One

The attacker swung his knife in a killing blow where Vashon's throat had been only moments before. The man raised his dagger high above his head to strike again, but Vashon dashed aside and grabbed his opponent's down-swinging arm and used the man's own momentum to flip him on his back. With a brutal twist and sickening popping sound, his assailant was on the ground howling in pain, his arm lying limply at his side. Vashon had just enough time to get his sword free, blue steel glowing in the moonlight, as five more men came rushing at him from all corners of the inn. As he backed out into the inn's yard where he would at least have the freedom of movement to fight them all, he counted at least fifteen men. It at last dawned on him that Kerrick commanded many more men than those who had sat at his table.

Realizing he was as good as dead if he waited for them to rush him en masse, Vashon used the only weapon he knew could defend him against a mob like this: surprise. He ducked at the last second as the first man reached him and threw the man over his shoulder where he landed hard on the ground. The man running at his back never had a chance as Vashon sprung from his crouching position, the flat of his blade clubbing the man on the ear. The man's eyes rolled back in his head, and he dropped like a stone where he stood. The remaining men slowed their advance and backed off warily, each realizing that this was no ordinary foe. Still, Vashon knew better than to give them time to gather their courage, so he rushed at them headlong, his sword swinging in intricate patterns as he charged into the group.

This was no ordinary man, indeed!

Kerrick's men could only curse and bleed as Vashon spun and moved among their number, his sword a bright blue arc in the night air. Every time one of them got close enough to strike him, he easily parried. They were slowly being picked apart by this stranger in black. As mere spectators, they would have applauded him for his talent with a blade, but, to their misfortune, they were very much participants in this battle, the tides of which were quickly turning.

Finally, realizing that no one man would be a match for him, they began to close in together, forming themselves into a loose circle and attacking Vashon on all sides. His blue blade continued to flash in the moonlight, however, beating back the ring of men around him with a skill and beauty none had ever witnessed. Just as they began to question whether or not they could win this fight, Kerrick and two of his men appeared at the corner of the inn, leading the man's black horse on a long rope. The horse reared and kicked, ears pinned flat against its head, but Kerrick, attempting to subdue the animal, kicked it square in the ribs with the heel of his boot. The horse's screeching neigh pierced Vashon straight through the heart, but knowing he couldn't take his eyes off of his attackers for even a split-second, he yelled out, "Striker, away!" The sound of its master's strong command jolted the horse, and Sunstriker kicked free of Kerrick's grasp and fled into the night.

Meanwhile, Vashon was holding back the mob, when he misjudged his footing on a slick patch of mud and went down, barely parrying a blow meant to remove his hand from his arm at the wrist. Refusing to surrender, he was pulling himself to his feet when Kerrick quickly made his way into the fray and rapped Vashon sharply on the back of the head with his sword's hilt. Vashon's sword slipped from his hand, and he fell face-forward into the mud.

"You didn't think I'd let a no-good spittoon of a man like you backtalk me and get away with it, did you now? Shame we gotta kill such a fightin' soul, though I'm sure you can rightly 'preciate even y'own meaningless death at the hands of a fellow practitioner of carnage." He booted Vashon onto his back and positioned his dagger point-down over his heart.

"Excuse me," came an unexpected voice, "but isn't the hour a little late for this kind of bloodshed?" The old man from the bar had ambled out the front door and was now striding directly into their midst, gently scolding the men as if they were children caught up in horseplay.

"Mind yourself, old prune. You ain't invited to this party," said Kerrick, removing his dagger from Vashon's chest just long enough to wave it threateningly in the old man's face.

"Just seems like a waste of good bait to me, don't you think? If I were you, which I'm obviously not, I would lay the man in the woods in front of the garrison. There's a full moon out tonight. When the Beast comes down to eat him, you and your merry men here can kill it. It's the perfect plan. But if you've got a better plan, be my guest. After all, like you said, I'm just an old man, and this is no business of mine."

The men looked at one another, and revelation flashed across their faces as the seeds of the old man's plan took root. They envisioned themselves riding back into the town later that night, bathed in glory, the Beast in tow. Kerrick took his dagger from the man's chest and re-sheathed it as he looked at each of his men in turn and gauged their mettle for the task ahead. Finally, he shrugged and said, "Bring him, then. And bring the old fossil along, too. I'd hate for him to miss his own show."

But as he turned around, he found that the old beggar had long since vanished into the night. No trace of him could be found as the men yoked their prisoner behind one of their horses and set out towards the Beast's castle in the misty woods.

Chapter Twenty-Two

Two boys peered out at the garrison in the distance. They had been planning and daring each other for weeks to come out here to see the Beast for themselves.

"I guess as long as we have this Beast repellent you stole from that old woman's cart in the market, nothing can hurt me, can it, Michael?" Timmen asked while nervously fingering the strand of garlic cloves and chicken beaks around his neck.

"Nope. We're well protected by these charms. Besides, you don't really think I'd let anything happen to you, do you?"

His fears assuaged, Timmen boldly stepped from the shelter of dangling walnut branches and took a few steps forward before stopping and motioning frantically for his cousin to join him. From here, the garrison was easily visible through the mist and fog, out of which they both imagined a dangerous monster might fly to devour them at any moment.

The eerie hooting of an owl in the trees nearby startled them as they turned to look at one another, eyes wide. They took one last look at the keep and quickly turned back towards town. Dark as the night in the forest was, and so caught up were they in the night's terrors and their defiance of them, that neither noticed the trap that was barely covered by leaves in the path before them. Suddenly, both boys were pulled from the ground in a rush and found themselves hanging upside down, back-to-back, nearly seven feet from the ground, a rope securely tied to their ankles.

The boys' momentum carried them in lazy circles above the ground. They spun about, wondering how they were ever going to escape their predicament. Timmen's eyes suddenly widened as, on the fifth pass, he thought he caught a glimpse of something not there before, something darker than even the night itself. He nudged Michael in the back to get his attention. "Did you see that?"

he whispered. But before Michael could answer, they found the spinning had suddenly stopped, and Timmen was face-to-face with the Beast, which now held them suspended by the rope over the leaves and pine needles of the forest floor.

"Don't you boys know it's far too late to be out in such a dangerous place?" The voice sounded nothing like the trembling boys had imagined a monster's would. It held a slight musical quality, and if they hadn't been so busy crying and screaming, they would have recognized the tone as not malicious but reproachful, as every word was punctuated by the sharp rap of a long claw on Timmen's forehead.

Desperate, Michael brandished his string of garlic cloves in front of the creature's face. His movement was cut short, however, as one huge paw grabbed the strand, pinched off a clove and promptly popped it into its mouth, which was lined with dagger-like teeth.

"Mmmmm, delicious! Everything tastes better with garlic," it announced as it drew the strung-up boys closer to its face. It sniffed them over with the quick, short snuffles of a curious hound dog. "What do you say, boys? Care to stay for dinner?"

They both let out anguished screams of "Help! Beast!" and "Please don't eat us!" while the creature before them stood there and chuckled heartily with its head tilted back.

"Fortunately, I've already eaten tonight. You two should go home and—"

Its remonstration was cut short as the faraway sound of men moving through the woods reached its sharp ears. The mood changed quickly as a low growl emanated from deep within the Beast's chest. With a snarl, it abruptly sliced through the rope that held the boys in the air, letting them fall the short distance to the forest floor. They lay frozen in place, too scared to realize that they might actually survive the encounter.

"Go!" the Beast commanded. "This is no place for you. I have pressing business I must attend to. And in the future, you should both be more careful."

Leaving them in their consternation, the Beast turned and was gone in the blink of an eye, moving much faster than any animal either boy had ever seen before in the direction of the enchanted castle.

Chapter Twenty-Three

By the time Kerrick and his injured men made their way through the woods, finally arriving at the spot they decided best for them to set their bait, a slight moaning had begun to emanate from their bound captive. The men knew he would begin to stir soon, and none of them seemed too anxious to face the man again, bound or not. Kerrick held up his hand and instructed two of his men to pick the captive up and lay him in the center of a clearing that was ringed with trees of gnarled oak and walnut. They would wait under the cover of the leaves for the Beast to come and claim its prize, and that would be the end of it.

The men withdrew into the black security of the concealing branches and watched their lure in the clearing. Kerrick silently hoped that they hadn't damaged him too badly to serve as sufficient bait. After he had struck him on the head, several of his boys had put in a few licks as revenge for their wounds. Those blows, along with the injuries he had sustained from being dragged behind a horse over rough terrain for several leagues, would have killed any other man, but they all knew that, whoever this stranger was, he was no ordinary man.

The men got edgier as the minutes wore on, with no sight or sound of any of the forest's other dangerous inhabitants. One of the men, the first to go down in the previous battle, could finally stand it no longer and looked away from the injured man to focus his eyes on the forest canopy.

Something moved in the brush immediately to his right, and he raised a hand to notify the others that he had located the area where the Beast was hiding. The movement grew more intense, and loud grunting and snorting emanated from the spot. Suddenly, a huge black boar burst from the brush and headed directly at them, but before it reached the first line of defenders, its body was riddled with arrows.

"That was the biggest boar I've ever seen! Something must have spooked it," the man said to the next in line.

The look his companion gave him was one of quickly dawning comprehension. They turned to look at the spot the boar had come from and screamed in horror as a large part of the darkness detached itself from the forest and hurled itself at them with supernatural speed.

Their plan had backfired; they had become the hunted, not the hunters. The remaining men and their leader fell into chaos as the Beast moved among them like a giant specter, wreaking violence and destruction at every turn. The first man was pulled from his horse, and the others struggled to free their weapons and defend themselves before they suffered the same fate. Screams reverberated throughout the clearing as the Beast launched itself from the man's still body on the ground and tore into the remaining men like a creature bent on revenge.

The next man swung his sword in a killing stroke towards the monster below him, only to stare as the Beast twisted as quickly as any trained warrior and took him from his horse with one great swipe of a monstrous paw. The Beast grabbed the man as soon as he hit the ground and held him like a shield as arrows from two of his companions thudded soundly into his back.

Before the men could reload their bows, the creature was upon them in a flurry of claws and teeth. The first swung his bow at the Beast's face in defense, but it was caught in the Beast's giant maw and snapped in half with one crunch of its massive jaws. He then found himself hurling through the air and into a tree across the clearing. His friend, seeing what befell his comrade, tried to flee the scene but was quickly run down by a creature that moved like a lion but was the size of one of the great bears rumored to inhabit the ice floes of the far north. He would have been finished off just as quickly had it not been for Kerrick's intervention.

Much more level-headed than any of his men, and having survived more than one fight in his life, Kerrick had the good sense to simply move out of the way and avoid the creature's first rush. His stream of curses filled the air at the bad luck which had led them to fighting a losing battle against a creature out of a nightmare. He knew that if he had any chance at all of surviving, he would have to await his opportunity to escape. As for his men, it was a common understanding that following a man such as he entailed certain dangers. Besides, men such as these were easily replaceable, and he wouldn't make the mistake of bringing so few of them the next time he came to this place—that is, if he could somehow manage to survive this night.

He saw his chance as the Beast went to finish off the second bowman. He lunged in with his short sword at its unprotected side. Lightning fast reflexes met him as the monster simply swung the man in its arms against Kerrick's sword arm, stopping his blade and breaking his arm in several places. Before he knew what was happening, a giant paw appeared from the air and clubbed him to the ground, slashing his face with razor-like claws. As he tried to get back up, he found himself staring into a pair of fiercely burning eyes which radiated the most rage he had ever felt from another living thing. The paw landed on his chest, and its claws slowly extended an inch or so into his flesh, pinning him to the earth.

"You have a choice, stupid man," barked the Beast. "Either you take your men with you and leave this place, never to return, or stay your present course and die. I would decide quickly if I were you."

"We'll leave, but I promise you, one day I'll be back, and we'll face each other again. I give you my word." Kerrick's words somehow carried their malicious intent, despite the fact that he was gurgling on his own blood and slowly suffocating under the weight of the Beast.

"And I give you my word," the Beast returned, "that that will be your last day alive. These are my woods, and any who enter answer to me. You have seen what I will do to protect my home. Do not mistake my letting you go for weakness. You have been warned. Now gather your men and leave here if you wish to see the sun on the morrow."

The claws were removed, and Kerrick struggled for breath as his men, who had slowly roused themselves, came over to help him up. As they neared the clearing's edge, Kerrick gave orders to seize the prisoner, but as they grabbed the figure in black, the Beast interceded.

"He stays, as does his sword," the Beast growled, turning to Kerrick's men who held Vashon's possessions. "Leave here now, One-Eye, and pray our paths do not cross again."

The men hobbled from the clearing, and the Beast slowly bent over Vashon and began to inspect his wounds. It looked up as a rustling of branches announced the arrival of the old man from the inn, leading Sunstriker calmly behind him.

"How bad is he?" the old man asked as he freed the horse to examine its master.

"His wounds are deep, Vinquist. Though I do not doubt your skills, it will take all that you possess to heal him. I see you were kind enough to bring his horse. I'm sure he would thank you for that if he were awake."

"Oh, yes, Sunstriker and I are old friends, aren't we, boy? We have a long history together, the three of us." He held his hands over Vashon's still form until they began to emit a white glow. He then ran them over Vashon's body for several moments, discerning the severity of his injuries.

"His body will heal. He is stronger than most. It is the wounds done to his heart and spirit that will take time and effort to mend. Are you up to the task, my friend?"

In answer, the Beast hoisted the man up with a gentleness that belied its great size and, with the wizard and horse in tow, set off towards the castle gate. Lights had begun to glow in the upper windows in anticipation of the master's return.

Chapter Twenty-Four

The nightmare was the same as it had been since it started, except for one key difference. Instead of merely watching the incident unfold, Vashon now found himself an active participant. He was the star puppet, and someone other than he was pulling the strings. He knew how this play would end but could do nothing to stop it.

Alaric Vashon twisted and turned in the fresh bed sheets. The fever raged, wracking his body first with blasts of cold, followed by unbearable heat. Bette and the Beast listened from his bedside as he tossed and turned, murmuring the terrors he was reliving and occasionally crying out loud. Both wished they could do more to help him but knew that they had done for his tortured body all they could and that the fight was now his own. The greatest swordsman that had ever lived now faced his greatest foes without a weapon in his hand, and so he lay, in sweat-covered sheets, turning his head from side to side, unwilling to face the inevitable. There would be no escape for him, however, and he finally surrendered to the forces he could no longer resist.

Spiraling down further and further as his fever burned hotter, he saw a man he had called his best friend from childhood riding alongside him at the back of a column of men. Vashon and his comrade rode together in a cloud of dust as they talked on a warm spring day.

"You know, Alaric," Duncan said as he attempted to peel an apple while he rode, trying in vain to keep the dirt and grit from spoiling his snack, "I honestly can't believe I let you talk me into this again." Finally giving up, he cut the apple neatly in half and gave one half to Sunstriker and the other to his own horse.

"It's because you would be bored without me, Duncan. You know that," Alaric replied with a sideways grin at his friend, who somehow always knew how to lift his spirits when things were at their worst.

"Oh, that's right. I would be, wouldn't I?" he quipped, returning Vashon's

grin as he stood in his stirrups, shielding his eyes with one hand, trying to see over the column of dust, men and horses in front of them. "Come on, Alaric, why are we still with this lot? You can feel it as surely as I do—these are bad men. Why are we helping them?"

Vashon had, in fact, thought much on this subject over the past couple of weeks, as Duvaliet, Kragen and Vigan Marsh made their distaste for him and Duncan quite clear. Being a fairly good judge of character, he knew what kind of men they were, knew that if you kept company long enough with men like them, all it would bring you was hardship. The only thing that had kept him with them this long was a promise he had made to Duvaliet's father to try to make something of his weasel of a son, and once Vashon had made a promise, he seldom broke it.

These men, however, had pushed him to his limit. From the first day they set out together, the men had made it abundantly clear that they merely tolerated the presence of Vashon and Duncan as a concession to Duvaliet's father who still held the keys to his Dukedom and all financial provisions in his iron fist. Vashon and Duncan rode at the back of the column and at night made their campfire away from the other men. Unwanted outsiders, trapped in an ever-closing circle of men who did not like them, they made do as best they could.

When they stopped to rest, Duncan and Vashon would gather all who showed a willingness to learn and teach them what they could in the ways of combat. Not teach them everything, no, but how to stay alive just a little bit longer than their opponent in a fight. Vashon was the obvious choice as a teacher, having built a reputation as the best swordsman in the land, and Duncan came along in the package deal. It didn't hurt that he was quite a swordsman himself, though not many would know it. His glib tongue and quick smile helped him avoid many fights. They taught the men to fight while Duvaliet and his two generals watched from a distance, pretending not to really care how they trained the men. Vashon, however, knew these men as warriors and knew they noted every move and the progress of every man. They didn't miss much, those three.

He had also decided that, promise or no, he no longer wanted to be a part of this—this survey of lands and vassals, this culling of unruly landowners and any who might stir up dissent. Vashon had seen one too many townspeople "taught a lesson" as Duvaliet was so fond of saying, laughing with his mouth, while eyes reflected the true cruelty lurking within his tiny visage.

"All right, Duncan—at the next village, while everyone else is asleep, you and I will leave. It will be dawn before we are missed, and by then we'll be too far gone for them to find us. Besides, we aren't the easiest men to track down if we don't want to be," Vashon said with a smile, glancing to catch his friend's reaction to this piece of news.

"Are you serious? We're really leaving?" The look on his friend's face brought a hearty laugh out of Vashon, and he was reminded of how fond he was of his friend. They had been playmates as children, and their friendship had only strengthened over the years, as each grew into manhood. While Vashon had grown up practical and, at times, overly serious, Duncan showed a great love of life and had a gregarious spirit that could lift even the most dour individual around him. They made a natural pair, and Vashon was glad Duncan often accompanied him on these journeys.

"Yes, Duncan, we're really leaving—tonight perhaps. If I am not mistaken, we should be coming up on the next village any time now, and I'm sure that will provide them another chance to stop and resupply for the next leg of their journey. Yes, old friend, like you, I've had enough of this evil to leave a bad taste in my mouth for months, and life is far too short to be wasting it with this lot," Vashon said as he gestured with a hand at the column of men in front of them.

"Now you're beginning to sound like me," Duncan beamed. "I was beginning to think all this time you've spent around me over the years had been wasted. I'm glad to see you've learned a little something, Alaric," he said as he took another apple from his saddlebag and cut into it, humming to himself contentedly, knowing they would soon leave this distasteful business behind them.

Over the next half hour they were both so caught up in their plans for leaving that neither one of them really noticed that the rear ends of the horses in front of them kept looming closer and closer until they were almost riding right over the men directly ahead of them. It appeared that Vashon had been correct in his estimation, for they had arrived at the next town, which lay on the outer fringe of the great forest called Bitterknot.

It was a small village, much like many others they had visited on their travels. The town, famous for the furniture that came from its craftsmen, was flanked on its north side by a forest of dark-wooded trees. If worked properly, as it was by the village woodworkers in the tradition handed down for generations, the knotted wood could provide a beautiful chair, or table, which polished up to a dark brown-black color, the knots in the wood giving each piece its own personality. The riders arrived to the sounds of saws and anvils, as the village men plied their craft, while the women and children gathered in the main square to see who had come with such a retinue to their humble steading.

Vashon and Duncan reached the front of the column as Duvaliet finished telling the villagers who they were and what their purpose was here. Nervous glances passed between those gathered. They had heard of Duvaliet and his reputation. The saws had stopped, and men wearing heavy leather aprons stepped out of their shops and eyed these new visitors with wary glances. Looking over, Vashon saw Duncan smile at a young boy hiding behind his mother's back, his hand nimbly darting out to catch the apple Duncan had tossed to him.

His eyes wandered toward the rear of the column and watched in growing anger as two of Duvaliet's wagons pulled up near the main shops and his men *began busily loading up everything in sight, just as they had done in so many other towns.*

"Pay, Duvaliet! Pay these people for it," Vashon told him, having finally had enough.

"You insolent pile of—" Duvaliet began, before a small voice cut him off.

"Look, Mommy, that man is small just like me," the boy with the apple laughed as he tugged on his mother's dress, pointing at Duvaliet's back with his other hand.

Duvaliet immediately stopped his horse and turned it around to stare at the child. "I'm sorry, sir. Please forgive him. He doesn't know any better," the boy's mother begged as she hid her son with her own body from Duvaliet's calm gaze. Too calm, Vashon thought, fearing the storm he had been trying to avoid had finally caught up with him.

"What a charming boy you have, madam. Vigan, burn the village to the ground—and bring the boy to me," he said calmly as he turned from the woman. A terrible grin came over Marsh's face as he lit a torch and threw it onto the nearest thatched rooftop, watching in delight as flames shot up moments later. The others followed suit and began lighting torches of their own, moving like a wave among the homes and buildings of the town, spreading fire wherever they went.

Vashon moved to intercept these men, to stop this at whatever cost, but Duncan was quicker this time. He didn't hesitate. When Duvaliet gave the order, he immediately loosed his sword and began hacking and fighting his way through the men towards Vigan Marsh, knocking burning torches out of hands as he went. Most of the men didn't even realize they were being attacked, so intent were they on destruction, and Duncan moved through their ranks quickly. They soon realized they had an enemy among them, though, and began to circle in on him. To their misfortune, they forgot Duncan was not alone, and many fell from their saddles before realizing that Vashon had entered their midst like a fell wind.

Vashon having finally fought his way to Duncan, they moved together towards the largest group of men busy lighting torches and handing them to the others.

"Well, Alaric, looks like we waited just a little too long to take our leave. As soon as we get those torches out, we should r—"

The rest of Duncan's sentence was cut short, as a spear, thrown by Vigan Marsh's considerable might, caught Duncan square in the chest, lifting him from his saddle and depositing him several feet away on the ground. He lay still and unmoving. Vashon stared in horror before vaulting out of his own saddle and rushing to his friend's side.

"Duncan—No!" he cried as he tried to stop the flow of blood coming from his friend's chest. But there was no answer; Marsh's throw had met its mark. Vashon let out a scream that put a halt to the chaos enveloping him. Both fleeing

villagers and rampaging soldiers alike paused as the man in black leathers closed his friend's eyes and climbed quickly onto his horse.

He turned his gaze from Duvaliet's men and sought out his two largest threats. He wheeled Sunstriker around to face Kragen, who had drawn his crossbow and was notching it with the bolt intended to end Vashon's life. Kragen looked up in surprise to see Vashon draw his dagger. As Kragen raised the crossbow to fire, Vashon's dagger struck the wood of his bow with a hollow "thunk." Its force knocked the crossbow back in Kragen's hands, so that it pointed directly at his face when the catch mechanism gave way and released the deadly bolt. Only by jerking his head to the side in reflex did Kragen save himself. The bolt screamed past his ear, dragging itself along his face as it flew towards the clouds. He clutched his other hand to his bleeding face and galloped off before Vashon could finish the job, blood dripping between his fingers as he fled.

Vashon then turned back to the man with whom he had the largest score to settle and charged directly at Vigan Marsh, unsheathing his sword as he went. The larger man sat astride his horse, war axe in hand, waiting for the chance to prove once and for all that he was the better of the two. As he drew near, Vashon grabbed his sword's hilt with both hands, steering Sunstriker with his legs, preparing to attack. At the last second, Marsh swung his axe in an arc meant to decapitate Vashon, who ducked quickly and brought his own sword up, making a jagged cut all the way up the larger man's forearm. As Vashon circled for another pass, he noted that all of Duvaliet's soldiers had stopped their burning of the town and had now taken an interest in him. Weapons drawn, they charged, and he was caught between wanting to avenge his friend's death and his instincts that told him he was far too outnumbered to continue.

He swore vengeance in his mind for Duncan, and hearing his friend's last words of "we should run" echoing in his ears, Vashon turned Sunstriker and tore through the underbrush, hoping to somehow evade the many men loudly following after him. As he galloped past, he saw his friend's peaceful face, frozen in time by a boar's spear, and heard Duvaliet's laughter chasing after him on the wind.

Chapter Twenty-Five

Bette's mind reeled with the impact of all that she had seen, heard and felt. She walked slowly away from Vashon's doorway, hand to her head, trying in vain to staunch the headache swiftly imposing its will on her. She had done all she could; if he was to recover from the wounds inflicted on his body and heart, then it would be by his own doing. The Beast had stayed behind and was now sitting in silent vigil by his bedside in case he should wake and need something.

Dragging her thoughts from Vashon's plight, Bette focused on the many tasks requiring her immediate attention. She never dreamt that keeping an entire garrison of people in order could be such hard work. In truth, she grudgingly admitted, she hadn't really given any thought to what would happen after she and the rest of the town's workforce deserted their homes and came here, simply on a wizard's advice and a baker assistant's hunch. And now that everyone had somewhat settled in, they seemed to regard Bette as their leader. She suddenly found herself responsible for keeping everything running smoothly.

If only Vinquist had stayed longer to help, she might have had some further inkling as to what she was supposed to do. But he only came around from time to time for short visits to see how things were going, never offering any advice. When she asked him once, in exasperation, why he didn't help her or tell her what to do, he only replied, "Because, dear Bette, you seem to be doing a far better job than I ever could." Then he patted her cheek in that infuriatingly charming manner of his and walked out the door.

Things settled into a kind of routine for the people of the garrison—her people, Bette reminded herself, since they all looked to her for guidance. She tried to explain to them that they were their own people now and didn't have to listen to anything anyone told them to do or take direction on how to live their lives, but they stubbornly shook their heads. So accustomed were they to following orders that they needed and trusted her to do what was best for them. Freedom and autonomy, after all, were completely foreign and new to them. They were at a loss, and many longed for the supervision and order they had left behind in La Croix. Re-building these people's sense of community and teaching them to govern themselves and their neighbors was a difficult and tedious task. After several weeks, however, she was beginning to see results, which brought a smile to her face in spite of her aching head.

The people's progress was manifesting itself in small ways: the cooks baking the bread for the day without her prompting, men starting badly-needed projects to repair the castle that had so long been neglected, women helping each other with their daily tasks as they all settled into their new home. As the people began to taste freedom, a joy grew among them that they had never known until now. Still, in spite of their new-found initiative, Bette found herself responsible for the general well-being of the people. She barely had a moment's rest between settling arguments and helping out wherever she could.

On top of everything else, Vinquist had shown up tonight with this stranger, injured and in need of care. He was obviously someone special. Before Vinquist left to "take stock of some matters," he instructed her to do all she could to see to the stranger's comfort. More than once Vinquist said he was relying on her and Sophie to pull Vashon through. Saying no more, he headed back out into the night to return to La Croix and see how events had unfolded there since they had left.

Bette found herself wandering the halls of the citadel, not really paying any mind to the tasks around her, but wondering what Vashon's appearance would mean to the other exiles of La Croix. She could sense the winds of change blowing their way and hoped that they would not sweep away what little stability the people had gained since their arrival. After several idle moments, she headed back upstairs to check on their charge just as he let out another cry.

Chapter Twenty-Six

The next day, following Vashon's arrival at the fortress, a massive storm blew in off the sea. Outdoor activities were curtailed for the day. Some simply sat at windows and watched the rain pour down. Others busied themselves cleaning areas that had been abandoned for centuries. All knew these tasks merely served as temporary distractions from what really filled their minds. They were all thinking about the man who had entered their private world so unexpectedly the night before and what changes his arrival might bring.

While the storm assaulted their home, Vashon slept in his bed, high in one of the towers overlooking the sea. His fever burned hot throughout the night, and he relived many moments of his life. He felt the wooden sword his father put in his hand at the age of five. He heard his mother laugh as she danced with him, then saw her, serious this time, as she taught him the Dance. He revisited other memories as well: his first meeting with Vinquist as a young boy at his parent's cottage; traveling in the company of the wizard, learning the mysteries and intricacies of the world; his sworn oath of protection given in the Elven glade in Avereen, their capital; and, most painful of all, he lived and died again and again with Duncan, knowing the spear was coming, but powerless to do anything to stop its flight. He remembered with shame his time spent running, from anything and everything. Finally, flashes of lightning illuminated a soft bed where he was laid to recover by a monster out of a nightmare so terrible that he knew his fevered mind was taking its toll on his senses.

He surfaced several times throughout the next day and a half, his mind clearing long enough for him to draw breath and open his eyes to take in his surroundings. He found that he was, in fact, in a soft bed, covered in a down blanket, in a sparsely furnished room. He wanted to rise so that he could look out of the room's solitary window, but he could not find the energy.

These bouts of consciousness never lasted long, however, and he returned to the cocoon of sleep, his dreams and nightmares his only companions in this feverish world.

Once, he awoke to find Vinquist sitting by his bedside in the same patched cloak he always wore, holding his hand and quietly mumbling some spell. Another time, he found a middle-aged woman sitting at his side, patiently wringing small sips of water from a cloth into his dry mouth and over his cracked lips. As his eyes caught hers, he tried to speak, but she gave him that motherly smile and said, "hush, child," as she pushed his head back onto the pillow, where sleep would find him again. And then there was the girl—or young woman; it was hard to tell exactly which title fit her better. He awoke to find her sitting on the bed beside him, brilliant blue eyes studying him, not wavering when she saw him awake and returning her gaze. She smiled at him, and in some deep part of his heart, where he had allowed no feelings for a long time, a door began to creak open. She wiped his brow with a cloth dipped in cool water and sent him off to sleep with that smile of hers, causing his dreams to be a little more pleasant than they had been before she entered his world.

The worst awakening came for him in the middle of the next night when his fever had reached its apex and burned its hottest. Covered in a cold sweat, he had been tossing and turning, trapped once again in Bitterknot. Only this time it was he who threw the spear, laughing while Duncan, fallen from his horse, asked, "Why, Alaric?" He became aware of a burning sensation in his left leg and opened his eyes to find the cause of his distress. He saw through blurred vision the monster from the night before leaning over him, concentrating on his leg. With silent horror, he watched it raise one huge claw and neatly slice open an area on his leg, where he could see that a piece of branch had been embedded as he was dragged through the woods. The wound had become infected. After the Beast made its incision, it removed the piece of wood. His horror turned to shock and amazement when the Beast licked the wound several times, cleaning it in its own way. Primitive but effective, he thought as he felt the pressure releasing in his leg. About that time, it must have sensed him watching it, for it shifted its gaze to his face. As Vashon tried to focus on the creature's eyes, he fought the rising tide of unconsciousness that came to carry him away once again. The hint of familiarity, the sense that he had seen those eyes somewhere before, haunted him until he awoke the next morning.

Sunlight, absent the day before because of the storm, began the new day by shining brightly through the window of his room. Vashon first felt the warmth on his face and spent several languorous minutes lying there, letting the warm rays refresh his body. The second thing he noticed was that he could think clearly, a signal that his fever had at last broken. His excitement over having conquered his fever in the night, however, quickly gave way to an assortment of aches and pains resounding all over his body as he remembered the events leading up to his arrival here, wherever "here" was. He could only imagine the worst as he pictured his body a mass of cuts, bruises and scrapes. Despite the pain, he was anxious to get up and look at his surroundings, so he slowly opened his eyes, letting them adjust to the light.

The first thing he saw was the girl who had sat patiently beside him on the large bed, staring at him with those blue eyes in a way that made him want to smile back at her despite the way he felt.

"Good, you're finally awake. I was beginning to wonder if we were going to have to spend another day watching you lie there. I, for one, am tired of sitting here, so as soon as you feel up to it, we'll get you up and about to work out some of that soreness you must be feeling, eh?" she said as she reached for an object on his bedside table.

"Where am I?" The thought rang clear as a bell in his head but came out as a hoarse whisper, as dry as two twigs rubbing together.

The young woman smiled indulgently and brought a cup to his lips, from which she gave him several small sips of cool water. After he drank enough to sate his thirst, she took the cup away and helped him to raise his head up on the pillows so he could sit in a reclining position.

"Thank you, my lady," he said as she put the cup back on the nightstand and returned her gaze to him.

"You're welcome, and you may call me Sophie. I am no one's lady—not that I am aware of at least."

"Well then, Sophie, I give you thanks again. Now where am I, and where are my things? My sword and my pack?" The last bit he asked with a small hint of panic in his voice as he realized the magnitude of losing his sword and belongings.

"Relax. Your things are on that chair over there, your sword included. As for where you are, you are in a once-abandoned garrison several leagues travel from La Croix. I, along with the Lady Bette and many of the town's workers, have come here seeking refuge from a town in which we had no place. As soon as you are well enough, I would be honored to show you around your new home."

"My new home? I am sorry, Sophie, but you don't understand. I have to get moving as soon as I possibly can. Men hunt me—dangerous men. I would do well not to stay in one place for any length of time. I need to see Vinquist as soon as possible and then be gone before I endanger you and these people any longer," he said as he began to push away his covers and rise from the bed.

"Wait! You are certainly in no shape to be getting up and moving around by yourself. You can see Vinquist when he gets back. I think he said he had some business to attend to in Carne. He left you a note on top of your things. I'm sure it explains things better than I can," she said as she smiled shyly at him.

"In Carne? To see Jacoby? I need to go with him," Vashon said.

"I think he intended for you to stay here and heal. He said he would be back as soon as he could," she replied, holding her hands out in front of her to stay his progress.

"And just what makes you think that he wanted me to stay here and not go with him?" Vashon asked impatiently.

"Well, for one thing, he took your horse," she replied calmly, a small smile creeping over her face.

Alaric Vashon did something then that he had not done in quite a long time. He laughed.

Chapter Twenty-Seven

When Sophie left the room to find him something to eat, Vashon slowly began the painful process of testing each sore muscle and readjusting his body to moving about. Never one for being idle, he didn't want to stay in his bed any longer than he absolutely had to, and as long as he was stuck here without his horse, he figured he might as well make himself useful. He reminded his aching body that there was too much to do to simply lie there and wallow in his own discomfort.

He pushed back the covers and slowly swung his legs over the side of the bed where he sat panting for a moment, realizing for the first time the extent of the damage that had been done to him in the brawl. He gingerly put his feet on the floor and stood up and stretched his entire body. He glanced at his bedraggled image in the full-length mirror next to the chest on which his clothes and sword rested. Shock crossed his face as he studied his profile, noting the numerous scars and bruises that covered his body. The new scars showed up red and angry, while a patchwork of older, white scars marked a hard life spent traveling and fighting. Every one of his scars told a story, and he knew he wouldn't be the man he was now without them. He grimly nodded as he accepted that his body would now have one more tale to tell.

He looked at his belongings that lay on the chest and saw that everything was there, just as Sophie had said it would be. He noticed new patches sewn into his neatly folded black leathers. He wondered if it was Sophie who had mended them and reminded himself to thank her when she came back. The thought of her coming back gave him a strange feeling, and he found himself wondering who she was. How could she affect him so after only one meeting, for which he was barely conscious? He sighed as he resigned himself to focus on one thing at a time and began to once again take stock of his belongings.

His sword lay on top of his clothes, still in its scabbard, which was much scarred and notched from long use. He wondered that the men who had attacked him had not realized its value and taken it and was grateful for its safe keeping. It and Sunstriker were the only two possessions he truly cared for, and it appeared that both had made it through this trial with him. His body would heal quickly, as it always did. By then, Vinquist will have returned, he hoped, and could tell him what was going on here. Thinking of his old friend, who was more like a second father, brought a sad smile to his face, and he realized it had been far too long since they had traveled together. He wondered if Vinquist had heard the news of Bitterknot and Duncan's death. He wanted to tell him everything that had happened so that the old wizard could put things into perspective for him. He frowned, knowing these things would have to wait a while longer, until the other man returned.

When he took his sword out of the scabbard to check the blade for any nicks or scratches, an old habit he knew to be unnecessary because this blade didn't scratch, he found a note lying on top of his clothes. Knowing immediately who it was from, he set the sword down and eagerly opened it. He read,

My Dear Alaric,

I know you must be wondering where you are and how chance brought you to this place. Know you are safe, for the time being. I trust Sophie and the Lady Bette implicitly and so should you. Theirs is a tale worth listening to if you find yourself in need of a good story in my absence. I thank you for the loan of Sunstriker and promise to return him, hale and healthy, to you. He and I are old friends, as you know, and I relish the chance for us to travel together again. I go to Carne to see our good friend Jacoby and regret that you could not come along, but destiny pulls us in different directions this time, my friend, and you have some tasks to do in lieu of my return. I want you to know I have seen what befell you in Bitterknot and mourn the loss of Duncan with you. He was, as are you, like a son to me, and you and I shall sing his song of farewell together when this is all over. I want to remind you that all loss is not sorrow and all sorrow is not loss. There is far more to the story than you know, and, in time, you shall have all of the pieces of the puzzle. In the meantime, make the most of your time at the garrison and get to know those there and their story. Let your body and your heart heal themselves and wait for my return. Along with these things, I ask one more favor of you, and I know that it is no small thing but beg you to trust me in this. I have no doubt that you have met the young lady, Sophie, already. She is very special and near to my heart. While I am gone, Alaric, I would like for you to teach her the Dance. I lay my trust in your hands, my friend, and eagerly look forward to the day when we can meet once again. Until that day, I remain yours and always,

V.

Vashon closed the note back upon itself, wiping away the tears that had run down his face upon reading of Vinquist's sorrow at Duncan's loss. He knew his old friend felt it as keenly as he did and longed for the day when they could properly send off their friend as befitted one such as he. He also felt a twinge of irritation at the request to teach this girl the Dance. The wizard couldn't know what he asked of him in this, thought Vashon as he placed the note back on top of his clothes.

Further reflections on the matter were halted as the door to his room opened and Sophie entered, carrying a tray which held a bowl of steaming broth, a piece of bread, and some fruit, which set his mouth to watering. He couldn't remember how long it had been since he last ate.

"What are you doing up?" she asked as she sat the tray down at the small table in the room, pulling out a chair and pointing at it, her stern expression telling him to sit down and eat if he knew what was good for him. He obeyed without hesitation and laughed nervously at the imperious look on her face. He slowly took in the broth, beginning the long and arduous process of healing his body.

"I see you found your things and Vinquist's note," she said inquisitively. "Did he say what you are to do while he is gone?" As she spoke, she began making his bed, not wanting to appear overly interested.

"Yes he did—and he wants the impossible, is what he wants," he said quietly as he helped himself to another mouthful of ale and began formulating a plan for the massive task ahead.

Chapter Twenty-Eight

Vashon felt refreshed after eating everything Sophie had brought to him, even sopping up the last of the broth with the last bit of bread. Having finished and relishing the feeling of a full stomach, he leaned back and closed his heavy eyelids, only to open them seconds later when he felt her gaze upon him. For a moment, they simply stared at one another without any words to poison the silent contemplation between them. Eventually, he smiled at her, and she smiled back, saying, "Bette said that once you have eaten you should have a bath. Then I am to show you around if you are up to it. Well, actually, she only mentioned the bath, but since you're up, I thought that we might as well make the most of your time here."

She picked up the tray and carried it out of the door, while he grabbed his clothes and followed her into the hallway. He took note of everything he saw as they traversed the halls of the garrison, his tracker's senses immediately alert. He promised he would have Sophie show him everything of this place after he had bathed. They passed many people who smiled at her as they approached, although the smiles Vashon received were fewer and more cautious. Nevertheless, he returned all greetings in a courteous manner as they made their way to the bath chamber.

"I have a question," he said when they had reached the door. "Who are these people, and where did they come from?"

"All of your questions will be answered in good time. For now, enjoy your bath and relax. I will return when you are finished, and then I will show you the rest of the grounds and tell you a little about what is happening here and who these people are."

Flashing him one last smile, she left the room, closing the door behind her. Eying the steaming tub of water and knowing how good soaking would be for his aching body, he disrobed and entered the tub gingerly. He lay there for what seemed like an hour until the water began to cool off and his aches and pains started to abate, and then he turned his attention to the task of washing off the accumulated layers of dirt and sweat that covered his skin.

When he had finished, he dried himself with a soft towel and put his leathers back on, noting that not only had they been stitched up, but that they had been cleaned as well. They felt very good over the linen shirt that Sophie had put with them. For the first time in a long time, he felt more like himself. When he opened the door leading to the hall, he saw Sophie walking towards him with a middle-aged woman by her side.

"Well, well, Sophie told me you were up and insisted on seeing some of our home, so I thought that I would come and meet this man Vinquist spoke so highly of for myself. I am Bette, and it is a pleasure to meet you," she said as they began walking.

"The pleasure is mine, Lady Bette, for it seems I owe you much," Vashon said as he grabbed her hand, kissing it as if he were greeting a lady of great royalty. This made Bette blush, which was something she could not remember doing in a very long time.

As they walked through the garrison, Vashon listened in amazement as Sophie and Bette took turns telling him their tale and describing how things worked here. He, of course, knew of Vinquist's travels through towns such as this but had to admit that he never really thought about what happened to all of the people of such places. Now he saw the fruits of his friend's labors. In one room, many women sat knitting and repairing clothes. Men had turned one of the barns outside into a massive smithy, and the sounds of hammers striking anvils filled the air as they plied their craft. Bette and Sophie explained that, in this place, no one was greater than another. They had all experienced enough subservience in La Croix. They all lived together, everyone contributing to the common good, while they established their new home.

He added to their tale by telling them what he had seen of the town as he passed through, and they were truly surprised at the change wrought there in their absence. As they made their way back inside, he asked about Sophie and her role here. His eyes grew big when she told him who she really was and explained that her life as Sophie du Rochelle had ended on that day in the market. Then she laughed. He would have to get used to surprises, she told him. He laughed back, noticing how good it felt to be around people who made him feel alive again.

Soon, the sun began to make its journey out of sight, signaling the approach of nightfall, and Vashon began to feel his body tire. Bette and Sophie led him back to his room, where he promptly collapsed into a cloud of soft linens. They both wished him a good night, and he succumbed to the call for sleep before they had even fully closed the door behind them.

Awaking with a start several hours later, Vashon sat up in bed and looked out his window to see the night sky, the full moon shining brightly. Realizing that his racing heart would prevent him from going right back to sleep, he put on his boots and opened his door, entering the hallway to do some further exploring of his temporary home. He walked through dim, torch-lit hallways and made his way to the first floor. There, he found the main kitchen and helped himself to a glass of cool water and piece of fresh pie that one of the cooks who had risen early to start baking bread for the next day offered him. Thanking the cook, who had introduced himself as Isaac, Vashon left the kitchen and headed quietly down a hallway that they had not entered on their earlier foray.

He stopped in front of a door that was opened just enough for him to see the flickering shadows cast by a burning fire within and slowly opened it and stepped into the room. Looking around, he could see he was in a small library, built not for grandeur, but practicality and use. A fire burned brightly on one wall, and several chairs sat in front of it. He was browsing the titles of the books on the shelves when a rumbling voice stopped him short.

"I see I'm not the only night owl. I'm happy to see you up and about, Vashon." The voice, almost a growl, sounded from a chair that was hidden in the shadows next to the fireplace. He turned towards the sound, not knowing what he would see, and found himself straining to make out a dark form—one he thought existed only in his dreams.

Chapter Twenty-Nine

Vashon could only stand, frozen in place, and stare at the massive creature that was sitting in a chair by the fire. His initial reaction was of fright, his first thought to either find a weapon of some sort or flee. But he then realized that he was helpless against this thing that could easily dispatch him at will. Curiosity filled the void left behind by his fleeting fear. Entranced, he stared in mute fascination at the dark outline of the creature that, if his ears were not deceiving him, was laughing at him.

"Is this how you respond to one who saved your life and helped nurse you back to health, Vashon?" the Beast asked with a deep chuckle.

"I … I'm sorry," Vashon stuttered. "You took me by surprise—as I am sure you do most people, if you will pardon my frankness." Vashon was finally gaining his bearings enough to respond coherently. The Beast, gesturing with its massive paw, invited Vashon to join him, and Vashon cautiously took the adjacent seat.

"No apology needed," the Beast said in a gentle rumble. "I find your frankness refreshing. Most people—even those who live here, who know me by now—don't like to dally in conversation any longer than necessary." The Beast leaned forward into the firelight, giving Vashon a better glimpse of his new acquaintance. Vashon stared in awe at the Beast's massive size; its head towered over the top of the chair it sat in, and its massive body more than filled out its generous width. It had to be almost eight feet tall and was covered head to toe in a bluish-black fur. It was heavily muscled, but moved with a snake's grace. Its head was almost the size of a cart wheel, with ears that pointed up and an enormous jaw that revealed razor sharp teeth in its laughter. A pair of luminous eyes regarded Vashon with both intelligence and humor. To his credit, Vashon did not flinch but met the Beast's gaze squarely with one of his own as they took one another's measure. Obviously satisfied with what they found, they both leaned back in their chairs and continued their conversation.

"And what of those not of this place? What happens when they talk to you?" Vashon asked curiously.

"Alas, those conversations never go very well. Most people leave either screaming or speechless. It's a real shame, though. Even I need someone to confide in from time to time." The tragic note in the Beast's voice, coupled with the sly wink of one great eye, struck Vashon's humor and both of them settled into a fit of laughter that soon had Vashon wiping tears from his eyes.

"I am in your debt," Vashon said with a levity that indicated how serious a matter he felt this. "What is your name, friend?"

"I have held many names over the years, most of which are lost to the sea and the sky, but you may call me Beast, if you insist on naming me. My title, however, is now and has always been the same. I am called the Protector," the Beast replied.

"Well, Beast, I am Alaric Vashon—though I gather you already know this. For what you have done for me, Beast, I am at your service. Any time you feel a need to call upon me, I shall be there."

"Thank you, Vashon. It has been long since any have spoken to me as friend," the Beast replied, sincere gratitude audible in its voice.

"Do you know where Sophie is, or if she is awake? I was looking for her before I came here, but the door to her room was closed, and no one answered when I knocked," Vashon said.

"That is because she is my ward, and I must protect her. When she is resting, none may see her. Although," the Beast added, noting the look of dismay that crossed Vashon's face when he was told of Sophie's unavailability, "I'm sure she would be pleased to show you more of the keep tomorrow."

"I would like that very much," Vashon said as he began to rise from his chair. "I should bid you good evening. I did not mean to intrude on your time. Having slept so much lately, I find it hard to sleep through the night and thought a walk might help to ease my mind."

"Then if you're not overly tired, perhaps you would like to stay and talk awhile longer. I think neither of us has anything other to do this night but keep each other company. That is, if you don't mind. It's been a long time since I have gotten to simply talk with one I can call friend," it added as an afterthought.

"Actually, I think good conversation would be very welcome right now," Vashon said as he smiled and sat back down in his chair.

"Good. Perhaps you would like to have some of this fine red wine from La Croix. I have it on good authority that it happened to be the Duke's personal favorite. Since he's not here for us to toast his health and prosperity, we shall have a toast for his daughter and hope she finds her own happiness in this place." And the Beast poured two glasses, which they raised in silence together, and they drank to Sophie's health.

———————————

Several hours later, their bottle of wine long empty and sleep finally beginning to lay claim to Vashon once again, he said his farewell for the evening to the Beast and headed back towards his chamber. They had talked long through the night, and Vashon had been very impressed with the Beast's knowledge of history, warfare and a wide array of other subjects. They had shared ideas, dreams and philosophies and traded stories of their pasts. When he finally made his way to the door and turned to say good evening, the Beast stared at him from its chair and said, "Sleep well, Alaric Vashon, and sleep safe knowing that while you are here, you too fall under my protection. No harm will come to you, Sophie or these people. You are all under my watch. If you wish to talk more, whenever the moon is full, you have but to look and you will find me. Until our next meeting, friend, good night."

As he walked the halls of the keep, the dark blue of the twilight slowly fading to dawn's first hint of steely gray, Vashon thought of Duncan and all the times the two of them had spent together talking, much as he and the Beast had tonight. His heart heavy at the loss of his friend, he opened the door to his room and lay on the bed where he fell immediately asleep, no longer able to fight off his exhaustion.

As he slept, he once more dreamed of his friend, only not as he last saw him in Bitterknot, but as he had always known him—smiling, laughing, drinking, fighting and bringing out the best in Vashon as he so often did. That night he was visited by his friend again and again as they re-lived their time together, and it did his heart good to remember the man he had called brother. For the first time since he began running those many months ago, Alaric Vashon slept soundly and safe.

Hours later, a young woman's hand opened his door quietly, and Sophie peeked in with her deep blue eyes, finding him sound asleep, a peaceful smile across his face.

Chapter Thirty

"I must admit, that was one of the finest meals I've ever had," Vashon said as he sat back, placing his hands over his full stomach. He and Sophie had just finished a picnic lunch on the lawn of the garrison, and now he threw his head back to bask in the afternoon sun. Their lunch, which rivaled any meal he had ever eaten, consisted of cold chicken spiced with a seasoning so flavorful that every bite danced on his tongue, pears cooked in a light cinnamon sauce, more of the dark bread from the kitchen oven, and a soup made from fish caught fresh from the ocean the previous night.

"I'm glad you find our food agreeable since you ate enough for three," Sophie laughed as she looked at their empty dishes. "The people who helped prepare our meal did work in a town, sharing their gift with many, but they did not make themselves rich in the process. The men and women here came from La Croix, and all toiled away for nobles and wealthy merchants. They, along with the smithies, tailors, artists, seamstresses and others who live here, were the true heart of La Croix, and it's in them that the magic of the town resides," she said as she began gathering up their dishes to take back to the kitchen.

"But what are these people going to do now that they have left La Croix and their homes and work?" Vashon asked as he took the stack of dishes from her and began to walk back towards the keep.

"That is entirely up to them. They only have to learn that their futures now lay in their own hands, not in the hands of their employers or of a greedy Duke like my father. Once they learn to be free, they can do anything they like with their lives," she said.

"And you? What will you do now that you have left your family and the only home you've ever known?" he asked her.

"These people have been more my family in these last couple of months than my real one ever was, and this has been a far greater home to me than the mansion where I grew up. As for my life after this point, let's just say that it is a work in progress and that I am sort of making it up as I go along"

"Well then, Sophie, it seems that you and I have one more thing in common," he said as he held the door for her.

Life settled into a steady rhythm for Vashon at the keep, and he relished the feeling of belonging somewhere again, even though he knew in the back of his mind that once Vinquist returned things would change again. His body healed itself day by day, and after weeks of resting and good food, he felt nearly himself again and wanted to help out in whatever way he could as a way of saying thanks to these people for all they had done for him. Bette, of course, said that no thanks were necessary and that any friend of their rogue wizard was welcome in their home. Vashon insisted, however, and threw himself into whatever task he could find. Sophie often laughed as she spied him about the castle either moving things around, washing dishes or cooking (which proved so disastrous that he was only allowed to do it once). The chore he excelled at the most, however, was caring for the horses, which came natural to him. Vashon relished the simple opportunity to let these menial tasks absorb his thoughts, and slowly his mind began to heal itself as had his body.

Most of his free time was spent in Sophie's happy company. He was amazed at her love of life and the exuberance with which she took in everything she saw or did. She peppered him constantly with questions about his travels and all the things he had seen and done. She was most curious about the Elves and Dwarves and their way of life—so much, in fact, that Vashon began teaching her the most simple elements of their languages, of which she proved a natural student. Sophie was like a sponge, soaking up every bit of information he had to pass on, and Vashon slowly became infected with her love of life, as did most who spent any time around her.

The problem still remained that Vinquist had laid upon him the task of teaching this young woman the Dance, and Vashon, after sitting up many nights trying to figure out a way to make this impossible task possible, was no closer to the solution than he had been when he first read the note.

Chapter Thirty-One

Life for Vashon and Sophie continued this way for nearly an entire month, and they found a joy in each other's company that neither had ever experienced before. One day, as he stood in the doorway to the kitchen silently watching her peel potatoes for the evening meal, the women around her laughing at some joke that she had made, he found himself smiling. He thought of how wondrous this girl was who had come into his life and of all the different ways she made him feel. A memory from childhood brushed his consciousness. He remembered how he and his father had come in from their morning lesson at swordplay and found his mother busy setting the table for their morning meal. Vashon had hurried in the door and given his mother a quick hug and kiss before running off to put away their practice swords. As he reached the doorway to the kitchen, he had turned around to look at his parents one more time and saw his father still standing in the same spot watching his mother, wearing the same smile that Vashon now felt on his own face. He shook his head at the memory, left the doorway, and headed down the hallway to the room he had set up to begin practicing his swordplay again.

He had discovered the room on one of his many forays throughout the keep. Exploring the premises was more than a pastime for Vashon. His years of fighting and training had instilled in him the need to know every in and out of any place he dwelled should he ever need to escape or fight his way out. The practice room was fairly large and empty of anything but a few faded tapestries and some suits of armor. Vashon pushed these to the side along the walls, clearing the entire room for freedom of movement. A balcony ran along the top of the room, accessed either by a stairwell at one end or from the next upper level of the keep. This room had been intended to host balls, plays and other festive occasions, but his needs were much simpler. He found, stored away in a chest that was partially hidden by a picture of men hunting a bear, several swords and shields, which he polished, probably for the first time in centuries, until they became usable again. Once that task was done, he practiced the Dance.

His father had taught him swordplay. Aidan Vashon, without equal in the blade, had drilled into him from a very early age the various stances, moves, countermoves and positions of fighting with a sword, but it was his mother who taught him the Dance. She whirled with him in the yard outside their cottage in the summer and then inside when the weather turned cold, teaching him how to move as gracefully as if he were walking on ground as thin as eggshell that would crack beneath his feet if he missed a single step. At first he had thought it silly and complained to his father that he would better spend his time learning to fight than learning to dance, but his father had merely smiled indulgently (in that annoying way parents do) and told him to mind his mother. Then one day, before their evening meal, he went outside for his dancing lesson and everything changed.

His mother stood in the ring of trees where they usually practiced, but instead of her house dress, she was clad in loose-fitting breeches and a linen shirt. In one hand, she held the thin sword she kept in a chest in her bedroom. In her other hand, she held the sword with which Vashon practiced. She tossed him his sword, saluted him, and said, "Defend yourself, if you can," then launched into her attack.

His fighter's instincts took over, and his father's training served him well, but Vashon barely blocked his mother's blow before she had taken one step to the side, gotten inside his guard, and sent his sword flying.

"How … how did you do that? I didn't know you knew how to fight," he said. "Will you teach me?"

"Alaric, my love, what do you think I have been doing all this time? You have learned the Dance, and your father has taught you how to use a sword. Now, we join the Dance to the blade," she said with a smile.

For the following months, she worked with him on moving smoothly, on making his partner (or opponent, if it came to that) move where he wanted her to go, and on how to strike quickly and evenly. When she deemed him ready, on the day of his final dancing lesson—his eighteenth birthday—he walked out to the usual grove of trees. Both his father and mother stood, swords in hand, waiting for him to join them. They didn't have to say a word. He already knew this was a test and welcomed the challenge. He was surprised when his parents' friend, the wizard they called Vinquist, stepped out of the trees and bowed to them all, taking a seat on a stump to observe the match.

"I hope you don't mind if I observe your trial, young Alaric, but your parents thought I might like to bear witness for you," Vinquist said as he lit his ever-present pipe and sat back to watch the spectacle.

And what a spectacle it was. None would have believed who had not seen it for themselves. These three skilled artists moved and struck with speed and grace unmatched by any others in a dance of deadly beauty. Vashon quickly recovered from the surprise of playing to an audience, even if it was just a friend of the family, and engaged his parents at once as they attacked, coming at him from both sides. Vinquist watched the exhibition in amazement. The sheer sublimity of the family's movements and parries, the way in which they moved both separately and as one, brought tears to the wizard's eyes.

It ended abruptly. Vashon spun in-between the twin attacking blades of his parents, their swords missing him by inches, and disarmed both of them in a single motion before either knew what had happened. He smiled as they both turned to face him, looks of pride and admiration on their faces. Silence filled the glade. Only the heavy breathing could be heard after the sound of ringing steel had stopped. At last, Vinquist's applause broke the reverie. Vashon's parents hugged him tightly. When the father had picked up his sword, the large blue blade gleaming in the sunlight that shone through gaps in the green canopy above, he walked over to his son, got down on one knee, and held out the blade in his open palms. Vashon's young mind could not register what was happening.

"Go on, Alaric, you've earned it today," his mother urged.

Alaric Vashon reached out with timid hands and took his father's priceless sword that Aidan had always joked was made for him by an Elven prince. Vashon felt it for the first time and smiled at the way it felt in his grip. He raised his father up, thanking both his parents a hundred times over, and they all, including Vinquist, headed into the house, where they sat down to a fine meal, the kind they would all remember fondly for the rest of their lives. Throughout the entire dinner, Vashon never once let the sword off of his lap, wondering at his good fortune that such a thing could come to be his. Soon after he set out on his travels with Vinquist, the first of many times they would journey together.

Alaric Vashon, in that abandoned room in a garrison by the sea, recalled his parents' lessons well as he moved and spun about the room. As he remembered the joy of the Dance, he resigned to tell Sophie that night that they would begin her training the next day. For good or ill, she would learn the Dance. He worked with his blade, an artist at home in his craft, until the light of the rising full moon shone in through the windows.

Chapter Thirty-Two

Following his practice session and a bath, Vashon walked towards Sophie's room, mentally rehearsing how he would tell her of Vinquist's request. Having thought of and discarded many different ways of broaching the subject, he gave a mental sigh of frustration and abandoned his efforts. He finally concluded that she was his friend and that he had no reason to be nervous around her, although the way she looked at him sometimes brought a funny feeling to his stomach. He would simply advise her how they would approach their lessons and start as soon as possible.

He had to admit that this past month at the garrison had done wonders for his wounded spirit. He had the time he so sorely needed to heal without the distractions or interruptions of the running that had consumed his life for months now. He had been able to lose himself in his friendship with Sophie. He knew that their relationship would surely change once he began training her, but he hoped that their new friendship would remain intact. The Dance was sacred, and he had never taught it to anyone, much less someone who had never before held a blade. Even Duncan, who was his oldest friend and one of the foremost swordsmen in the world, had never requested that Vashon teach him the Dance. Training Sophie was going to be something that would take as much out of him as a teacher as it would her as his student, and the task before him loomed large and unassailable in his mind.

He was so caught up in his thoughts of Sophie's lessons that he failed to notice that something was stealthily looming over him in the dark hall as he approached Sophie's room. A quiet voice behind him stopped him dead in his tracks, his hand reaching out to knock on the closed door.

"Looking for someone at this late hour, Vashon?" the Beast's hearty rumble greeted him from out of the darkness. He turned to see the huge thing move from where it had been concealed in the shadows, into the torchlight.

How anything that big could conceal itself without being noticed in this hallway was beyond him, but he quickly shook such thoughts aside and smiled up at the Beast, realizing he had missed it in the past month.

"I was looking for Sophie. I have something important that I need to talk to her about," he said.

"Have you forgotten our conversation so readily, Alaric, or have you been too busy practicing your swordplay that you failed to notice that tonight marks the first night of the full moon? Vinquist must have skimped on your astrology lessons. Sophie is resting tonight, but perhaps you might accept my company instead? I'm sure whatever you have to ask her will stay on the shelf a while longer and will be as fresh in your mind in the morning," the Beast said as it put its large paw on Vashon's shoulder and led him away from the door and back down the hallway.

"You're right—it can wait until the morning. Maybe by then I will have figured out a better way to say what I need to tell her," he agreed.

"I would go with the simplest and most direct way to say anything. But then again, that is my way, not yours. I'm sure you will figure it out—you seem to be an intelligent lad," the Beast said with obvious affection in its voice.

"Where are we going? I don't remember looking over this area of the keep before," Vashon remarked as the Beast grabbed a lit torch from a brazier in the wall, holding it out in front as they made their way through piled-up crates and boxes that were covered in a thick layer of dust. No one had made it to this wing of the keep in recent times.

"There are some things you have yet to see in this place, Vashon. It shouldn't be long now," the Beast replied in a quiet voice.

They headed through storerooms filled with boxes, crates and various other items, all covered in the same layer of dust. Vashon tried to memorize the paths they took, so that he could come back to examine these things more closely, but it was hard to form a path in his mind in this dark place, and it seemed as though they were walking in circles. At last, he gave up, resigned himself to the Beast's guidance and followed in silence.

He almost walked right into the back of his guide, so suddenly did it stop and blend in with the darkness around them. Only the halted progress of the torch indicated that they had reached their destination. Vashon walked forward to join the Beast and saw that they stood over a curved stairway leading into the deeper parts of the keep. With a glance to make sure Vashon was still there, the Beast held the torch before it once more and proceeded down the stairs and into the shadows below.

How long they walked down those steps he couldn't guess. Time seemed to have stopped for them this night. When they at last came to the bottom, the Beast pointed forward with its torch and walked towards what quickly showed itself to be a closed door, hidden in the darkness. When they reached the threshold, the Beast looked at him and pushed it open.

If he had expected a loud creaking noise, Vashon was to be disappointed, for the door swung open smoothly on its hinges with barely the slightest grating sound. As they entered the room, they found armor and weapons stacked upon each other. These seemed to be of a different make than those in the store rooms upstairs. Implements of war from ages past stood in various positions around the room. Chests lay open, spilling scrolls so ancient that they had become yellow and brittle with time. As he slowly looked around, Vashon saw on one wall, mounted and snarling, the largest boar's head that he had ever seen. Startled, he backed away from the creature's vicious countenance, first in shock, then in sorrow, as he remembered the day in Bitterknot. He saw Duncan thrown from his saddle, a boar spear protruding from his chest. Holding his hands in front of him and trying in vain to protect himself from the visions which assailed him, Vashon backed towards the door, only to be met with solid resistance as he backed directly into the Beast's still form.

"Why did you bring me here?" Vashon asked, sorrow plain upon his voice.

"Because not all of your wounds have completely healed, Alaric. You still have a small ways to come until you can forgive yourself for what happened that day. You must confront your fears and overcome them if you are to be the man you once were. This is the final part of your healing," the Beast said quietly.

"It was my fault. He would still be alive if it weren't for me. Following me got him killed. Not to mention all the villagers who died that day. What did they ever do to deserve such a fate? I should have stayed and fought for them, instead of running for my life, which I've been doing ever since," Vashon said, tears streaming freely down his cheeks.

"Duncan would not want you to wallow in your misery at his loss. You were not responsible for his actions. He simply did what was in his nature to do. You could expect no less," the Beast said in an even tone that calmed Vashon.

"What if I told you that his death was not in vain and that in running that day you actually saved the people of that town? Would that change how you feel about things?"

"What do you mean 'saved the people'? The village was destroyed. I saw it. Duvaliet's men burned it to the ground while I ran. I'm sure they didn't stop there. I know them—traveled with them. I saw the look on his face. He would not have been satisfied until he exercised his anger on the town," he said.

"When you ran after Duncan fell, all his men gave chase after you. They lost you after a short while. As I'm sure you know, none of them possessed the hunting skills that they would have needed to track you, and they gave up and returned to town. Duvaliet ordered them to move on and left the town alone. The buildings set aflame while you were there were the only ones that burned. Through Duncan's sacrifice and your actions, the people of the town were spared. Buildings can be rebuilt; lives cannot be so easily repaired. And thanks to your actions that day, they didn't have to be. Duncan died a hero's death, and the people there showed him all the honor he deserved in his burial. You saved Bitterknot, Vashon. You did not destroy it."

Hearing this shook Alaric to the core. He had been running so long from what he thought had happened in that place, and to now hear this creature telling him that he and Duncan had saved the people of Bitterknot relieved him of a heavy burden that he had carried upon him ever since he took his first step as a hunted man. He knew Duncan would want him to go on living, free of this shroud of guilt and grief, living for both of them. He smiled as he looked up into the hooded face of his friend.

"Thank you," he said, mere words unable to express his gratitude and relief.

"Vinquist wanted you to know and said I would know when the time was right to tell you. He wanted to tell you himself, but obviously he has pressing business elsewhere. He wanted you to be free to move forward and said he had given you an important task to complete before he returned. I was to make sure you were fit to the task. Do you think you are?" it asked as they turned and headed back up the winding stairs.

"Yes ... yes I do, and first thing in the morning, I will find Sophie and begin her training, though how it will go is in fate's hands," Vashon said.

"Well, since you are free for the rest of this evening, shall we see if we can find any more of that fine red wine. What do you say?"

"After you, my friend. After you."

As Vashon turned to close the door behind him, he could have sworn he saw Duncan standing there, smiling at him and giving him a wave of farewell. When he blinked his eyes to clear them and looked to that spot again, however, his friend had gone. Vashon shut the door and turned to follow the Beast back up the stairs, humming to himself the tune that Duncan had hummed as they rode into Bitterknot.

Chapter Thirty-Three

" ... and that is how I came to be in your father's town a month ago and what led me here to you and this place."

Vashon finished telling Sophie the story of Bitterknot and of the subsequent months spent running from Duvaliet's men. He also told her, over breakfast, of his conversation with the Beast the previous night and how it had changed him. He felt whole for the first time in a long while and up to facing whatever challenges came his way. Having finished his tale, he sat back and watched as the different emotions played across her face.

Sophie couldn't believe what this man had gone through and the weight he had carried in his heart for so long. Her sorrow at hearing him tell his tale out loud for the first time showed plain on her face. But that quickly fled, as clouds flee before the sun, when she caught him smiling at her. She returned his smile, seeing that he was at last at peace.

"Thank you for sharing that with me. I know it must have been hard," she said as she poured herself another cup of tea.

"I thought since you told me your story that it would be unfair of me not to show the same trust. You have become a great friend to me, Sophie ..." He paused, unsure of what to say; "... and I have something else I need to tell you today," he finished.

"Go on," she urged him.

"Vinquist, in his letter, charged me with teaching you something. He said we should be finished by the time he returns, though I don't see how that is possible. But he was adamant about it nonetheless, and I just wanted you to know," he said as he took a sip of his tea.

"It sounds important, whatever it is, and I trust you, Alaric. I know you wouldn't let any harm come to me. If you think it is as important as Vinquist does, then I am ready to learn whatever it is you must teach me," she said.

"I will try to be a patient teacher. To be honest, though, I have never taught anyone these things, and they have never been taught to anyone outside of my family. It may be hard," he cautioned.

"Well, when do we start?" she asked.

"There is no time like the present, as my mother used to say. Shall we, my lady?" he asked as he got up and offered her his hand. He was pleased to note that she didn't release his grip until they arrived at his practice room.

"Here you will learn the Dance," he said as they entered the spacious room.

"Vinquist wanted you to teach me to fight? With a sword? I've never even held one before," Sophie said, uncertainty in her voice.

"No, not to fight, but to dance. It is so much more than fighting. It's art; it's love; it's war—it's everything and every feeling, embodied in motion," he said passionately as he tossed her a thin, wooden sword. She snatched the weapon from the air and gripped the leather-wrapped hilt tight in her hands. "There," he said, "now you have held a sword. Shall we begin?"

"Good, now, what would you do if I attacked you like this?" Vashon said as he launched a low attack, aimed at Sophie's knees, which she nimbly avoided, knocking his practice sword aside as she did. He had to admit, she had learned a lot in the past month.

She had learned at an amazing rate. Vashon was constantly awed at how naturally—or even supernaturally—the steps came to her. For someone who had never even handled a sword before, she soaked up the nuances of swordplay the same way she soaked up everything else she put her hands and mind to, and from their first few lessons, it became clear to Vashon that Sophie had the makings of a dancer of undreamt potential.

He often came to the practice room, unheard, and watched as she practiced on her own the moves and motions to better herself for their next lesson. When the next lesson came, she was always a little better than the one before—a breath quicker, a little stronger—and the time came, after several weeks of training, that he found he wasn't teaching her anymore, but that she was learning on her own, improvising on and performing variations of the moves he had shown her. From then on, they simply sparred during their sessions, Vashon occasionally correcting her or demonstrating a better way to execute a certain move. Mostly, as of late, he found himself pressed to keep her from getting inside his guard.

Sophie's prowess as a swordswoman advanced at such an alarming rate that Vashon knew she was born to handle a blade, just as he had been, and as he wiped the sweat out of his eyes, preparing to engage her next attack, he marveled that Vinquist saw in her the potential that no one else could, least of all Sophie.

He knew one thing: the past few weeks had been some of the happiest of his life. He and Sophie basked in each other's company, rarely leaving the other's side, even outside the practice room. He slipped to the left, barely avoiding her sudden lunge, and laughed as he engaged her blade and they whirled about the room before an audience of children who had snuck onto the balcony to watch the grand spectacle, a wonder they would tell their own children of many years hence.

Vashon knew great happiness and safety in this place. He reveled in the thought that the men who hunted him were separated from him by vast spaces of time and distance, and he imagined that their chances of finding him dwindled with every passing day.

Chapter Thirty-Four

Muddy boots rested squarely in the middle of the massive oak desk where the Duke of La Croix had sat mere months before. The man to whom the child-sized boots belonged reclined leisurely in the exiled Duke's ornate chair, lying back so far that only the top of his head, balding and gleaming in the late evening's lamplight, could be seen over the desk's massive frame.

"I am growing very weary of sitting around and waiting for this ... this so-called beast to come out. Why don't you just let me start at the entrance to the woods and walk towards the middle, killing everything that moves until I get lucky? Seems like a good enough plan to me." The sarcasm directed at his companion couldn't be missed in Vigan Marsh's voice as he sat on a couch in the corner, calmly picking lamb from his teeth with one of the Duke's finest gold-handled daggers.

The only answer he received was a small throwing knife which landed with a "thunk" a mere inch away from his left ear, pinning one of his red braids to the wall. Kragen hadn't even looked up from where he calmly sat, examining a small crossbow that fitted on the wrist and fired six-inch-long bolts. It was a gift he had gladly helped himself to from the small chest of arms in the main hall—one he had quickly mastered by shooting holes, from various distances, in the family portraits found throughout the palace. With only a small flick of his wrist, he had thrown the blade with pinpoint accuracy.

"You missed, friend," the giant said through clenched teeth as he gave a yank and freed the dagger, together with a large hunk of red hair, from the wall. He quickly gave the little knife a toss into the air, caught it by the blade, and sent it flying across the room to land in the seat of the chair directly between Kragen's legs. Kragen calmly reclaimed the blade and slid it back into place next to its five mates in the brace that enclosed his left forearm.

"Looks like your aim's getting better, Marsh. Maybe I've rubbed off on you a little bit. Stick around for a while longer and see what else I have to teach you." Kragen gave the bigger man a humorless smile and a wink before returning to his newfound toy.

"Those tiny blades of yours aren't any use in hands this big. However, I do have a larger blade here I could throw next time if you like." He calmly pulled his six-foot broadsword and smiled as he laid it across his lap and began to hone the already razor-sharp edge for effect.

"Would you two stop acting like spoiled children. I swear—turn you loose in a few villages with permission to steal, kill and destroy and you are happy as pigs in a rut. But hole you up in a fine house like this one for a few weeks and you're ready to gut each other for lack of things to do—ridiculous!" Duvaliet, who had since been aroused from his catnap, barely raised his head from the maps rolled out before him. He was studying the nearby lands, especially the nearby woodlands where they had not yet gone, and where he believed their quarry lay. He calmly took another sip from his glass of fine brandy and began drawing different sized radiuses over the map with a compass.

"I honestly don't know how you drink this stuff. It all tastes like swill to me," said Marsh who stood peering into the Duke's liquor cabinet. He opened a dusty bottle of rum and began sniffing at it suspiciously. After satisfying his curiosity, he took a swig directly from the bottle and promptly spit it out upon the bearskin rug on the floor. He then smashed the bottle against the wall in the corner, its pieces falling atop a pile of broken glass where he had broken a half dozen others. "Give me a good keg of dark ale over this garbage any day," he mumbled as he rummaged through the cabinet for his next likely victim.

"This garbage, as you call it, is some of the finest brandy I've ever encountered in my travels. Not that it matches what my—er, my father's lands produce every year, but still not bad. What you have thrown in that corner is probably worth a king's ransom, so stop wasting my brandy or else I'll have our quiet friend over there help me throw you against the wall to see what comes out when we do. Do we understand each other?" The anger of the Prince slowly became evident as he addressed the larger man. While anyone else of Marsh's stature would have laughed at the smaller man's threats, he knew better than to bait his current employer, so he backed away from the liquor chest and began pacing the room.

The last few months had worn the three men's patience down to a very thin layer, and each exhibited new symptoms of restlessness as the days progressed. Their voyage across the sea hadn't been the sort of thing tales are made of, but at least the captain of their vessel had been capable enough to get them through without much excitement. Money and influence such as theirs easily afforded them the luxury of proper travel. But the only excitement during their several weeks at sea had been the day that Kragen had come to the sudden realization that he had never hunted a shark and dived into the water holding a piece of meat from the casks below in one hand and a long knife in the other. Now, after what seemed like an eternity spent in the safety of this abandoned palace, Kragen proudly wore a string of shark's teeth around his neck.

It had been Duvaliet's decision to land at the town several miles away from their actual destination of La Croix. He said they would be better prepared for whatever lie in store for them if they took a couple of days to feel out the local landscape and listen to any rumors or gossip that was circulating in the surrounding villages. It had proven a smart decision indeed, as the situation in town had changed greatly since they had set sail nearly two months prior. It was whispered that a monster prowled the streets of the town at night, though none had actually seen it, and it was further said that any who crossed its path were made its slaves and never heard from again.

Duvaliet had quickly dismissed these ramblings as pure myth that had been conjured up by the country folk, although he suspected that some other truth lay below these exaggerated tales. More interesting to them, however, were the rumors that the town had become a haven for thieves, mercenaries and cutthroats, and that no decent person would ever set foot there again.

"Sounds like our kind of place," Vigan Marsh said brightly as they came at last into view of the town where the long rope of destiny had been leading them for the past several weeks.

For his part, Duvaliet said little as he eyed what he thought would surely become the next addition to his ever-growing lands. Doubt still nagged at him, though. They had crossed the ocean for several reasons: the hunt for Kragen's beast, to escape his father's scrutiny for recent "indiscretions," and last but not least in his calculating mind, to settle the score with Vashon. The last reason gnawed at him like a great thirst that could never be quenched until he had his blade at the throat of the man who had once traveled within his circle and eaten at his table, only to betray him when his guard was down. But no matter how many times and how many different ways they asked about a tall man wearing a black cloak, bearded and mounted on a huge black horse, none of the people they encountered could remember anyone matching his description.

Knowing that had any of these people seen a foreigner like Vashon they would have certainly remembered him, Duvaliet feared that the trail had grown cold. Thus, they made their way into La Croix. Everything they had heard about the place seemed to have once been true, but the beauty had become quickly undone by the new residents. Unsavory characters eyed them suspiciously from house windows and darkened alleys, as if their looks

121

alone would be good enough to scare off this new threat. Those who were savvy enough to have made it this far in life living outside the law, however, recognized the danger that these men brought with them and kept their distance.

It wasn't hard to find the place they would set up shop. The Duke's mansion, though slowly succumbing to the decay that afflicted the rest of the town, was the ideal location of power and prominence. Duvaliet suggested that they and their small company of soldiers settle in before taking stock of the town.

As they rode through the mansion's front gate, a large man in furs came galloping towards them with three of his guardsmen close behind. He informed them in no uncertain terms that he was the new lord of these lands and that any who wished to take up residence here would have to clear it with him first. Otherwise, he warned, they should vacate his property immediately if they knew what was good for them.

Duvaliet had calmly looked at Marsh, who with a sinister grin drew his axe from where it lay crossed over the long sword on his back, rode his horse directly next to the man's, and lopped his head off with one great stroke. His men, in shock and disbelief at their leader's abrupt end, realized too slowly that they should have run when they saw these men enter the gate. Dumbly, they tried to free their weapons from their scabbards but never had a chance as the thin man in dark green leathers began moving his arms in abrupt, hypnotizing motions. When they looked down, each man found a small knife embedded in his chest. They slipped out of their saddles and into the quiet embrace of oblivion and were not even paid a second glance by the three men and their company as they rode up to inspect their new lodgings.

Following that incident, none of the other mercenary leaders or hunters challenged the new sword slingers in town. Most simply accepted that someone bigger and badder had come along to take charge of things, just as several had done before them. Of course, Duvaliet noted on the eve of their second day that Marsh had impaled the severed head of the home's last occupant on top of the gate, which so far seemed to be keeping would-be intruders at bay.

Several weeks had passed, and Duvaliet had set up a network in town for gathering information about events and preparing for the hunt. However, time was dragging along inexorably, and all of the men longed for some sort of excitement to break their boredom.

As chance would have it, while Duvaliet was busy racking his brain for ways to keep his men from killing each other, the distraction they so sorely needed came their way in the form of one of the rightful heirs of the estate, who was now returning to his father's ransacked palace. Brendan, eldest son of Duke Meirmont Rochelle, had made the unfortunate choice of cutting short his mission to gather men who could help save his poor sister from the foul Beast's clutches, for he would soon discover that his timing could not have been worse.

Chapter Thirty-Five

"What in the seven hells is the meaning of this? And who do you think you are?" was the first thing the young man said as he was led into the study by one of Duvaliet's men. The trio had been alerted to his presence by the commotion they heard outside.

The three stared in mild agitation—mixed with a tinge of amusement—at the foppish young man who stood addressing them in such an irreverent manner. After receiving several sideways glances from Kragen and Marsh, Duvaliet got up from the desk and walked over to the intruder. But finding that he had to crane his neck back just to look the tall man in the eye, the short prince retreated several feet.

"I'm sure you have a name, and I'm sure you think you have a purpose here," said Duvaliet.

"I am Brendan du Rochelle, son of Duke Meirmont Rochelle, lord of these lands and owner of the estate in which you and your companions are both unwanted and unwelcome. I am sure that you have a name and think you have a purpose here, and I demand answers." He stood in the middle of these three dangerous men with hands on hips, lecturing them as a parent would a gaggle of belligerent children.

"Who we are is of no real concern of yours, boy. All you need know is that we are not the kind of people to take lightly. We appropriated this house from its most recent owner. Perhaps you met him on your way in."

"That's my handiwork," the giant man with red hair said from where he sat cradling a huge battle-axe in his lap.

"Yes, I'm afraid my associate here can be a little overzealous when it comes to property negotiations, but I cannot deny the effectiveness of his methods. I am called Duvaliet by those who know me best, Prince or master by all others.

The large man there is called Vigan Marsh, and that brooding fellow staring down a crossbow at you is Kragen."

"Ha! The infamous Duvaliet, Kragen, and Vigan Marsh, all come across the far seas and sitting here conversing with me in my father's study—that's quite a jest, gentlemen. Very well, if that is to be your game, I am pleased to make your acquaintance. I am called Brendan by my family but am, in all truth, King of the little Faeries." Saying this, he gave his best mocking grin to the man standing not far from the ground in front of him.

A storm broke behind Duvaliet's eyes, and Brendan received a surprisingly quick and strong fist to the stomach that dropped him to his knees.

"Impudent little cur! I give you a chance to be civil and perhaps leave here with your life, and in return you mock me? Very well. We are who we say, and whether you choose to believe that in the short remainder of time you have left is up to you, but I will not tolerate any insolence from you." Duvaliet visibly calmed as he addressed Brendan and hoisted himself up onto the edge of the great desk to continue the questioning.

"I'd not make him angry again if I were you," Kragen dryly remarked from his seat several feet away. "Just a word of advice—not really for your sake, but for my own. You see, I have the beginnings of a terrible headache, and if I had to listen to your screams for the next several hours, I don't think it would help my situation much."

Brendan had managed to bring his head up and was spitting blood on the rug between gasps of air. Tears had begun to freely roll down his face, and he began sobbing and begging for mercy, all vestiges of the haughty young man that had entered the room quickly dissipating.

"Now then—we have some questions for you, Master Rochelle. We have come quite a long way to your pathetic little town and have yet to find what we're looking for. I hope your answers meet my satisfaction. If they do not, I will have Marsh here" he gestured to the giant who had moved directly behind Brendan and was gripping his shoulders with hands as large as boulders—"break every bone in your body starting with your feet and working his way up. That way your brain, the only part of you that could possibly be of any use to me this night, stays conscious until the last."

The only answer from Brendan was a renewed round of sobbing as he squirmed his way around in the larger man's iron grip, futilely seeking some form of escape from his current situation.

"And if you still do not give us the answers we seek, then I shall have to let Kragen here join in the fun. Trust me, son, you do not want that to happen. I've seen his work before, and he can be quite … inventive."

Kragen's mouth quirked up a little on one side—the closest he ever came to smiling. He removed one of his knives from the brace on his arm and began honing its edge against a whetting stone, never taking his eyes from Brendan.

"Please don't hurt me. You can take anything that you want. There are many fine things here, and I'll tell you everything that you want—just don't hurt me anymore, please." The nobleman saw a glimmer of hope—hope that he might make it out of this situation alive if he played his hand right.

"Fool!" Duvaliet spat at him in response. "We have already taken whatever we want. Thank you for your magnanimous offer, though. I am growing weary of this and want some answers. What happened to this town? What happened to your father, the Duke? Where is the rest of your family? And what, if any, is the truth to the matter of this Beast we have heard so much about?"

"My father was driven mad after my sister was taken away by the Beast that you mentioned. Several months ago, a series of events here in town led to Sophie being abducted by this Beast, right around the same time that a wizard was seen passing through. My father spent all of our wealth luring men here to kill the Beast and rescue his workers from its foul clutches, but none that came were equal to the task, and eventually it turned my father mad. I have not seen him in some time. I have just returned from seeking help from people in nearby regions."

At the first mention of the Beast, a spark of interest lit in Kragen's eyes, and he sat forward, intently listening for any detail or clue in the man's ramblings that would aid him in the hunt to come.

"Soon after her disappearance, I led a squad of men to the bastion, which is the abandoned citadel in the middle of the woods three leagues from here. We were attacked in the fog before we even entered the castle's shadow, and we never had a chance. One minute we were alone in the woods, and the next the Beast was in our midst wreaking havoc. It moved so fast that you could barely make out its form before it was upon you. I survived and returned to tell my father of the events. He sent out notices on every ship and posted signs in every tavern for leagues around, promising a large reward to any who could defeat the Beast and rescue my sister. Soon, mercenaries and hunters—men like yourselves—began to appear, and their stain slowly spread over my once beautiful town. That is how things came to be as you find them now."

"You have done well, son of Rochelle, except for one small detail. There are no men like us. Remember that." Then, without the slightest change of expression on Duvaliet's face, he turned to Marsh and said, "I believe that this man is telling the truth. Break only one finger on his left hand."

"Wait, I thought that you said … Aiieeeee!" The Prince's pleas were quickly cut short by his screams of pain and the sickly popping sound of his finger being quickly bent in an unnatural direction. Duvaliet waited patiently as his cries subsided into whimpers, and then he renewed his questioning.

"Tell us more about this castle in the woods," he requested amicably.

Brendan sat motionless, whimpering, until Marsh shook him by the shoulders, shocking him into speech.

"Yes ... yes the castle. It is located in a clearing almost three leagues from here, hidden by a wall of wild rose bushes. It has some sort of magic spell cast over it that makes it only visible under a full moon. We have searched long for it at other times but only found ourselves wandering in circles."

"A full moon, you say? That's only a few nights hence," Kragen said as he began to stir in his seat at last.

Duvaliet remarked curtly, "I know when it is, thank you. It seems you'll have your hunt after all, Kragen. One more question, though, Lord Brendan. An acquaintance of ours, a big man with a very large horse and fancy-looking sword, may have passed this way. Do you know anything of such a man?"

"I haven't heard anything about a man like that passing through; I've been abroad for some time now. I'm sorry, but I have no answer for you."

Duvaliet nodded to Marsh, who released his death grip on Brendan's shoulders and hefted him up as one would a small child, setting him once again on his feet.

"Thank you, Brendan, son of Meirmont, for your aid. You have been most cooperative. Now leave. You are—how did you put it?—unwanted and unwelcome here. This house belongs to me now. Be glad you survived this night with your life and remember who you met here. Now get out of my sight." He motioned towards the door before returning to his map-covered desk, determined to locate this mysterious citadel.

As Brendan was leaving, he ignored the screaming voice of good sense that told him to leave immediately and get as far away from these men as possible. He hesitated at the door then turned to address the small man once again.

"I hate to push my luck here, but the sword on the desk ..." He pointed at a blade with gold wiring around the handle, set with a very large ruby in the pommel; "... it's my family blade. It belonged to my great-great-grandfather and has been passed down to the men in my family for generations. It would have been mine from my father in time. I beg for it back so that it may stay in my family." Confident that he had made a reasonable request, he drew nearer to the desk and waited for Duvaliet to place the sword in his hands.

"This sword here? A very lovely specimen," he said taking up the sword and moving to stand in front of the heir to La Croix. "You're right, Brendan. This sword should stay in your family. It belonged to your father, and now"— he stuck the point of the blade in Brendan's chest and pushed until the hilt of the sword rested flush against his ribs—"it belongs to you." Taking a step back, Duvaliet calmly watched as a look of shock stole over Brendan's features and the light faded from his eyes. After only a few seconds, he slumped to the floor and closed his eyes for the final time.

Duvaliet looked up and noticed Kragen and Marsh making their way around the body and out the door. "And just where do you two think you're going?" the small man demanded of his two lieutenants.

"To find some bait—can't hunt for a Beast without the proper bait. We'll send someone to clean this up on our way out." Without waiting for any response, Kragen slid out of the door, his boot heels echoing hollowly down the long, marble corridor as he headed to the front door of the house.

Marsh shrugged and followed his companion. Duvaliet nudged the body out of his way with his boot and turned his attention back to his maps. He wondered if he and Vashon would meet again before the hunt was finished.

Chapter Thirty-Six

The atmosphere within the Inn of the Lucky Merchant had changed much in the months following the disappearance of the Duke's daughter. But the clientele, however less dignified, was no less thirsty and still provided a steady business for the man who had named himself innkeeper. Sitting in his usual spot at one end of the bar, spreading vast tales of how he alone would kill this Beast—once his arm healed, that is—was Kerrick One-Eye.

"Just wait! That mange-ridden mutt'nhead 'll get its comeuppance. Hidin' in the shadows, the coward. 'Fraid to show its repulsive face. Ha! No one, man or beast, gets the better of Kerrick One-Eye and lives long—no one." His companions, numbered considerably fewer since the deadly excursion into the woods, said nothing. They had become used to Kerrick's rants ever since "the incident," as they referred to it, and knew better than to bait him when he was in this dark of a mood. They silently sipped their watered-down ale and nodded in mute acquiescence to his ramblings.

Suddenly the door opened, and in walked a dark man with a thin, black goatee. He wore green leathers and a black cloak, the hood up to protect his face from the evening's rainstorm. Immediately the man took down his hood and removed his cloak, tossing it across the nearest table, and made his way to the bar.

Normally no one would have paid much attention to a stranger's entrance, but ever since Vashon's appearance, they had become even more wary of newcomers. More than one unfortunate drifter found themselves hauled out back and beaten for the simple fault of entering the inn without knocking. The men's eyes were dulled to the way the man in gray moved like a predator; oblivious to the dangerous man he in fact was, they saw no more than a run-of-the-mill intruder in their midst.

Kerrick noticed the stirring all around him as everyone in the bar turned to stare at this stranger, who had an apparent disregard for his own safety.

"Humph," Kerrick muttered to himself, "another idiot needs a schoolin' in good manners."

Kragen drew to a halt six feet from the men who now stared at him with open malice. He had marked every man as he walked into the building and knew that, while they might be dangerous in a group melee, none would beat him man-to-man. "Good," he mused as he prepared his speech to recruit some of them to his cause, "They seem to be in the mood to fight. Maybe a bit of sport would do me some good after weeks of being cooped up with nothing to hurt."

"Gentlemen," he announced. "I'm here to offer a payment of ten gold crowns upfront for any man willing to join me in my hunt for the Beast. We leave in two nights' time for the woods. Anyone willing to join must submit to my command and the command of my two partners, no exceptions, no questions asked." He stood and waited for some response from the gathered men or from the big fellow wearing the eye patch who seemed to be their leader.

"Tell me, stranger, what's to stop us from killin' you and takin' your money right here and now, no questions asked?" said One-Eye. His companions laughed. "You ain't welcome here. 'Sides, you got a devil's prayer of catchin' the Beast. Can't kill what you can't see—'til it's right on top of you, that is. What, you think a scrawny twig of a man like you's a better hunter'n me? Y'aint the first gangly fool tuh come through here in a fancy getup, thinkin' money 'n pretty swords'll bring you luck. Not two months ago, a man cut from the same filthy cloth as you came through here, ate my food and drank my ale—thought himself better than us, but we took care of him and that big stinkin' horse of his."

"Big man? Long, dark ponytail and black beard, with a black horse and fancy-looking sword?" Kragen asked.

"What's it to you?" Kerrick replied. "He your long-lost dandy?"

"Tell me, did your men happen to kill him somehow?" Kragen asked, ignoring Kerrick's attempt to provoke him.

"Not exactly, though he's good as dead. We used him as beast bait. Last we seen of him, that slobber-flingin' fiend was haulin' him away—probably to eat."

"That, my nearsighted friend, was a big mistake. You should have killed him when you had the chance."

"Can't you hear, gangly? I said he's dead—beast droppings!"

"I somehow doubt it," said Kragen, turning to the other men. "The price has just been raised to fifteen gold crowns. My offer stands for two more minutes, gentlemen. How say you?"

"I speak for these men, and the answer is no," said Kerrick. "You made a mistake struttin' in here alone tonight. Take him out back and kill him," he said to his faithful men, then he spun back around to face the bar and sipped on his beer.

As the two men on either side of One-Eye made their move, each reaching for the handle of the his weapon, Kragen made two whipping motions with his fist, and they both went down with daggers in their throats.

The next three in line at the bar hesitated just a little too long, and two more fell before they knew what was happening. As the men on either side of Kragen began to close the circle, he started attacking in a blur of hands and feet that quickly put four more of Kerrick's men on the floor, either moaning in pain or unconscious. Kragen was rising from where he had just broken the leg of a particularly large man with a move he called the leg scissor, when a young man who had been hiding in the shadows ran at his unprotected back wielding a wicked looking dagger. But the young man never even came close, as he was propelled forward from the force of a broadsword, thrown from the doorway with precise accuracy. It landed in his back with such force that it nearly cleaved him in two. A lightning strike illuminated the doorway, in which stood the biggest man any of them had ever seen.

"Is there any fun left for me?" Vigan Marsh's rumbling baritone filled the room as he addressed his companion who was calmly retrieving his throwing knives from the bodies by the bar.

"Damn it, Marsh, I thought I told you to wait outside."

"Well, it sounded like things were getting exciting in here, and Duvaliet would probably appreciate it if you didn't kill all of the men that we need."

"Did you just say Kragen?" interrupted One-Eye. "The Kragen? Then that would make you ..." Kerrick One-Eye turned his narrow gaze upon the larger man.

"Vigan Marsh, at your service." Vigan made a mocking bow to the men, while bending down to remove his sword from the young man's back.

"Now then, I think my friend here made you an offer. Time's up. What say you, One-Eye? Are you and your men up for another run at this Beastie?" Marsh asked.

"I guess you leave me little choice. I only hope for all of our sakes that you have a better plan than that old drunkard did last time," Kerrick said as he downed the last of his beer.

"Oh, I think we can manage something. Come to the Rochelle mansion tomorrow to receive your pay and instructions," Marsh said. When they turned to leave, they nearly collided with one of their captains as he entered the inn at a rush.

"What in the world are you running for, Captain?" Kragen asked as the man caught his breath.

"It's a message from Prince Duvaliet, my lords. He says to return immediately. We've found the son of the Duke."

"We know that already, you fool."

"No," said the captain, "the other son."

"Well," Kragen said, "this just keeps getting better and better. I'd hate to keep our good Prince waiting. Shall we, Vigan?"

Chapter Thirty-Seven

"Now, let me get this straight. You say your name is Cass Rochelle and that you are a minstrel of some renown?"

"A bard actually. A minstrel simply sings songs for people to hear. A bard sings songs and tells stories," Cass corrected Duvaliet politely for the second time.

"Yes, yes, whatever you say." Duvaliet threw his hands over his head and flung them about in exasperation at the tone in his latest detainee's voice. "Now then, you are Cass Rochelle, a bard of great repute, younger son of the Duke, and you have been traversing the land gaining fame and fortune, and, on top of all that, you have returned home triumphant from your travels in order to rescue your ill-treated sister from the clutches of your controlling father?"

"Good," Cass sighed in relief. "I was beginning to think we were not communicating very well. Now that you know who I am and why I am here, perhaps I might inquire as to who you are and what you are doing in my family's house?"

The two guards holding on to either of Cass's arms during the entire exchange instinctively tightened their grip on the man. They knew what a mood the Prince was in and expected a blow to fall any minute on their unsuspecting charge. Wincing inwardly, they both tried to look elsewhere as the Prince flew out of his chair and came around the huge desk to meet his prisoner face-to-face. The Prince's attack was interrupted, however, by the sound of the door to the study opening and a familiar voice.

"I tell you what, Vigan. We leave for a short while, and our good leader here has already happened upon another son of the Duke. I'm beginning to think you people breed like rabbits, boy. I wonder just how many of you will crawl out of the woodwork before the day is over?" Kragen asked of Cass, while giving Duvaliet a sidelong glance, as if to ask what this was all about.

"There are only three of us. I have an older brother named Brendan—then there is me and a younger sister named Sophie."

"No, I'm afraid you had a brother named Brendan," Duvaliet sneered as he nudged the pair of boots protruding from behind the side of the desk; "there is only you and your sister now, and if you can't keep a more civil tongue in your mouth than your brother, then I'm afraid dear Sophie might become an only child before the sun rises tomorrow."

Cass gasped and tore himself away from the guards' grip to rush to see for himself the gruesome sight of his brother lying on the floor with a look of bewilderment on his face, their father's sword still sticking out of his chest. "What have you done with Sophie?" he demanded of the three men staring at him.

"Easy, boy—bravado will only get you killed here," Marsh cautioned as he placed one of his massive hands on Cass's chest to prevent him from coming any closer to their leader. "We have not seen your sister, nor will you find her in this place. I take it you haven't heard the news? Well then, sit down," he said, not really extending an invitation as he shoved Cass into a chair, "and we'll tell you why we're here."

Suddenly, it was Duvaliet who was the bard, spinning the tale of their journey and filling in the gaps with fragments he had pieced together from stories told to them by others. His face was animated, and he made broad, exaggerated gestures with his arms and hands as he spoke. And this went on for some time.

"… and that is where you managed to find your way into our story, young Rochelle. Your sister was abducted by a beast living in the woods near town; your town is overrun by sell-swords and thieves; your father has gone mad; we are here to kill the Beast and hopefully get revenge for a wrong done to us many towns away; your brother got himself killed, putting you next in line for the Dukedom; and you are sitting in my study where I find your usefulness waning. Any questions?" Duvaliet took a breath and then took another drink of brandy from one of the decanters he had managed to save from Marsh.

"I … I don't know what to say. I've been away for so long. I only wanted to come back and take my sister away. Now that I find things as they are, I don't know what I'm going to do. I suppose I will go to the garrison and see if I can rescue her. Yes, that is what I must do. Thank you, gentlemen, for the information. I'll take my leave now, if you please." Cass hurriedly got up and tried to make his way to the door, only to be blocked by the massive form of Vigan Marsh casually leaning on the door frame.

"Now, now, lad. We didn't say that we were through with you, did we?

You get to leave when and if we say so," the big man growled as Cass went back and sat down in the chair again.

"You're not like your brother," Duvaliet remarked as he studied Cass over the lip of his glass. "I don't really see how you were related. We have a lot in common, you and I. We're both handsome, we both have siblings who are nothing like ourselves, although I plan to personally strangle my brother when I get back home, so perhaps I can understand a little bit about sibling differences after all."

"Sing us a song, bard," Kragen drawled from where he had been sitting quiet for the last several minutes. "You claim to be one of the best in the land, and our ears are about as noble as you're likely to find in these parts, so why don't you favor us with a nice ballad? If we like what we hear, we let you go, with our best wishes in finding your sister. However, if we do not like what we hear, you'll wish to share your brother's fate before the night is over."

Cass looked from one face to another, trying to see if there was any other way out of his current predicament, but he could tell from the resolve he found on the three men's visages that if he was going to get out of this house alive and ever see his sister again, he would have to sing for it.

So Cass cleared his throat and shared his gift with the men in the room. He opened up with a rich voice that washed over them so strongly that even they found themselves caught up in his song. Caught up, that is, until they realized two lines into the second verse that Cass had chosen to sing for them the newly-made "Ballad of Bitterknot."

The giant astride his horse sat and bled,
the dark one, crying, turned and fled,
and the little one stomped his feet, face red.

Lost in his craft as he was, Cass did not notice the darkness steal across their faces. They let him continue, but Duvaliet had taken the lute from Cass's pack and was running his hands over its polished wood frame. As the third verse came to an end, realization struck Cass more profoundly than any blow ever could. The line about how the valiant Alaric Vashon had fought them off had already slipped from his mouth before he could stop himself.

Pain exploded in his head, and he abruptly wished he hadn't opened his eyes to see his favorite lute crashing towards him as Duvaliet gave in to his anger. Cass fell to the ground as blood poured down his face from where the instrument had gashed his head. His vision ran in a sea of red for moments as he convinced himself that this was how his life was going to end, all for picking the wrong song to sing for three of his most unappreciative critics ever.

"Stand him up, Marsh," Duvaliet panted as he knotted his hands into fists, preparing to unleash some of his pent-up fury on Cass's bleeding form.

As he hauled Cass up from the floor, even Marsh's eyes widened a bit at his liege's sudden loss of temper, and he shot Kragen a look of surprise. They'd seen Duvaliet angry before, but he had always been able to rein it in. This was a blind rage, and Marsh didn't think the lad would live through the night. His thoughts were broken as Duvaliet struck Cass four times in rapid succession. The first hit slammed into his nose, making a sick squelching noise, and the next three landed on his stomach, ribs, and kidney. Cass slumped limply to the ground into a whimpering heap.

"Again, Marsh. I said stand him up. Do not let him go until I tell you to," Duvaliet said with a deadly quiet.

As Marsh's big hands picked him up to face Duvaliet, Cass's survival instincts kicked in, and he vowed he would not lie down and die for these men like some animal in his own house. Feigning unconsciousness as he was hoisted to his feet, he threw his foot out in a lightning-fast kick aimed at the smaller man's groin. The sudden pain in his foot told him he had connected with his target. His heart leapt in triumph as he heard the Prince groan and go to his knees, and the big man momentarily let go of his arms to help his liege.

Cass didn't even consider stopping for his things as he sprang for the door and threw it open, heading towards the main entrance and out into the open safety of the night air. He had only gotten five steps when a sharp pain in the back of his right knee dropped him like a stone. Turning to see what had happened, he saw the handle of a small knife jutting out of his leg. The blade was buried several inches into the meat right at the bend of his leg, making any further attempts at escape futile.

"That was either very brave or very stupid," Kragen said as he walked up and, with one smooth jerk, removed his knife from the back of Cass's leg, wiped it on the front of Cass's tunic and replaced it in his brace. Both men turned in time to see a limping Duvaliet coming out of the study towards them, Marsh directly behind him.

"You have just earned yourself the privilege of being our guest for the evening," said Duvaliet between groans. "We will see just how deep we can explore the depths of your pain. I hope it was worth it, Rochelle." Duvaliet panted as he caught sight of an old man shuffling down the hall in the other direction towards the mansion's kitchen. The old man had been there since they had arrived at the mansion and had apparently been part of the original household staff. Duvaliet had kept him on as he knew where everything they might need was located, and because he seemed to know the value of keeping his mouth shut and doing what he was told. Grimacing through his pain, he pointed a finger and yelled at the man.

"You there! Come here and take this man below until we deem it time to deal with him later on this evening. Find one of the rooms below and lock him in it. No one is to go in and see him until we are ready to continue our talks with him. Do you understand me, old man?"

"Yes sir, I understand very well. Come, lad. Let's get you out of this hallway. We can't have you bleeding all over the place. I'll just have to clean up more blood. One dead Duke's son is all I can handle for one day." The old man quietly slipped an arm around Cass's shoulders and, with strength belying his frail appearance, led him around a corner and out of sight of the three men.

Cass's mind reeled in panic over the events of the past few moments, and it took him several turns in the hall to realize that he was not being led below ground as Duvaliet had ordered.

"Where are you taking me?" Cass demanded as he turned to get a better look at his guide.

"Shhh, child. Quiet now, or they will hear, and then I'll never be able to get you out of here undetected and alive. Do as I say, and old Vinquist will set things aright, dear one."

Cass's eyes widened at the mention of the name that he knew from many of the songs he sang—a name of power. He turned awestruck eyes to once again look at the man leading him.

They stopped as they entered a pantry storeroom full of bags of flour, kegs of salted beef and mounds of potatoes, and Cass slipped from the man's arms to the floor, his hands immediately going to his bleeding leg and head. Vinquist made sure the door was shut tight behind them, and when he turned to once again face Cass, his appearance was not that of a feeble old servant but of a tall man with long hair and beard, cloaked in black, with a nimbus of power surrounding his form.

"There isn't much time, so I'll have to do the best I can right now and finish healing you later," the wizard muttered as he bent over Cass's prone form and placed hands glowing with a faint white light over his head and leg. The wounds were suffused with a warm feeling and closed over themselves in a matter of moments.

"Now then—your sister is indeed alive, and I am going to send you to her. I'll let her explain the rest to you. Out this door is a horse, saddled and ready to ride. All you have to do is hang on; he knows the way to the citadel. Don't worry about being seen; I've seen to that. Just make it there in one piece. Your body has sustained massive damage and needs more care than I can give it right now."

"But how...?" Cass began, until the wizard's hastily raised hand stopped him short at the sound of faint voices coming down the hall.

"No time. When you get there, tell your sister and Vashon"—Cass's eyes widened as yet another name from many of his songs came to life—"Tell them who these men are and that they will be coming in two nights' time, so be ready. I'll see you again soon. Now go, Cass, and be safe."

Vinquist opened a hidden door behind one of the casks of salted beef that led to the sweet night air which, after the events of the past two hours, smelled like rain-washed freedom to Cass. Directly in front of him, he saw a brown horse saddled and ready to ride. Wearily, he climbed into the saddle and prayed he could stay in his seat until he found his sister.

The wizard crept out unnoticed behind him, concealing their exit place as he went and silently hoping he had given them all enough time to prepare for the coming storm before it would break two nights hence. Looking at the nearly-full moon, he moved through the woods in the direction of the citadel, wondering what he would find upon his arrival.

Had he lingered in that same spot only a moment longer, he would have been greeted with the sight of a shadowy figure slipping through the same door he had exited only moments before and disappearing into the waiting darkness within.

Chapter Thirty-Eight

Meirmont Rochelle walked through the same woods behind his estate that he had traversed many times. After a good dinner, and with a full stomach, he would meander through the comforting paths among the trees and shrubs and meditate on the condition of his prosperous town. This night found him repeating the ritual that had become habit to him during his many years spent ruling La Croix.

He had been walking the pathways of the forest for some hours, when his stomach's protests told him the time for his usual repast had long since passed. Mumbling to himself how good it would feel to sit before a roaring fire with a nice glass of wine or two, along with a brace of roasted pheasant and those pickled beets of which he was so fond, he hitched the collar of his fine cloak closer about him and set off for his estate to enjoy his evening meal.

His boots of polished black leather made little noise as he moved through the underbrush, and none of the animal residents of the forest bothered him on his way to the side door he had taken to using as of late. It seemed to him that all the living creatures of his lands recognized him as lord of this place and paid him silent homage as he traveled amongst them. He smiled a grand smile and patted his silken doublet over his stomach in anticipation of the meal he knew would be waiting for him when he reached his destination.

There it loomed only a couple of hundred yards in front of him, his own private entrance to his secret lair within the estate. He smiled at his servants' training—that they had anticipated so well their master's arrival and had left the door open for him. Quickening his pace just a bit, he hastened to the door and, taking one last look about him to make sure no others marked his secret entrance, slipped inside and became only another shadow consumed by the darkness within.

Even though the dark suffused the room and drowned out any use of sight, Meirmont knew by heart where his secret lay. Taking two steps right and then four steps forward, he let out a small grunt of approval as his waist bumped against the barrel he knew would be there. Grabbing the top of it in his hands, he gently slid it to the side to reveal the trapdoor beneath, with only a small piece of rope marking its location. Meirmont chuckled at his own cleverness and wondered at his good fortune to have such a place of solitude when everyone else desired to be in his presence.

Raising the hatch and sliding first his left and then his right foot onto the ladder below, Meirmont felt his way by touch alone down the dozen sturdy steps of the ladder until his feet touched onto the solid stone floor below. Looking with satisfaction to make sure the trapdoor had closed well behind him, he grabbed one of the torches off of the wall to his right and lit it in the already blazing fireplace. As it illuminated the scene before him, Meirmont took in his surroundings and smiled.

"Yes indeed," he thought bemusedly to himself, "I truly am a lucky man."

The fire roared strongly in the fireplace, giving its gifts of light and heat to the small stone room. In front of the fire was his favorite chair—not the nicest he owned by any measure, but the one he had always loved to sit in and reflect on the events and politics of running a successful town. Set on a small table were two tapers, which he quickly lit so that he could survey the meal before him. Crackling pheasant, the skin brown with a sweet glaze and still steaming, sat in a platter of pan-fried apples. A hunk of strong white cheese lay on a side platter with a large loaf of freshly baked dark bread and newly-churned butter. A golden wine goblet sat next to a bottle of his favorite white wine, a vintage that came from far overseas, nearly impossible to find in these parts of the world. Pulling the stool out and preparing to dig in for his evening feast, Meirmont felt a sudden urge to look at himself in the mirror on the opposite wall before his dining commenced.

Looking at the fit man before him, no longer young but still healthy in mind and spirit, he gave a satisfied nod and went to turn back to his cooling meal, when a cold voice, no louder than a whisper, stopped him in his tracks: "Rochelle, look with unclouded eyes and see what you have become." He watched as the image before him faded into that of a decrepit man, unkempt, deathly pale and filthy.

Had he not been so deep underground, surrounded by several feet of stone and earth on every side, everyone above would surely have heard his scream.

———————————————————

Vinquist stopped dead in his tracks, not a mile from the estate. He had to find a fallen trunk to lean on, as his power had suddenly drained from his body. Although it was restored seconds later, he was left feeling dizzy and disoriented. He had experienced the same feeling when waking from his nightmare so many months ago, and the same presence had flickered across his consciousness, and then just as quickly it was gone. He now knew why fate had brought him to this town, and he knew that the journey was a long way from over.

He reminded himself that he had imprisoned the dark one a dozen lifetimes ago and that it must be old age that was slowing him down, making him sense things that were not really there. But try as he might to convince himself otherwise, he knew the true cause of the sinking feeling deep within him. While it lacked its full power and came like the yawning of a sleeping giant in a distant cave, another storm had begun brewing this night, one that could soon threaten to drown all he cared for in this world.

He would have to look into these things when time permitted. For now, however, he had to focus on the task at hand. He steadied his resolve that there was still much work to be done before all was played out in this time and place. He stood up, brushed himself off and once again resumed his trek through the woods towards the waiting citadel—towards Vashon, Sophie and the interlocking destiny that had brought them all together.

Had anyone been watching his retreating form they would have noticed the slight shiver that wracked his body as he turned a fleeting eye to the western sky before he turned again to the path ahead. They also would have noticed him finger an age-old scar that ran over his heart. The flesh had long ago healed, and only a faint line remained visible, though the wound beneath now ached as it had not done in a very long time.

Frozen in place, Meirmont could not avert his eyes from the horrifying image in the mirror, a ragged beggar, beard and hair gone wild with lack of upkeep and clothes tattered and stained, mere rags on a famished and skeletal frame.

In one hand, instead of the wine glass he believed he was holding moments earlier, was a dirty, cracked bowl containing a small amount of soured beer. In his other hand, gripped with white knuckles, was a single golden coin, worn smooth from constant rubbing. As the voice in his head commanded him once more to look more closely, he turned in horror and stared at his private room of solace. No fire burned in the fireplace. Only a few charred sticks and a small pile of ash gave notice that a fire had ever been lit there. His cozy chair in front of the fireless pit was nothing more than an empty crate. Worst of all, though, was his discovery of what awaited him—or rather what did not—on his dining table where he had hoped against the horrible certainty brewing in his mind that there truly was a grand meal. The table and stool still stood as they had in his vision; however, in place of his lavish feast lay the remains of several rat carcasses in varying stages of decomposition and one bone-dry wine jug next to a rock-hard crust of bread and moldy rind of cheese.

Meirmont began to wail in fear and desperation. He crumbled to the floor where he lay in a fetal position, rubbing his coin with a ferocity born of terror, as if it were the only thing keeping him alive. It was then that the voice, which had remained silent while the stark reality of his condition was still sinking into Meirmont's enfeebled mind, resumed its whispering in his ear.

"Rise, Rochelle, and look at what I would show you. Things need not always be thus for you. We have both been wronged by one man, and together we may yet make things right. Rise and look in the mirror, Meirmont."

He did as he was bidden and slowly pulled himself to his feet. He then looked through the mirror into a time when things might be far different. At first he saw things that pained and enraged him: the disappearance of his daughter, the mob pelting her with refuse, his interrogation of the wizard, Vinquist. The face of a beast then flashed before his eyes, and he saw himself kneeling in front of Gaston, deranged and reduced to a sobbing babe in front of his eyes. But he didn't dwell on these painful scenes for long, for the image changed once again, and he saw himself become great once more, sitting on an ivory throne in a gigantic room of black marble while thousands bowed before him and hailed him as their leader. He saw himself standing before a pile of gold such as he had never before imagined, and lying on top of that treasure horde was the body of Vinquist, impaled on a black sword, eyes forever open in fear and surprise. Meirmont Rochelle smiled, dreaming of a day when he would be restored to his proper place in the world.

"Soon, Rochelle. I have not yet regained my true strength. It will take time, but our chance will come, and when the opportunity presents itself, we shall not be found wanting. But for now, it must be thus," the voice faded off, leaving Meirmont with a feeling of great contentment as he dreamed of what would come.

The vision vanished, and he was again himself, the very picture of wealth. He couldn't remember the last moments but was ravenously hungry. Straightening his silken doublet, he turned back to the table to resume his feast and pulled off a wing, letting the juices run down his chin, thinking all the while how wonderful life truly was.

Chapter Thirty-Nine

The sound of engaging blades rang sharply up and down the hall, and those doing their part to keep the citadel running gave pause whenever they came within earshot of the room where the two duelists had been practicing for the past hour.

"Good, now turn and thrust," Vashon said through clenched teeth as he sidestepped a parry and thrust so quick from Sophie that he would have easily been run through had he been any other man. Truth be told, he was hard-pressed to keep her attack at bay and barely glimpsed an opening in her defenses in which he could launch a counterattack of his own. Through the sweat that ran down his forehead, stung his eyes and tinged his tongue with salt, Vashon bared his teeth in a terrific grin and launched at her with a great overhead blow. Sophie nimbly ducked under his swipe and gave him a slap on his backside as she spun through his attack to face him on the other side.

Their lessons over the weeks had gone exceedingly well, and Sophie had, after all, learned the Dance.

And what a dancer she had become, Vashon marveled to himself as they moved through their graceful practice. Work throughout the keep frequently came to a standstill as the residents crowded the balcony running around the top of the practice room just to watch them. The Dance captured their attention, while the two on the floor swinging their blades and moving through the now familiar patterns never knew they had an audience, so enamored were they with their swordplay and each other.

As much as Vashon hated to admit it, Sophie had reached the end of his lessons. He had moved from reluctance to teach one who had never even held a blade before to amazement at her natural ability. She seemed to be born to fight and excelled in a way that only a few others he had ever seen could match. He could sense, however, a tension building and a pressure mounting as they both realized that the routine they had established over the past couple of months would soon end.

During the course of his time here at Sophie's Garden, as the keep had come to be called by its inhabitants, Vashon's soul, which he thought would never be whole again, had flourished in the presence of the woman laughing before him. During their training, he had grown strong again, and against all odds, he had learned to love in this hidden place. Of course, he still had to build up the courage to tell Sophie he was in love with her.

His reverie had distracted him just long enough for Sophie to gain the element of surprise. Instincts alone saved him as she launched her most cunning attack yet, and he backed away quickly, moving his sword in front of him in intricate patterns too quick for the eye to follow, blocking her every cut, thrust and lunge, but just barely. Quick as thought, she had backed him against the far wall. As he brought his sword against hers, pommel to pommel, he knew he had taught her all he could. Vashon grabbed Sophie's arm, pulling her close, and smiled.

She smiled back through the sweat that ran down her fair face, dark tendrils of hair pasted to her skin. Hers was not the cautious smile of one who is unsure of the next step, but the sure grin of one who truly knows the moves of the routine and relishes the next one she will make.

Ah, what a dancer she had become!

A sharp rapping on the only door leading into the room jolted them both from the spell they had cast about themselves. One of the townsfolk, formerly a rose merchant in La Croix, stuck his head in the door and made his way across the room.

"I beg your pardon, my lord and lady. I know you said you were not to be disturbed by any means while you are practicing, but I thought you should hear this as quickly as possible. A man just entered the grounds, injured and on horseback. How he found the place and got in unattended we can't tell, but he is a fright to see—bleeding and all. We thought you two should come and take a look as soon as we found out." Having conveyed his message, he simply crossed his arms and looked back and forth between them, waiting for them to follow him from the room to see for themselves why he had interrupted their dancing lesson.

"Do we have any idea who this man is or where he comes from, Marcus?" Sophie asked as she and Vashon slid their swords into their scabbards and started to follow him from the room.

"That's why we came to get you so quickly, my lady. It's your brother, Cass."

Before he could say more, she dashed down the staircase toward the reunion she had thought would never happen.

Vashon, hand still on the hilt of his broadsword, hesitated at the top of the stairs and looked down on the scene of Sophie kneeling in front of a man who lay on the ground. Judging by the resemblance they bore, he knew that this could only be the brother, Cass, whom she had told him so much about. After giving them a moment alone, he hurried down the stairs to meet Sophie's beloved brother for himself and also to find out how he had gotten into the castle grounds, on a horse no less, without anyone raising the alarm.

His priorities changed, however, when he finally got to the place where they sat and saw the condition of the man who lay in Sophie's arms. She could only cry over him, both in joy at his return and in shock at the condition in which they found him. Cass had obviously been through a great ordeal, and Vashon had seen enough men on the edge of collapse to know that this man didn't have long. Thus, he resolved to quickly find out all he could about the circumstances surrounding Cass's sudden arrival.

He laid a comforting hand on Sophie's shoulder to let her know that he was there if she needed him, but she didn't even look up from her brother's bloodstained face to acknowledge his presence. Cass, however, took his amazed eyes from his sister's changed appearance to look up at the large man who seemed so at ease around his sister, and his eyes widened as he grabbed Vashon's bare wrist and pulled him close, a sense of great urgency come over him.

"You must be Vashon. I'm glad you are here, just as he said you would be. He said to tell you that they are going to need you very much before this is all over."

"Cass, hush, dear heart," said Sophie. "All of that can wait. What matters now is that you are safe with us." He obviously was in no state to be getting this agitated, and the look of need in his eyes frightened her for what it might portend.

"Old man? Long beard?" Vashon asked, his gaze never leaving Cass's.

"Yes. Vinquist. He helped me escape and gave me the message to give to you. Brendan is dead, Sophie. I saw him lying in Father's study with my own eyes, murdered by the same men who did this to me. I would have joined him had Vinquist not gotten me out of there just in time."

Sophie, ever strong, showed no outward signs of emotion, but Vashon knew her well enough by now to realize that, under her calm façade, a fountain of unbridled rage boiled at the treatment of her brothers by these men, whoever they may be.

"We know Vinquist well, brother, though he has not been here in quite some time. It's fortunate he was there to help you, but I think it far from coincidence. Nothing that happens around him is merely by chance. But tell us, who did this to you? Who took over our family house and treated you so?"

"That, my sister, is the message I was to give to Vashon. Vinquist said to tell you that the three have somehow found their way to La Croix and will be coming this way in just two nights' time. He said to be ready—your test is at hand." And Cass gave Vashon's wrist a hard squeeze before he succumbed to unconsciousness.

Chapter Forty

"These men—Duvaliet, Kragen and Vigan Marsh—how exactly do we get rid of them?" Sophie asked pointblank. She and Vashon were alone again after seeing to Cass's care and comfort. They had not yet had time to discuss what his arrival meant and, more importantly, what the message Vinquist had sent them was meant to convey.

"You don't understand, Sophie. These aren't normal men like those who've come here before. These are hard men. I should know; I've traveled within their circle. That is what led me here. Bitterknot is thousands of leagues away and a lifetime ago, but I still don't know if their being here is because of me or for some other reason. But that point is moot now anyway. What does matter is that they are coming and we have only two days to get everybody, including you, safely away." Vashon sounded exasperated and perhaps a bit desperate as he tried valiantly to sway the headstrong young woman in front of him to his point of view.

"What I do understand is that these men have taken over my family home, killed one of my brothers and almost succeeded in killing the other one. Now I am told that they are on their way here, the only place I have ever truly felt at home, and you are sitting here telling me that we are going to run? I'm sorry, but I stay and fight. Whether you choose to stand with us—I mean me—is up to you." She stood with crossed arms, and tears of anger flowed freely down her cheeks as she spoke so harshly to the man she had come to care for so much.

"But these are not men we can defeat alone. They are not the normal trappers and mercenaries who have been so easily run off from these woods by the Beast's presence. They will not come alone either. They will have men with them—seasoned men who know how to hold their heads in a fight. Duvaliet is many things, but he is not a fool. Believe me, I do not want to run anymore than you do, but this is a fight I'm certain we cannot win, and even if we did, the cost in lives would be too high. I'm begging you one more time to reconsider. Please. Help me lead the people away from here while there is still time."

"All these past weeks, all of the lessons, what have they been for—for show and exercise? No, Alaric. You knew as well as I that we were training for something more. We knew that something was coming and that we needed to be ready. Now that day is here and you want me to run away? I'm sorry, but I cannot do that. I will stand alone if I must, but I will not leave."

"So you plan to stand alone against three of the most dangerous men I have ever known and who knows how many others they bring with them? This is madness, Sophie. I'm begging you one last time to reconsider. Think about all of those people down there and the lives that will surely be lost."

"Those people have only recently begun to live their lives out from under the yoke of someone like my father. I will not leave them to fall under another's rule so easily. This is their home now as much as it is mine, and I will fight to defend it. Besides, Alaric, there is one more thing you have forgotten. It is a full moon in two nights' time; I will not make my stand alone. The Beast and I shall do our best to protect these people, as we have done for so long now, whether we have your aid or not." And saying so, she hurried from the room before he could see her tears of anger and sadness.

Alaric Vashon, swordsman unequaled, quietly walked to the window overlooking the grounds behind the old citadel. He let his head fall into his hands as he surveyed the children playing a spirited game of "King on the Throne" while the women of the keep gathered up the laundry that had been laid out to collect the last rays of the sun. He knew that tonight, as they had every other night before, the people of this place would gather for dinner as a true community, unaware of the danger they faced.

"Life is such a funny thing," he thought. He had been running for so long from something because he didn't have anything worth fighting for any more. "You can never really escape the past, only outrun it for a little while before it catches up with you," he thought as he closed the latch on the window, and he turned and calmly walked from the room. "After all, what could be more worth fighting for than this?" he thought. "And I've been running from this fight for too long," he said aloud and smiled a sad smile. Not for one second did he disillusion himself that the coming fight would be anything but a bloody, savage affair. Vashon headed to the practice room to work a little more and sharpen his blades, for in two nights he knew he would face the dance of his life, and he intended to be ready.

Chapter Forty-One

The next two days were the sweetest that the people of Sophie's Garden could remember. The children ran and played, unfettered and un-reproached by the adults who didn't wish to ruin any of what might be their last moments of fun. Meals were a far grander affair than normal with everyone gathering in the main hall to share every moment together, laughing and eating as if they were kings. There was, however, an undercurrent of nervousness and trepidation, which they did their best to ignore.

At the head of the table during every meal sat Sophie, who laughed at the right times and carried on conversations as if the worries that assailed her mind did not truly exist. She had come to love these people very much, for they had become the true family she had never known. All through the next two days, she wandered the holding, always stopping to share a kind word and encourage others that all would go well. These men were no different than any of the others who had tried to take their home from them, she would tell them.

She spent several hours sitting at her brother's side as his body recovered from its terrible ordeal. He only surfaced from his unconscious state to take small, hesitant sips of water that his body sorely needed, and then he would lapse back into sleep. She longed to hear the story of what had befallen him in the many years since he had stood before the scared young girl she had been in their family house. She vowed to be there the moment he awoke, so that her smiling face would be the first thing he saw.

The one thing lacking in the next precious hours was the presence of Vashon. After Cass's revelation and Vashon's subsequent argument with Sophie, he had spent several hours in his chambers. Upon reemerging, he tried in vain to convince several of the people that they should flee while they still had time, that they could rebuild after this new threat had come and gone.

The only response he received was that they trusted their lady's judgment in the matter and that the Beast had always protected them in the past and would surely protect them now. If these intruders managed to find their way into the castle, what a surprise they would find waiting for them. The people of Sophie's Garden were not about to simply lie down and let some petty lordling from across the sea wrest their home from them without a fight. Their newfound freedom was too precious to be given up so readily, so they would stay and fight if need be and let the chips of fate fall where they may.

So here he was—knowing his lot was cast alongside theirs and that he would fight tomorrow. The battle he had been dreading these many months was finally at hand, and he could only hope that time had readied him. He spent several hours in his practice room by himself, going through the forms burned into his brain so long ago by his mother and father. If any had been watching him at his practice, they would have sworn to the end of their days that no man should have been able to move that fast. While Vashon sweat and spun and lunged against an army of invisible opponents who sought to take this new home away from him, Sophie watched him from the concealment of the shadows as she wondered what the morrow would bring.

Sophie regretted their harsh words, but there was no way to take them back. Thus, she and Vashon spent those last few hours apart, which was the last place that either of them wanted to be. She longed to run to him even now and tell him how sorry she was, that she never wanted him to hurt on her behalf, and above all else, that she loved him. But the rift between them was too fresh, and she could not find the words to mend it. Not knowing what else to do, she watched him dance, marveling at how he moved and silently praying that he would somehow make it through the next evening's fight, for she didn't know if she could go on without him.

The day sped by in a haze of laughter, nervous smiles, hugs and kisses freely given, and grim anticipation. Before the people knew it, the evening had stolen away the last of their sunlight, and the time for delays ended as all of the residents of Sophie's Garden lay down for one last night of peaceful sleep before their lives would be decided by the coming bloodshed.

Sophie kept vigil the entire night, sitting at her window and staring out at the night sky. She absentmindedly stroked the petals of a red rose and listened to the faint sounds of the man she loved finally going to his chambers after many hours of practice. When the dawn sky finally relieved the moon and stars from their shift watching over the earth, she had not moved from the spot. The first drizzle of rain began to fall outside of her window. She went down the stairs to give her people what comfort she could before she had to leave them in the hands of the Beast, hoping that those great paws would be enough to keep them safe.

Chapter Forty-Two

Long before the sun's rays crept into the edges of windows and the first cock's crow heralded the new day, Duvaliet was up and dressed, going over his plans for the evening's hunt. Never prone to oversights or missteps, he planned and re-planned so compulsively that his men thought him mad. But he simply liked for everything to go his way—as he had pointed out on more than one occasion, he lived to stand before them, while many who had gone against him did not. So his men, with the exception of Kragen and Vigan Marsh, simply resigned their fate to the hands of their leader and did as he bade them.

The dawn found the three of them, joined by Kerrick One-Eye and ten of his most trustworthy men, clustered in Duvaliet's study. This was the ninth or tenth such meeting in the last two days, and patience was in short supply. Kragen and Marsh knew their leader and knew not to say anything when he got like this. Kerrick, on the other hand, lacked their tact and could be heard muttering to one of his men and chuckling under his breath.

"Something amuses you, One-Eye?" Duvaliet stopped mid-sentence and asked.

Kerrick's men immediately cut their laughter short and looked away, unable to meet the smaller man's gaze.

"Everything 'muses me," said One-Eye. "More particular, though, I find it kinda funny how many times it's takin' you to 'member 'em plans of yours, when me and my simple men done learnt 'em the first time 'round. I think I speak for the rest of us when I say we're 'bout sick of all this plannin' business." Kerrick looked about for someone to come to his aid, but even his own men had moved to Duvaliet's side of the room and were staring at him as if he were on fire.

"I mean ..." he stammered, the wind taken abruptly out of his sails. "I just mean to say that we've got a lot of men here—seasoned men, not green lads who'll tuck tail and run at the first sign of trouble—and it's not like we're invading Crittendown Hold. These're common folk—bakers, smithies, women and children. Granted there's the whole Beast problem, but what else they got goin' for 'em? Some traveler who may or may not be Beast droppings by now? It's not like we're going up against Alaric Vashon."

Now it was Vigan Marsh's turn to laugh, followed by Kragen and then Duvaliet.

"What's so funny?" Kerrick said, angry at being the object of their joke.

"I told you, One-Eye, you should have killed him when you had the chance," Kragen said as he rose from his seat and smacked Kerrick on the back.

"Maybe this time you and your men will be more equal to the task, now that you've had the benefit of a little more planning. Either way, you'll all get your chance tonight, and we'll see who's laughing when things get thick," Duvaliet said with a wave of his hand that signaled the end of the meeting. Everyone got up and left the room, each having made a mental list of the extended preparations they had to make now that they knew whom they were truly up against.

Marsh and Kragen readied themselves in their own ways for the night's battle. They both knew that their men would do their jobs. That was what they had been trained for. The youths that each of them had been were long departed, and in their place were hard men who knew their roles better than any other. It was the new blood, however, that worried them.

"Reckon Kerrick's men will stand when things get heavy out there? I know we aren't exactly facing an entire army, but this is Vashon we're talking about, Kragen." Marsh put a name to his fears as they faced one another just inside the front door of the Inn of the Un-Lucky Merchant. The sign had recently been repainted in what looked like blood.

"Stand or no, the victory doesn't hinge on them, Vigan. I'm the hunter, and you can trust my judgment in these matters. Our men will stand and provide the support we need if it comes to that. All I need Kerrick and his men for is a distraction. They are expendable—just there to put more bodies between this Beast and us so I can do my job. Meat for the grinder if it comes to that—nothing more." Kragen turned to walk away from Marsh when a giant hand grabbed him by the arm.

"But it isn't just a Beast, and you know it. That's Vashon in there with it, and we both know what he's capable of."

"That's your fight, my friend—yours and Duvaliet's, not mine. My business is with this Beast." Marsh could hardly miss the manic gleam that had come into Kragen's eyes in the past couple of days. He lived for this sort of thing and only cared for his hunt—nothing else.

"Then wish me luck, brother, for I hunt far more dangerous game than you. I hope the outcome favors my hand, but only fate will tell. Until this evening"—Marsh extended his hand with no trace of the usual ill feelings that strained their relationship. Kragen took it and held it tight in his own iron grip for just a brief moment before looking the other man in the eyes and heading up the stairs without another word spoken.

The big man stood in the entryway like some massive statue carved out of granite. Finally, he cast one last look at the stairway and went to his chamber to retrieve his weapons before gathering the men. They would leave in just three hours' time so that this castle of Faeries could be found in the moonlight. He smiled a small smile to himself and headed down the hall, shaking his head all the while.

Alaric Vashon stood before the chest that had sat locked and silent in a corner of his chamber until this day. Always there, always waiting for him, he thought, not making its presence known because it knew he would come back to it when the time was right.

After finally fooling himself into believing his soul and body were safe in this place, he had finally been found by those from whom he had been running. He knew he was not their sole reason for coming here, but he still chided himself for the thought and pictured Vinquist riding beside him through a green forest far from here, lecturing him on the finer points of living.

"There is no coincidence, Alaric, my boy. All things fit into the grander scope of things, even though we may not always have the sight or clarity of wit to see it. Do not trouble yourself so when you cannot see the way. Simply follow your heart. It will always be your truest guide in these times and will not let you down, as might your head," he said as they rode along beneath the sun-dappled canopy of great oaks and elms.

"Were that you were here, old friend, for I could surely use some words of comfort about now," Vashon said aloud, not surprised when no answer came. He knew that Vinquist had to be somewhere nearby, and that thought brought him some comfort, as he knew the old man was tending to his own part of these affairs. He wouldn't be surprised to find him in the middle of all of this sometime later in the evening, so he relaxed a bit. Comforted by the sense that he would never be alone in the battles he chose, he opened the trunk at last.

The armor within was nothing special to look at, simply dark brown leathers scarred in many places where perhaps some blade had sought to bite into the wearer's skin. To Vashon, however, these were a part of him. A part, he had to admit, that he had missed greatly. He placed the leather greaves over his forearms and began lacing them up, sliding the twin daggers in place on their undersides, pleased to once again have the comforting weight against his skin.

When he had finished his fitting, he turned to look at the man he knew so well in a mirror that stood in a corner of the room. Tall, serious and dangerous, here was a welcome stranger whose presence would be sorely needed this night if these people were to preserve their way of life. The armor itself was not built for great protection. Blades seldom came close enough to men like Vashon to warrant full armor. It was simply there to turn away a glancing blow just long enough to buy him needed time. It had been made long ago to allow a full range of movement, without hindering the wearer, and Vashon wore it very much like a second skin. He stared at himself a moment longer in the mirror then tied his long hair back with a leather thong and threw his sword's baldric over his shoulder with a practiced, fluid movement.

Vashon spun around suddenly, sword hissing free of his sheath at the sound of his door creaking open. He immediately lowered its point and replaced it in his scabbard when he saw who entered.

"What are you doing here, Isaac? I told you to stay with the women and children and make sure everyone stays hidden and safe," Vashon growled, his exasperation clear in his voice, for before him stood not only Isaac, but a dozen other cooks, smithies and men of Sophie's Garden, all clutching knives, clubs, and even a couple of rusty swords that must have been found somewhere in the keep.

"We came to help," Isaac stammered. "The women and children are safely hidden away. They know not to come out. Bette is with Cass, tending to him, and we thought we could help tonight. This place is the only place most of us could ever call home. What are we if we can't defend it when the time comes?" Isaac begged.

"Alive, Isaac. That's what you are—alive. I appreciate your offer and understand your desire to defend your home, but this isn't some fairy tale where the villagers come out and help the heroes save the day from the villains. In our story, the enemy is evil incarnate and will kill you all without hesitation. Protect your families and yourselves. If for some reason I should fall, you all know what to do. Your homes are with each other, not in this place. As long as you draw breath, no man can truly take your freedom from you. Remember that. Go back to your positions, and do not come out for any reason," Vashon said.

"But we——" and Isaac got no further, as an ear-splitting growl filled the room.

"You will return to your rooms now!" The Beast's roar sent the men fleeing the room even before its echo died away.

"You really must teach me to growl like that one day," Vashon said.

Fading laughter was the only thing that answered him.

Before Vashon left the room, he went to the window that faced the woods and threw it open, letting himself be washed clean by the blast of night air the storm had brought. A slight drizzle turned to a steady rain as he watched, and lightning strikes created a stark contrast across the terrain before him. As he closed his eyes and let the cool rain on his skin calm his mind, he knew it would soon be time to leave. His eyes opened, and through the rain he saw the first of the line of torches winding its way through the woods nearly a league away.

"It begins," he thought as he closed the window and moved toward the door at last. He knew that she would have seen the lights as well and must be leaving her room to find him. There were words yet between them that needed to be said before they headed into the night.

The Beast left its chamber and paused to take in everything its heightened senses could feel. It could sense Vashon waiting for it just at the bottom of the steps— could feel his resolve and the dangerous air that he carried with him this night. It could feel all the people below and could sense their fear and their strength, which they had found together in this place, and which would either be lost or bought in blood. It could sense the men in the woods outside. It knew that they were dangerous men, much unlike those who had come before simply looking to make a name for themselves.

It felt Kerrick's presence among those gathering about the forest's edge, close to the relative safety of the trees where they waited to make their move. A grim smile and fangs the size of daggers gleamed red in the light of the torches that lined the stairwell's walls. It was a smile that would have made many children scream had they looked at it and not known the heart that beat behind that ferocious visage.

But it was also one that would make many grown men scream ere the night was over, the Beast knew. "Especially you, Kerrick," it thought. The thought sustained the grin all the way down the steps, the Beast making no noise until it came face to face with the man whose confrontation it had dreaded above any other this night.

"Looks like the time for running is at an end," Vashon said in a dead tone he had not used in the many months during his stay.

"This is not your fight, Alaric. I am charged with protecting this place and the people within—I alone. You can still slip out the back if you so choose. No one will think any worse of you if you don't stay and fight tonight." The Beast's gravelly tone came out flat, but Vashon thought he heard some new element woven into its thread—was that uncertainty he heard? He couldn't be quite sure and knew he couldn't dwell on it. There was business that needed tending to.

"How can you say that? Not my fight? These men have chased me halfway around the world, and I would hate to keep them from our appointment any longer. This is what I do—what I was born to do, and like you, I do it very well. This has been my home for the past months, these people my family, and without our help, they will only be slaughtered like lambs. I lived with the ghost of Bitterknot for too long, and it almost destroyed me. I don't think I could survive with this many people's blood on my hands knowing that I could have done something to prevent it. No, I stand with you tonight, and we will meet our fate together."

"Please then, do as I ask and stay within the walls and protect the people. I know they are well-hidden in the rooms below ground, but if I should fall, or if these men get into the castle somehow, you will have to lead and protect them. Please, Alaric, take care of yourself and don't do anything foolish," said the Beast as they looked out a large window overlooking the front of the citadel's grounds. There are so many of them, it thought as they stared at the numerous fires marring the landscape like wounds on a body. How will the two of us be enough? Then all of these thoughts were put aside when, as the Beast prepared to leave, Vashon's strong grip fell on one of its huge, furry forearms.

"Be careful, Sophie, I can't lose you now. You are too precious to me, and I don't think I would ever recover if I something were to happen to you. I love you." The last came out in no more than a whisper, but she couldn't miss the raw emotion in his words.

Her eyes widened in shock and understanding as his words struck her as soundly as any blow ever could. How long had he known, she wondered? She cursed herself for a fool and, with a snarl, tore her gaze from his and flew down the remaining steps before disappearing down a dark hall. It would be later in the evening, after much blood had been shed, before she realized she hadn't told him that she loved him back.

Vashon watched as one line of torches advanced upon the grounds, while many of them stayed back within the safety of the trees. "You always were a clever one, weren't you, Duvaliet?" he thought as he noted that the men now advancing upon the garrison were mere sell swords, much like the men in the inn who had attacked him that night. He watched in amazement as the Beast emerged silently in the middle of the advancing column of men and began to wreak havoc among them. This went on for a few moments, until he noticed the secondary line of torches advancing from the trees to join the fray.

Alaric Vashon pulled his sword free of its scabbard, held the flat of the blade against his forehead in salute, smiled and headed for the window.

Chapter Forty-Three

Hidden safely within the cover of the tree line nearly half a league from where Kerrick's men had stopped their advance, Duvaliet, Kragen and Vigan Marsh sat their horses spaced apart and waited patiently for the Beast to make its presence felt among Kerrick's unsuspecting men.

Despite knowing that the only response he would get from the thin man wearing his black leathers tonight would be stolid silence, Vigan Marsh, for the fourth time in the past ten minutes, whispered, "Do you actually think that getting the Beast to come out and fight will be as simple as sending in those fools as bait? You think we'll be able to just walk up as we please so you can put one of your fancy little arrows from your fancy little bow in its sorry hide and we can go home? Something smells wrong with all of this, Kragen. Surely you can feel it, same as I can?" Kragen remained unresponsive. In times like this, he entered his own world, not to be disturbed by anyone or anything. Instead, he held his intense gaze upon the field of play, hoping he had moved everyone into the right position. Of course, he too felt something was odd about this—his instincts functioned just as well as Marsh's—but he was already too deeply ingrained in this hunt to turn back or change course. He merely hoped they would have a few moments to take advantage of the inevitable deaths of the poor souls who would trade their lives for a pocketful of gold.

Duvaliet calmly sat on his horse and observed all that went on about him, knowing his true prey was not the Beast, but Vashon himself. Let Kragen worry about the stupid beast; he was sure the man would be more than equal to the task of taking care of the monster. He hadn't proven himself unworthy in the past, and he was sure that he could take care of one beast by himself, much less with a band of men fifty strong to support him. No, he would take his hunt into the keep, as soon as the opportunity presented itself, for he went after far more dangerous prey this night. They had a score to settle, and he didn't intend to leave accounts between them unsettled any longer. He just wished this blasted rain would let up. Duvaliet truly hated conducting business when he was soaked to the bone, but he had to play the cards dealt him, he thought.

Marsh kept his eyes on Kerrick One-Eye and his twenty men, who were now spread out in a tight line in the near distance. The rain had intensified, and their torches sputtered and flickered in the downpour. Flashes of lightning offered a grim vision of the nighttime landscape. The castle stood directly in front of them, a silent black specter that offered no comfort or warmth this dark night. Few lights could be seen in the windows, and those that could showed no signs of life within. The brief flashes of lightning cast shadows, which further spooked the already hesitant men who were terrified of what might be waiting for them in the dark. Marsh knew that if something didn't happen in the next few moments, they would either have to turn around or rush the castle and try their luck within.

As things worked out, he didn't have to wait much longer. The next lightning strike revealed a scene he could not drive from his mind no matter how hard he tried. The man nearest the eastern wall of the castle had turned to look back at him and the men with him in the trees. He waved his torch back and forth in front of his eyes, trying in vain to dispel any terrors the night might hold, when a figure appeared directly behind him out of the darkness. It rose to a height much greater than the man's own and possibly even larger than Marsh. The Beast grabbed the man by the back of his tunic, and the man's scream rent the night air as dagger-sharp claws dug into the unprotected flesh of his back.

In the next instant, the man was hurled through the air into another poor soul who had turned at the sound to see what was happening. The only thing he saw before he went down was his friend's face, contorted in terror, before it crashed into his own. Both men lay unmoving on the field, their torches lying sputtering on the pile of bodies. The men nearby barely had time to react before the Beast was upon them, and everyone who had drawn the unlucky duty of being on the front line found themselves fighting for their lives, as the wraith-like figure moved among them.

There was no time for the men to mobilize any sort of attack on the Beast. They simply defended themselves as best they could from the large figure in the flowing black cloak before them. But all were unequal to the task, as Kragen had anticipated, and their field of battle quickly turned into a bloodbath.

The men had said that the Beast simply looked to get its message across that they were not welcome on the citadel's grounds—that it had no intent to actually kill any of them, but only wanted to protect its land. Things were obviously different tonight. The Beast seemed to know that the rules had changed and laid into the men with a viciousness that was unparalleled.

Only half of Kerrick's men remained on the field when Marsh shouted the order for the rest of those hiding in the shadows to charge. They all fired their crossbows at the Beast as they ran, avoiding their fallen comrades who littered the grounds. Though their aim should have been true, none of the arrows struck home. The Beast either dodged the arrows with supernatural speed or simply grabbed its nearest enemy and held them in front of it as a human shield.

These men of Duvaliet's were no green soldiers or mercenaries, though, and had been well-trained not to panic in the face of danger, so they managed to form an attack against the Beast as they reached the site of battle. Trying to close in the distance between themselves and the Beast, they spread out into a V-formation and began to close in on and crush the monster. They managed to drive the Beast back towards the front of the castle but were not making any headway in defeating the thing. The number of wounded continued to grow, and one of his lieutenants turned to address Duvaliet at last.

"What are we waiting for? Now's our chance, sir. There's only one Beast," he said to his commander, who was busy staring at the window directly above where the fighting had moved to, his eyes caught by some movement within.

"No, lieutenant, there are two," he quietly said as the window came crashing out and a large man landed on the ground, giving a quick salute to the men staring in amazement at this new figure who had miraculously appeared in front of them.

Death, it appeared, had decided to take on two forms this evening, and the men surrounding the Beast screamed at last in terror, as Vashon's sword began to sing its horrible song in the night. They began to fall like wheat as he danced among their number.

Chapter Forty-Four

Alaric Vashon felt nothing but calm as he flung himself out of the window and landed in a quick forward roll, coming to his feet with sword in hand. The nearest opponent dropped as Vashon's sword knocked away his blade, and he received a sharp elbow to the temple before he even knew what hit him.

If anyone had ever asked him what he felt when immersed in battle, Vashon would have simply described it as a feeling of utter peace. "Though the world may be tearing itself apart piece by piece all around you, you stand alone on your own private field of battle, the only occupants being yourself and the nearest opponent, the sole actors on a stage performing for only yourselves." For few had walked the earth who could fight Alaric Vashon and survive, and of those who had survived engaging Vashon in battle, none were eager to repeat the incident. He was an artist, and that night, amidst a backdrop of screams, raindrops falling as heavy as the moon's tears lit by crackling forks of lightning, he created his masterpiece. And there are those who sing about it to this very day.

Vashon knew that Sophie, or simply the Beast, as she believed herself to be, fought for her life only a few yards from where he rose from his crouch. He knew he had to fight his way to her and get her back inside the keep where they could regroup or at least take away the advantage those bowmen of Duvaliet's had out here in the open. He noticed the line of torches moving in quickly from the tree line and watched in dismay as the men, moving within the torchlight like deadly fireflies, began to fire their crossbows in Sophie's direction.

Vashon had time to note the figure sitting on horseback calmly watching the fight from a distance. "No, Duvaliet, you never were a fool. I didn't expect

I would get the honor of killing you out here in the open. You always waited to claim the victory until you were sure it was yours. But we will dance together, little man, before this night is over. I promise you that." He effortlessly evaded a clumsy thrust from one of Kerrick's surviving men and spun back around with a kick that caused the man to double over in pain, before he was finished off with a hard smack from the flat of Vashon's blade.

The Beast, had it not been so outnumbered, would not have required Vashon's help at all, as she was a terror to behold. The men had finally been given some direction by Duvaliet's trained troops and had gathered in a half-circle around her, herding her steadily back against the stone wall, where she would either be crushed between their ranks or killed by a projectile that somehow slipped through her defenses. Already there were tears in her black cloak, as well as blood, although Vashon didn't believe that much, if any, of it was her own.

Vashon did not hesitate to throw himself full force into the rear row of men, his blade singing as it flashed too quickly for the eye to follow. Wherever he swung his black blade, it found its target, a disarming blow here followed by a strike to the back of the head there. Vashon found that he did not have to kill all who came within the sweep of his blade to advance his cause. He found no joy in killing these men and only did so when it was absolutely necessary. He knew they were men blessed with good ability who had the misfortune of serving an evil master who sought to use their gifts for his own good.

Only one man remained directly between himself and the Beast, the others having been pressed to the outside of the fight by the ferocity of both attacks, and he hesitated one moment too long on which opponent he should engage first. Vashon feigned a thrust at his chest, which the man barely parried before being caught from behind by two massive paws. The sound he made as she spun with him in her arms and threw him against the castle wall was quite sickening. The Beast, it appeared, did not share the same compunctions that restrained Vashon when dealing with foes, and both Kerrick's and Duvaliet's men had suffered greatly for it.

As soon as they found their way to one another, Vashon and the Beast fought alongside one another, both able to anticipate what the other would do next. They fought back to back, turning and moving when necessary without a single word spoken between them. Their bond went far deeper than mere physical presence, and they became one fighting machine which would have decimated the men before them had things continued in their current state.

Instinct alone saved the Beast, as she sensed the crossbow bolt only moments before it would have slammed into her chest, ending their valiant stand right there. She managed to move to the left at the last possible instant, and the bolt hit her in the shoulder, ripping through flesh, fur and cloak and bouncing off of her shoulder bone before falling to the ground. She gave an earsplitting roar of pain that seemed to shake the very foundation of the castle. Clutching her wound, she looked around for the one who had been lucky enough to do any damage.

Vashon didn't have to look far to find the only one he knew to be capable of hitting her where all others had failed. He turned to find the Beast gazing with fire in her blue eyes at a spot in the trees nearly fifty yards away. He looked and saw the barest glimpse of Kragen, well-hidden by the branches, staring right back at her as he quietly reloaded his crossbow for his next shot, which Vashon knew would not miss its target as the first one had.

He knew that they had to get back inside the garrison now if they were to have any chance of winning. He grabbed a handful of cloak and fur on the arm that had not been injured and hissed into her ear.

"It's too dangerous out here. It won't be long before they realize they only need to charge and distract us for their arrows to find us, and then everything will have been for naught. As good as we are, I don't want to dodge arrows all night long in the rain. You go around back and enter by one of the hidden doorways. I'll keep them busy long enough for you to get away, and then I'll lead them inside by another door. Hopefully we can meet somewhere inside where we'll have the advantage again. Now go, Sophie," he yelled as he pushed her away; "Go before it's too late!" Then he launched himself anew at the men who were quickly coming their way.

Sparing one last look as Vashon as he danced his way among his opponents, the Beast turned and ran around the side of the garrison. She headed toward the entrance she intended to use in the back, noting on her way that the man who had shot her, the one she knew to be Kragen, had left his spot in the trees and was probably tracking her.

Her mind preoccupied, she barely noticed Kerrick One-Eye in her haste to reach the door and was taken aback when she found him pinned to a large oak tree by one of his own men's arrows, a look of complete shock and disbelief on his face as he stared down at the bolt jutting so prominently from his chest, holding him in place against the tree's slick bark. "Pity, Kerrick, that I could not have been the one to fulfill our bargain, but you were warned. My woods—my rules. This was all brought on by your stupidity," she thought as she grimaced at a wave of pain that emanated from her shoulder and headed off toward the castle.

Suddenly, a voice in her head halted her progress after only a few steps. "Wait, stop, and think. He can still serve some purpose."

Knowing where the voice came from and realizing it spoke truth, she turned once again to look at Kerrick's form lying against the tree, and an idea began to take root in her mind. She smiled her terrible smile, fangs glistening with rain in the moonlight.

It would be to Kragen's misfortune, as he tracked the Beast to that same spot a few moments later, that he didn't notice the small hole in the tree's bark where Kerrick had been held fast.

Chapter Forty-Five

"Excuse me, but you're blocking my view of things," was the last thing the guard heard before Vinquist's staff hit him sharply across the back of the head and dropped him to the ground, a frozen "o" on his lips from the warning he was about to scream. The wizard settled in among the trees where the man had been so inconspicuously hidden moments before and watched as Vashon and Sophie, or at least a part of Sophie, fought for their lives in front of the castle door.

It hurt him terribly that he couldn't aid them in their battle against Duvaliet and his men, for he knew these were likely to be their match in a fair fight. Although he could march himself down to the castle walls and lay waste to these men who thought they had a claim on this land and its people, he knew that this had to be Sophie and Vashon's stand. He knew their mettle and gauged them more than equal to the task. He only hoped that they believed enough in themselves and in their love for each other to see the sunrise on the morrow.

After a long pause, Vinquist said to himself, "Then again, maybe it wouldn't be breaking the rules if I helped out … just a little bit."

His meditation was abruptly interrupted, however, by an unexpected voice. "That's the third one you've taken out in the past five minutes. Did the other two not have quite the vantage point you wanted on things?"

A smile crept its way through his massive beard, and Vinquist turned to look upon one of the few people alive who could possibly sneak up and catch him unawares. His grin broadened as he saw a thin man, tall and fair, with hair that seemed to repel the raindrops seeking to plaster it to his head. The man had tall ears ending in points. In a scabbard slung across his back was a sword Vinquist had seen many times before and knew all too well.

"You must be getting slow in your old age, Vinquist. I never would have been able to creep up on you like that fifty years ago," Geren said, his affection for the older man clear in his tone.

"Bah, this rain makes it impossible to hear anything, much less an Elf who doesn't want to be heard. I actually knew you were there the whole time—I was just waiting for the right moment to surprise you, Geren."

"Sure you were, old friend, sure you were," Geren said. "Now then, you didn't answer my first question: what are you doing out here in the rain knocking sentries out? I would have expected you to be in the middle of things, eyes ablaze, and men falling under your staff."

"Would that I was fighting alongside them," he motioned to Sophie and Vashon, now fighting back to back in front of the castle door. "But there is some far greater power at work here, and even I know not to stand in the way of destiny. Much more is being decided this night than the lives of the people living inside the garrison. So I stay my hand and wait, like you, to see what the outcome may be. Now then, Geren, what exactly are you doing here?"

"Watching over things for my father. You know how he always wants to stay informed of events of import, and he likes for me to keep an eye on Vashon. He is like a brother to me, and I would not see him come to any harm that I could prevent. I, too, can feel the pull of destiny in this, old friend, and would see this played out."

"I would have made my presence known when I came through town, but I suppose I wasn't treated with too much hospitality in La Croix, was I?" Vinquist said.

"Sometimes anonymity is the safest way to go, even amongst friends. Besides, I may have another reason for being here," he said glancing at the Beast's snarling form.

"The sword?" was all Vinquist asked. No other words were needed.

"Yes, the sword. I've finally found its owner. After all these years, I can't let her get away without what is rightfully hers. I have only kept it safe until my heart told me I had found one worthy of carrying it. I only hope that she can make her way through the night." Geren's eyes held a hint of hope and a deeper concern, as his gaze caught that of the other man.

"Then let us see what part we may yet play this night, my friend," Vinquist said as he grabbed Geren by the arm. The two made their way back through the trees, toward the side of the citadel, the driving rain seeming to part before them. Their eyes never left the Beast and Vashon as the two fought their way through the mass of men and made their way back toward the inside of the keep.

"And besides," Vinquist said as he pointed at a man hidden in the trees twenty yards away, "I think the view might be better over there, right where that guard is standing. Shall we see if he will kindly share his spot with us?"

Chapter Forty-Six

An overwhelming sense of triumph sent small shivers through Kragen's frame, and victory sang in his blood as he came to the spot where he last lost sight of the Beast. He knew he had hit it—its scream had told him that much—but with the cacophony of sounds and movement, he wasn't quite sure how much damage his bolt had done. As he looked at the large smear of blood running down the tree's trunk where it must have stopped to rest, he considered that his aim must have been better than he first thought. A feral grin lit his face as he noticed, even in the downpour which had assailed them this past hour, the dark trail of blood leading away from the tree and into the night toward the castle wall.

The thrill of the hunt sustained him and perhaps clouded his judgment a bit. Had he not been so intent on his quarry and the excitement of such a long hunt finally coming to a head, his greater sense would have told him that he had only struck the monster a glancing blow and that there was no way this much blood could have come from that wound. As caught up in the moment as he was, however, Kragen merely notched another bolt into his crossbow and headed into the night in a tight crouch, sensing his prey waited only a short distance away.

It was a short walk from the tree to the castle, but it took several minutes for him to cover the distance. He moved ever so slowly, so as not to draw attention to himself in case the Beast had the good sense to look back and see if it was being followed. He had hunted all his life and prided himself on being able to sense what his prey was thinking. And once he had placed his mark on them, they experienced a blind panic and could only think about their need for survival, which overpowered all other senses. He paused at the entrance to the stairwell and noticed that it led not into the castle proper, but down into the bowels of the structure, away from where Duvaliet and Vigan Marsh were likely to penetrate the fortress. A path led him down where he could see the blood trail following the rock wall alongside the steps. He put a hand to the stain and pulled it away, sticky and dark. Taut as the crossbow string which foretold the Beast's demise, Kragen turned the corner and disappeared into the keep.

Kragen half expected this to be some kind of trap, that he would find a dozen armed men waiting for him as soon as he turned the corner, but all he found were a few sputtering torches on the walls and bags of flour, salt and wheat piled upon the floor, bearing mute witness to his finest hour. It was almost disappointing. He grabbed one of the torches off of the wall, noting how it spit and hissed as though even the keep's walls could not keep the damp of this night out, and looked about the room for the blood trail he knew must be there.

And there it was—winding along the far side of the room, high up on the wall, the blood still running down in rivulets where the Beast had begun to lose too much of its precious life source. The thick blood descended gradually down the wall, and Kragen traced it back to where he thought the Beast must be leaning more and more for support. He smiled and wound his way between casks of salted pork and bags of wheat, following the trail into the next room, sensing the end of his hunt at last.

The next room seemed to be a long-abandoned armory. Several suits of armor of an age long forgotten still stood at attention, though covered in a fine layer of dust. A tapestry on one wall showed a scene of a wizard looking out across a great chasm, glowing staff in hand and tears in his eyes, as all about him a great battle raged and men died. Kragen paused to look at it just briefly enough to wonder that he did not know the story the rug depicted, but then chided himself for letting his mind wander. He moved away from the swords and axes that hung on the wall and went back to the blood trail, which led him to a spiraling staircase tucked away behind a small pile of crates in the far corner of the room.

Holding his low-burning torch out into the stairwell to make sure he would not be surprised by anything waiting below, he followed the trail on the wall down the winding staircase and into the darkness. No torches hung on the walls to aid him on his passage, as if even the spirits of the castle wished him no good luck this night. This didn't bother him much, though, for he thought that only fools relied on luck and that he had not survived this long in his line of work on anything other than his own instincts and skills.

Anticipation built into a crescendo within his mind until he thought he might not be able to contain himself. He began to move more quickly, knowing from the amount of blood on the wall that the Beast must be waiting for him to finish this in the room at the bottom of the steps. He rechecked the draw on his crossbow as he rounded the last corner and took the last several steps all at once, landing him in a small hallway in front of a door carved out of the rock, the room beyond concealing all of its secrets from him in darkness.

He hugged the wall now as he stepped into the room and let his free hand trail along the blood, savoring the sweet feel of his imminent victory. He cursed in irritation as his torch began to burn lower and lower, succumbing to the encroaching darkness. "Just a bit further," he thought, as if he could keep the flame burning by sheer force of will alone.

The torch held out for just a few moments more, until Kragen reached a spot in the wall where the blood trail began to dip towards the floor, where he could imagine the Beast slumping towards the ground, bled of life. Placing the torch in a sconce in the wall, from which it could only illuminate a small portion of the room, he willingly made the sacrifice of the comfort of a bit of light for the ability to have both hands free.

One hand to the trail on the wall, still sticky, he made his way slowly, savoring every step to the final corner, around which he knew the Beast must have finally fallen. He steadied his crossbow with both hands and stepped away from the wall as soon as he could sense the figure lying slumped against the wall directly in front of him. He was surprised that he couldn't hear the figure drawing breath and wondered if he had come too late, if it had slipped away from him before he had a chance to make the kill. He knelt closer, eyes widening in shock as he realized just why the one on the ground drew no breath in this chilly air under the keep.

He recognized Kerrick One-Eye at once. Even though the torn figure lying at his feet had taken a severe beating from being dragged along the walls of the keep all the way down the stairs, Kragen could see that he had been done in long before by the arrow still protruding from his chest. Before he could flee the room and climb back up the stairwell to safety, Kragen felt breath, hot and fetid, on the back of his neck and sensed a giant presence directly behind him.

Knowing he might have only one chance to attack, he spun to bring himself face to face with his attacker so that he might have a split second to fire his bolt, but something deep inside him told him that the game had already been won—and not by him. As he began the spin, a huge paw grabbed him by the head, squeezing with such force that he immediately saw stars. Suddenly, he was lifted off of the ground as if he were nothing more than a limp doll and hurled across the room into the wall. The thing that surprised him most about this sudden turn of events was the fact that, although he should have fallen, his feet still dangled several inches above the ground, some unseen force holding him up.

Alas, he soon discovered what was keeping him elevated from the ground, as he lowered his eyes and found himself impaled on a pair of boar tusks, which were sticking four inches out of his stomach and holding him in place like some great trophy. He felt no pain, though, nor regret—only a great acceptance that he had finally been beaten at his own game and that he could not have desired any other way to leave this world. A small smile, devoid of any falsehood or trickery, came over his face as blood ran from him in deep rivulets onto the floor below. He managed to give a small bow to the eyes that glowed at him from the darkness, an acknowledgment to a great foe of a victory well-won. The darkness swelled about him, and he began to sink into calm waters, which quickly swallowed him up and carried him away from his body. As his spirit took its final leave, a voice spoke from just inches away.

"Your problem is that you were thinking like a beast, while I was thinking like a human. The hunt is over. You lose."

He could only wonder at the very end that the voice was not the gravelly roar of the Beast he had hunted this entire night, but rather the lilting tones of a young girl, very much tired and very much filled with both sadness and joy. And then he thought no more, as the darkness could be denied no longer, and he slipped free, having lost his final hunt to a quarry far greater than he had ever imagined.

As Sophie turned to head across the room and back up the winding staircase, she heard a voice that stopped her in her tracks.

"Sophie—come here, child."

She slowly made her way to the standing mirror in the corner to face her greatest fear in all of this and, hopefully, to find herself before it was too late and help the man she loved.

Chapter Forty-Seven

Vashon spared a sparse second to consider whether Sophie had made it safely into the keep, hoping that she had fared a little better in her ingress than he had. A blade from one of the three men in front of him almost slipped through his defenses. Silently wishing her good fortune, he caught the man's blade on the pommel of his sword and drove the elbow of his other arm into the man's temple, dropping him immediately to the ground, leaving one less attacker following him through the inner halls of the keep.

While Alaric Vashon may have had no equal in matters of the sword, things change quickly when one is fighting more than one opponent. When there is a steady stream of opponents throwing themselves only too readily at your blade three and four at a time, even the greatest blade masters may find themselves hard-pressed not to give ground. At least he had the advantage of not having men shooting at him with bows and crossbows here inside the keep's walls. Duvalier's men were no fools, and they knew these passages were far too narrow to try to take him down without serious risk to themselves. Their progress was marked by a growing trail of bodies of those ill-fated to meet with Vashon's blade. The men followed him through the keep's halls and passageways, always looking for an advantage to overcome their quarry.

At least the residents were not getting involved, thought Vashon. In fact, he had seen no signs of the people since he had entered the keep. "That's good," he thought, "they actually listened." He deftly knocked aside the blade of the soldier closest to him and smashed the man in the face with his fist, destroying his nose with a sound that was sure to disquiet the others who were still harrying him throughout the halls. The man fell back amongst the rush of his fellows, screaming and clutching at the crushed mass of flesh that was once his nose.

Realizing he could not run forever throughout the keep and that he would eventually tire, Vashon knew of one place where he could tip the scales in his favor, hopefully giving Sophie enough time to find her way back to him. He immediately stopped dead in his tracks, turned, and rushed shoulder-first into the new leader of the pack who had replaced the soldier whose moans of "my nose, oh, my nose" could still be heard far down the hall. The soldier didn't even have time to react to Vashon's about face and subsequent charge; he never stopped to consider that the tables could be turned so suddenly. All the air left him in a rush, and he went to the ground gasping for breath. The two men in the second line had the advantage of a split second's warning as they saw their comrade go down. Both of them raised their swords to skewer Vashon so that they might put an end to the chase, but they were not equal to the task. Before their blades could begin their downswing, Vashon rolled between them, his blade cutting one's tendons behind the knee and his elbow hooking the other man's leg, dropping them both where they stood in the hallway.

Before any of the others could muster an attack against him, Vashon was up and away, leading his slowly diminishing group of pursuers down a side hallway and toward the room where he and Sophie had spent so many hours together these past weeks. It would be in that room where he would put the finishing touches on his masterpiece. If this fight was to be the end of him, he would make such a glorious end of it that minstrels would sing about it long after. He turned his thoughts away from the verses of the death ballad that were composing themselves in his head and reminded himself that he would far rather hear someone sing the "Victory of Vashon" in some tavern one day than he would live on through song alone. He resumed his parry and retreat form of defense as he led the men, numbering only six now, toward the practice room.

About halfway down the corridor marked with ancient and molding tapestries, alarm bells went off in Vashon's mind. Instincts honed to a keen edge through years of diligence and training were the only thing that made his eyes dart to the right, toward an open doorway, where he thought he saw something small rapidly retreat back into the shadows. He prayed it was just his mind playing tricks on him, that he hadn't just seen a young boy, the same one he had played ball with in the courtyard days earlier. Hoping his pursuers hadn't caught a glimpse of the movement either, he turned and ran full speed toward the open door to his training room at the end of the hall. The men chased in after him, the door closed behind them, and there was once again silence in the corridors, the battle muffled by the heavy oak door and the thick stone of the keep walls. The silence lasted only a moment, however, before two sets of boot echoes could be heard coming down the hall toward the door, one light—almost the sound of a child's foot—and the other great and heavy, as if a draft horse had somehow found its way into the castle and gotten lost.

The two sets of steps stopped twenty feet from the door, and the breath of the two men could be clearly heard filling the hallway. Vigan Marsh turned and looked down upon the bald head of Duvaliet and simply asked, as he began re-checking the clasps on his armor and unbuckling his giant sword, "Well, it's your call. Where do we go from here?"

A cruel smile lit Duvaliet's face as he glanced at the room where the man he hated as no other was easily dispatching his men. He looked back down the hallway where he, too, had seen a small shadow disappear in a doorway.

"From here, Vigan, we go our separate ways. You go in there and kill Vashon for me once and for all. He has eluded us far too long. I am going to obtain some insurance, just in case things start to turn nasty for us at some point in the near future. It always pays to have a second way out, Vigan. Come find me in the main ballroom when you are finished with Vashon—and fare thee well." Duvaliet said the last as he clasped hands with the big man, his hand entirely disappearing in the giant's large hand.

"All I can do for you in that room is buy you a little time. I'm not sure how much, but hopefully it will be enough. I've felt this fight coming for some time—felt it in my bones—and I already know how it will end. It's my destiny, though. I wouldn't want to be taken by any other than him. At least that will grant me some reprieve from my role in this mess. This was a mistake, Duvaliet. I can see that now."

Releasing the smaller man's hand, Vigan Marsh, whose name was enough to evoke feelings of dread in any he had ever faced, couldn't hide the cold sweat that broke out on his brow or quell the empty feeling in the pit of his stomach as he put his hand on the doorknob and entered the room.

Duvaliet watched his back disappear into the doorway before turning and heading back the way they had come only moments before in search of the one thing he knew would even the playing field between himself and Vashon.

Chapter Forty-Eight

"Sophie—come here, child." The voice that echoed inside her head left little room for discussion as it emanated from the standing mirror in the corner of the room where Kragen had met his end only moments before. Sophie straightened her back and approached the mirror cautiously, head low like a doe seeking water, but wary of the dangers that lay before her.

She refused to raise her head as she stood before the mirror, instead staring at her naked feet on the dusty floor, dirty and splotched with Kragen's blood. "Not paws," she noted as she studied the limbs as though they belonged to someone else, "but my own feet."

"Sophie, look at me—at us, girl." The voice had a musical quality to its rumbling tone, and she could not help but look in the mirror directly at the source of her conversant. Her eyes, having adjusted to the dark, slowly made the long journey from the floor up the mirror. As she did this, she noted the huge paws, strong legs covered with hair, and the muscular torso. When she, at last, came to look at its eyes, staring back at her from a living nightmare, she was not surprised to find that they matched the singular deep blue of her own eyes. They stared directly back at her from the Beast's face. She noted the red wound on its shoulder, standing out against the Beast's dark fur, and looked down at her own bleeding shoulder. The throbbing had returned to distract her attention as soon as Kragen had died and she had heard the voice from the mirror. A small trickle of blood ran down her arm, making a greater contrast against her pale skin than it did against the fur of the Beast.

"Sophie, my time is at an end here. We have grown much together, but now you have reached the final test. You must do this alone. I cannot help you any further."

"But why? I still need you—these people need you to protect them. He needs you. I am not strong enough to do this alone." Tears now found their way freely down Sophie's cheeks. As she faced down the possibility of being severed from a part of herself, she feared she would not be nearly the woman she had become once she and the Beast were apart.

"You have the strength, though you may not know it yet. I have felt and seen much from you in our brief sojourn together, and I do not fear for you, dear one." The overwhelming tone of love and pride began to fill Sophie with hope, taking away her trepidation and fear and replacing them with the confidence and love of life that she had built within herself, layer-by-layer, in her time here.

"Must it be right now?" Sophie asked. "I fear there is more to do here, and I still do not know if I am up to the task." She wiped her nose on her bare arm, caring little for decorum at this point, although a part of her mind laughed heartily at the picture of her standing naked in a dark room and wiping her nose while talking to a mirror. "I will miss you greatly. You have become a part of me."

"I shall always be a part of you and yours, Sophie. Even though I may not make myself known and we shall not be as we have been, I will always be there in your times of need. Such bonds as ours cannot be sundered completely, for we have grown close, indeed, and I have had the pleasure of watching you become the beautiful woman you were always meant to be. I have seen such joy in you that it fills my heart to overflowing, and I have watched you love, Sophie. I felt your heart skip a beat the first time you looked into Vashon's eyes and have felt all of your feelings since then in your time together. And now he needs you—not me—so my task here is finished. I can protect you no longer. This fight is yours. But take heart, for all may still be well. Now go before it is too late, and do not forget me, dear one, for I will be with you always."

The note of finality in the Beast's tone connected in Sophie's mind, and she felt a presence withdrawing from herself. She began to bolster herself with the strength for what lay ahead. Raising her eyes to look once more in the mirror, she knew what she would find and smiled as her own reflection looked back, dirty and soiled, but alive and strong. She noted with a hint of surprise that her pupils seemed to have taken on a somewhat elliptical shape, a reminder that she would never be alone and that the Beast's strength would always be her own. Before she turned away, the image changed to one of Vinquist, bruised and dirtied, kneeling in a jail cell, spell flame casting shadows on the walls. His head raised from the spell, and his eyes held her own for just a moment, before he gave a faint nod, and the image dissolved again.

She turned and noted a plain linen shift lying in a crate, dazzlingly white despite the state of the other items in the room. She slid it over her head, not surprised to find it a perfect fit, and turned to the still form of Kragen to gather the rest of what she would need before she went back upstairs to aid the man she loved.

Chapter Forty-Nine

The picture that presented itself to Vigan Marsh as he opened the door to the room was very much the one he expected. Vashon stood directly in the middle of the floor, sword tip resting on the marbled tile, watching for the door to open. His eyes lit up with an expectant light when he saw Marsh's huge form fill the doorway, but he remained a statue, not moving from his place. The still forms of Duvaliet's men lay on the floor around him, some with small puddles of blood forming around them, though Marsh could tell from their shallow breathing that not all of them were dead, only dispatched from the fight.

"Well, well, looks like we're finally going to find out who's the better of us two, Alaric. It's too bad your friend isn't here to see this." The slight tremor in his voice undercut his bravado, however, and it was quite clear that this was not something he anticipated with a great sense of satisfaction. He knew how good Vashon was, knew it from the moment they had met in Duvaliet's castle those many long months ago. While most men respected his size and fighting ability, Vashon made it clear he considered him an equal, no matter what the difference was in their size. Marsh had seen him fight before, and no man could move the way Vashon could. None he had ever seen even came close. So while Marsh knew his size might give him a small advantage in this fight, he held no false hopes about the outcome.

Vashon lowered his sword across his body, relaxing into his fighting stance, and simply stared the larger man directly in the eye saying nothing in return. No words could come from his mouth that would do justice to what he felt inside. This man had killed his best friend. It was an act he was about to pay dearly for, and Vashon had no intention of making him wait any longer.

"You never were one for many words, were you? That's one of the things

I never really liked about you," Marsh said in one last vain attempt, hoping to somehow make Vashon angry, thus causing him to be vulnerable in his rage.

Seeing that no other words could prolong the inevitable, he slid his massive broadsword free of its scabbard on his back and raised his blade to his face in mock salute.

"Shall we, Alaric?" he asked as he moved quickly—much more quickly than a man his size had a right to—directly at Vashon, raising his sword behind his head as he ran, preparing for the blow that would cut his opponent in half.

"Good bye, Vigan," was the only response Vashon gave as the giant shortened the distance between them at an incredible rate.

When he came within ten feet of Vashon's still form, Vigan Marsh threw all of his considerable might into bringing his sword down in a sweeping arc that would surely cut his opponent in two. Marsh thought, as Vashon remained still as stone in front of him, that he may actually win this fight with a single blow and smiled as his sword continued its deadly arc downward. He was still smiling as Vashon caught his eyes, returned the smile with one of his own and took one step sideways, engaging Marsh's sword with his own when the point was mere inches from his face.

The move was executed so quickly and smoothly that Vigan didn't even have time to react as Vashon ran his blade down the length of his opponent's sword and twisted slightly as their pommels met, causing Marsh's sword to fly out of his hand. As his eyes widened, Vigan saw Vashon drop his own sword from his right hand into his left. Time seemed to stand still, and Vigan's body was unable to respond to his mind's screams to stop him at any cost. Frozen, he watched as Vashon drove his blade directly into his chest until the pommel rested against his midsection.

"That was for Duncan," Vashon said calmly, as if he were simply trying to lull a child to sleep.

"And this is for me," Vashon growled as he caught Marsh's own sword handle in his hand and rammed it home directly through his back, a scant few inches from where his own blade protruded from the front, so that the handle of Marsh's sword and the blade of his own nearly touched. The big man fell over sideways, the lifeblood spilling from his form to stain the floor around him.

Vashon walked over and pulled his sword free, not even giving the larger man another look as he wiped his blade clean on Marsh's tunic and slid it back in his scabbard before he left the room. He had seen no sign of Sophie but assumed that she had most likely resurfaced in the main hall, the largest room in the keep. Thus, he sprinted down the hall to find her.

When he got to the main hall, he threw the door open and froze in shock and abhorrence. The sight that greeted him was a scene directly out of his nightmares.

Chapter Fifty

"My, my, my, what do we have here? It seems to me we stood much like this the last time we met, you and I," Duvaliet said as the door slammed shut behind Vashon.

The smaller man stood in the middle of the great chamber where, once upon a time, lords and ladies must have dined and danced the night away at great galas. Now, however, only the checkered marble floor remained. In the center stood the man, and held fast in his arms was the child whom Vashon thought he had glimpsed earlier in the shadows. Duvaliet held a dagger to the small boy's throat.

"I must admit, Bitterknot had much finer scenery than this dreadful place, but I guess we have to make do with what we are given, don't we, Alaric?" Duvaliet smiled a snake's smile, the kind that a predator gives when it knows its prey has no more recourse for escape and there is all the time in the world to enjoy the imminent victory.

"Let him go, Duvaliet. This is between you and me. There's no need to involve an innocent child in this. Too many have died this night because of your ambitions. They have consumed you, little man, and I say we end this here and now, just the two of us, once and for all," Vashon said as he slid his sword free of its scabbard at his back.

"Ah, ah, ah—no, Alaric, I don't think that's how we'll play this game," Duvaliet said as he pressed the knife a little more sharply against the boy's throat, causing him to whimper in pain.

"Since it is you here and not Marsh, I assume you've done me the courtesy of killing him. I must thank you for that. He was getting a little too ambitious for his own good lately. If you hadn't taken care of it for me, I would have had to eliminate him after this was over." Duvaliet's body never shifted position as he spoke, and only the slight increase of pressure against the boy's neck betrayed any sign of the conflict playing itself out in his mind.

"That was a score I should have settled long ago. I could never make him fully pay for taking Duncan. My friend was worth more than all of us, and your giant killed him. And for what? For seeing that this is all foolishness. These games we play—with people like those in Bitterknot as pawns—it means nothing. For while you may gain power, wealth and prestige for a while, eventually someone more powerful, wealthier and more prestigious will come along and replace you, no questions asked. That is the price you pay for playing the game. I, for one, am through with these games, Duvaliet, and with you. I put Duncan's spirit to rest tonight. Now I'm ready to finish this between us so that I can start living again, something I hadn't done in a long time until I came here. Let the boy go, and we will finish this man-to-man." Vashon stayed his hand where it was, knowing full well that Duvaliet would kill the boy without hesitation if he felt it necessary.

"That's the difference between you and me, Alaric. I see through the mist to the truth of the matter. These games we play—they are a necessary part life. There are sheep, there are shepherds, and then there are wolves. The people—these people living in this citadel—are the sheep, just as the people of Bitterknot were sheep. They need people like us to keep the order of things. Otherwise, they'd have no idea of how to live their lives. Free of guidance or direction, they would simply stagnate. We, my friend, are what keep the world turning."

"That's the problem, Duvaliet. You claim to play the part of shepherd, but in truth you are the wolf, out to destroy the sheep to satisfy your own insatiable appetite. My eyes were clouded to the truth of the situation for far too long, but now they are wide open. These people can be left alone to live their lives. They must be, if they are to have any identity of their own—not the one that we give them, but one that they carve out with their own hands and hearts. I'm through running with the wolves. I've found my place, and it's here. Your tyrannical conquest ends tonight, little man. No more talk. Let the boy go, and I'll end it quickly for you. If you choose the hard way, then I can't be held accountable for my actions. After all, what else is a shepherd supposed to do when he finds a wolf threatening his flock?" Vashon started walking directly toward the boy and the man holding him.

"Very well, Alaric, let's do it your way. If you want him, here he is. Just put that big sword of yours down first, and then I'll let him go. Then we'll finish this, just you and me." Duvaliet's face showed the expression of one who knew well his fate and had finally resigned himself to it.

"Alright, I'll put it down, just let him go." Vashon's dark blue blade caught the light from the torches in the room and played a rainbow of shadows on the walls as he pulled it from its scabbard. Very slowly and against his better judgment, Vashon laid it on the ground in front of him and stepped back one pace, arms wide to show that he presented no immediate threat to the other man.

"You want him? Here he is," Duvaliet grunted as he shoved the boy forward. The boy stumbled to the ground and began to sob. The boy now a safe distance from his captor, Vashon reached around and drew a knife that was concealed behind his neck. He went to throw it and end this once and for all, but Duvaliet was prepared for such a move, and before Vashon could bring his arm forward to complete the throw, a small crossbow bolt thudded hollowly into his chest, two inches to the right of his heart.

The knife fell from Vashon's hand as a tingling sensation crept its way into his limbs and quickly spread through his body, so that he didn't even feel his body crash into the stone floor when he finally collapsed. His mind only dully registered the impact. He was in shock, a look of horror on his face.

"That's the problem with you, Alaric: you're still trying to save the village," Duvaliet said. He stepped over the prone form of the boy on the ground, holding up his arm that had the small crossbow attached to it.

"Like my new toy, do you? Kragen found one at the Duke's mansion. I thought it might prove useful, so I had one made just like it. Oh, and that numbness you're feeling—that would be the poison he put on the bolt. It should kill you in a few hours, but I don't think I'll leave you alive that long. You're just one last loose end for me to tie up here. You had the right of it, Alaric. I am a wolf, and you are a shepherd, but you've been with the sheep too long and have forgotten how the wolf thinks. It seems sad to me that we couldn't find common ground. What a force we would have made together. Oh well, things sometimes turn out differently than we wish, I suppose." As Duvaliet turned away from Vashon's bleeding form, lying still on the cold stone, four of his men appeared from behind the columns that ran down one of the sides of the hall.

"Finish him, then find me that Beast. I find the hospitality of this place waning and would very much like to return to the mansion before daybreak, Captain." The four men drew their swords as one and advanced on the prone warrior who lay paralyzed on the floor, his lifeblood leaking from his chest as he tried in vain to will his limbs to fight, move—to do anything other than lie there and resist his every command.

Eyes wide, Vashon could do nothing more than watch as his death marched towards him, and his only thought as they all lifted their swords to strike the killing blow was of how much he loved Sophie and of how he wished her a long life of happiness and freedom. He closed his eyes and waited for the blow he knew was coming.

"Enough!" rang out a shout with such force and authority that the four men couldn't help but obey and hold their blades mid-swing. Even Duvaliet stopped dead in his tracks and turned to face the source of the shout.

"That's enough, Duvaliet. Call them off, or I'll do it myself, and I don't think they would like that very much." Vinquist separated himself from the group of people that had silently filed into the walkway at the top of the steps to watch their savior fight for his life. He drew his cloak about him, moved down the steps and marched directly to Vashon, who could only stare at him, even his voice having abandoned him. Duvaliet's men looked at each other briefly and began taking several steps back out of the enraged wizard's path.

"The wizard, is it? It seems I forgot to tie up every loose end after all. You have ruined a show I have waited long to see. However, Vashon's death is already decided. No wizardry can call back the poison that courses through his veins." Duvaliet took several steps towards the two on the floor but kept his distance, knowing the wizard could end him with a nod of his eyebrows.

"Relax, my boy. I will see to it that things are set aright," Vinquist whispered with a sad smile and placed a hand over Vashon's wound, a faint light emanating from under his palm, as he attempted to heal the only son he had ever known. When he was satisfied that enough of the poison had been drawn out to hold Vashon awhile longer, he took his hand away and stood up, turning to face Duvaliet's men, who promptly dropped their weapons and fled the room.

"You will pay for this, Duvaliet, and dearly," Vinquist said as he advanced on the smaller man, who merely crossed his arms and waited, a smug smile on his face.

"But not by your hand, wizard," he spat. "I know something of your kind, and you are forbidden to engage in a duel as champion of another—something you seem to have forgotten. However, since I am nothing if not fair, I will allow Vashon a surrogate since he doesn't seem up to the task. If any among these"— he gestured with his thin bladed sword at the townsfolk gathered at the rail—"if any among them can defeat me, then his life is well won. However, if I am victorious, then he is mine." Saying this, he simply stared down the group at the railing, waiting for one foolish enough to step up and accept his challenge.

Two of the men moved towards the head of the stairway, clutching clubs and cooking knives. These were not warriors but craftsmen. They knew they had precious little chance of defeating a trained swordsman in a duel, but they also knew the wrong and right of the situation and would not stand to see the man who had fought so hard for their freedom slain like a lamb in front of them without doing something about it. Duvaliet laughed as the two foremost men stared at each other and began nervously inching their way down the steps.

"I will stand for him," arose a shaky voice from the back of the ranks of the gathered people. The two men stopped where they stood halfway down the stairs. The people parted slightly as the bandaged form of Cass Rochelle limped its way towards the steps, his body still not fully recovered from its earlier encounter with the navel-high villain. Where he had come from no one knew. The last time anyone had checked, he was still asleep in his bed which had been moved to keep him out of the grasp of the invaders should they make their way into the castle.

"Two men who have never held a blade and one Duke's son—a singer who should choose his songs more carefully. Quite the ragtag group you have standing up for you, Vashon, but at the very least, I'll get to finish what I started with the little lordling here. I still owe him for a certain kick. Come, boy," he said to Cass, "and meet your fate." Duvaliet pulled his sword and stepped back to allow Cass to descend the steps to where he waited on the floor.

Cass gave a weary look at Vashon and Vinquist and started down the steps towards Duvaliet's waiting form. Suddenly, the crowd behind him parted even more, and a fair voice spoke out above the din, halting Cass where he stood.

"Perhaps I would be slightly better suited for this, young master Rochelle." Geren's tall form separated itself from the crowd as he shrugged his cloak off, revealing green and brown leathers covering his lean form. He tied his long hair behind his pointed ears into a ponytail and pulled free the sword he had made all those years ago, its blade the twin of the one that lay at Vashon's feet.

Hesitation and fear showed themselves plain on Duvaliet's face as Geren began to descend the steps, stopping to flash Cass a smile as he clapped the Duke's son on the shoulder. He moved to the center of the floor where he would stand in as champion for his brother, if not by blood, then in name and in his heart.

"An Elf? No, no, no—this will not do. You have no place in this. This is between him and me," Duvaliet shouted at Geren, who merely smiled at the smaller man as he moved closer and closer to him.

"Fine then. If this is how it's to be, my huntsman should be here any moment, after he's taken care of your Beast, and then we'll have odds slightly more even," Duvaliet said as he backed towards the door, hoping to buy himself some time until Kragen arrived to help him deal with this new situation.

His feet stopped short, and he turned at the sound of something sliding across the floor. Kragen's brace of knives stopped directly at his feet, and he looked at the door as Sophie slowly walked into the room, throwing Kragen's small crossbow to land at Duvaliet's feet as well, noting the surprise on the man's face.

"I accept your challenge," she said as she pulled her sword free and walked towards the middle of the chamber.

Chapter Fifty-One

She walked across the floor, graceful and serene, while Duvaliet stared shock-still at the crossbow and brace of knives at his feet, his mouth opening and closing like a fish, unable to find the words to express what he was feeling. The whole time, Sophie never took her eyes off of Vashon, the man she loved now lying still on the ground, his eyes the only part of him that could still communicate. And in those eyes, she read everything he was thinking.

I'm glad you are alright.

Be careful—his size deceives.

Remember our lessons.

I love you more than anything.

Sophie knew she loved him as well, every part of her, the part that was Sophie and the part that was the Beast, now coinciding in her body, giving her strength and confidence in herself and in what she had to do. She pulled her small, somewhat rusty sword out of a scabbard she had found in the dusty room downstairs where the hunter hung on a boar's tusks, and then she finally turned to look at the small man who was responsible for all of the evening's pain.

"I said I accept your challenge. I will champion this man." Her voice was strangely flat. She had found that calm spring within herself—that one place of complete self-awareness in which time stood still—and she knew this was the defining moment of her life. Everything hinged on this fight, and every part of her welcomed it.

"A girl? A girl is going to be his champion?" Duvaliet asked first of the Elven prince who had stopped to stare in amazement at Sophie's form and then of Vinquist who knelt beside Vashon on the floor, awaiting this scene to play itself out the way it was meant to be played.

"And what have you done with Kragen? I don't know how you got these, but …" and he trailed off, noticing for the first time the small patch of blood that had stained through her white linen shift on her shoulder, exactly where Kragen had shot the Beast on the field outside. Like a shot, his mind was inundated by the dramatic revelation. "You mean that you're …" he couldn't get any other words out as she began to approach him, her sword at the ready.

Duvaliet, mustering all the strength that was in him to translate his panicked thoughts into words, spoke in a high-pitched voice to Sophie: "Alright! I don't know what kind of abomination you are, but I intend to find out. I'm not going to kill you—only hurt you a little bit. I might just take you back to my castle and keep you in a cage while I wait for the full moon to arrive. Or perhaps I'll sell you to the circus. What do you think, my lady Rochelle—how will you like being my pet?" Duvaliet could see in her bright blue eyes, which never revealed even a hint of emotion, that he had no more time to buy. The time of his making, or unmaking, was at hand, and he would have to fight his way out of this.

"My lady, I believe this belongs to you." Geren's voice halted her advance on Duvaliet. She turned to look at him, only to find him kneeling at the bottom of the stairs, sword in his hands held out for her to take. She gently walked over to him, pausing as she reached him, and laid one hand on his shoulder and the other on the pommel of the finest weapon she had ever seen.

"Are you certain?" she asked, her hesitation plain for all to hear in her voice.

"Yes, my lady, this is yours and always has been. It would make my heart sing to see you take it up and use it as it was destined."

"I thank you, from the bottom of my heart," she answered him in fluent Elvish, causing a surprised look from both him and Vinquist as she took up the sword and held it in front of her eyes, studying the way the light played across the thin, blue-black blade before turning back to Duvaliet.

"Shall we?" she asked Duvaliet. She turned to Vashon and raised her sword to her eyes in a silent salute, a student paying homage to her teacher, hoping to make him proud to have taught her in the craft.

And with no other words, the two launched themselves at one another, and the fight that would decide Vashon's fate was begun at last.

It was a fight that has been told and retold in both story and song many times over since then, and it was a wonder to behold. For Duvaliet, despite his small stature, was an excellent swordsman and had won many a tournament defeating bigger and stronger opponents who had underestimated him.

However, no battle he ever had could have prepared him for the duel he now fought with this young woman whose smile was constant, for while he may have been good with a sword, she had been taught by the best, and she loved the Dance.

No one else in the chamber spoke or made a sound. Only the ringing blades and the occasional grunt from Duvaliet penetrated the mist of silence that had settled over the room, as if time itself sensed the imminent importance of what was happening and took pause to watch the outcome. The outcome became more and more evident as the fight wore on and Duvaliet took on more cuts and blows that eventually slowed him down.

After only a couple of minutes, red marks criss-crossed on Sophie's white dress, and many on the balcony began to worry that she was indeed outmatched by the princeling. She continued to smile, however, knowing that none of the blood that patterned her shift was her own. Every time their blades met, she moved so quickly and fluidly that Duvaliet came away with at least one cut. She would slice his arm or strike at his inner thigh, and the blood began to flow heavily from his wounds. She could sense him losing strength and getting desperate, but she kept the smile on her face and continued dancing and weaving magic in the air with her blade.

It appeared that she did, indeed, remember her lessons very well.

Duvaliet had reached his breaking point, and Sophie readied herself for what would be his final assault on her defenses. As he launched himself at her with his sword making a straight line directly at her exposed throat, she deftly sidestepped, spinning as she did, and slapped his blade down with her own. She ended her spin with her back to him, and in the same motion ran her sword through the soft area under his arm, which allowed her blade to slide smoothly into his chest where his heart frantically beat its final beats.

His body slumped off of her blade, and he slid to the ground, a small trickle of blood escaping his lips. His shocked eyes stared at her as they lost their focus.

"I have learned to live with my Beast. I don't believe I can let you go on living with yours," she said as she stood over him for a few seconds longer, until he drew his last gasping breath. It was finally finished.

A loud cheer erupted from the hall as she set her sword carefully on the ground and ran over to check on the man she loved who was waging his own silent war for survival on the chamber floor.

Chapter Fifty-Two

The sun made its inexorable progress over the trees a scant few hours later, bathing the garrison in warm light. As the new day began to dawn, the people opened up all the doors and windows, allowing the spring sunshine to banish any lingering traces of the dark night before. After Sophie's battle with Duvaliet, she closeted herself in a room with Vinquist, Bette, Geren and Vashon's sleeping form, and the people they had both fought so hard to save could do nothing but wait for them to emerge from their seclusion to receive their due thanks.

In the end, it was Bette who took charge and gave them something to do instead of waiting outside of Vashon's room. She told the women that there was still a meal to prepare, as everyone was bound to be starving once the night's events wore off. The children she set about cleaning the halls and rooms of the castles where the battle had taken place, scrubbing blood and other marks off of the stone floors and walls. To the men, she gave the hardest task. They were to find as many tools as they could and dig graves for Duvaliet's and Kerrick's fallen men. The wounded had escaped at some point in the early dawn hours, with those who could not make the journey on their own aided by their comrades who still had strength left in them. None of the dead had been taken with them, so eager were the soldiers to escape this place. Many, however, would be running from the memory of what happened here for the rest of their lives.

After she got the women started in the kitchen preparing the midday meal and extricated a few weapons from the hands of some over-curious children who were vigorously re-enacting the previous night's battle, Bette made her way to see how the men fared on their grave digging. She couldn't resist taking the path that would lead her past Vashon's door to see if she could glean any new piece of information on how their savior fared from his wound. She was

189

rewarded by the emergence of an exhausted Vinquist, quietly pulling the door closed behind him so as not to disturb any within. As Bette caught his eye, no words were necessary. The look she gave him voiced her concerns and those of all her charges.

"We have done all we can for him," Vinquist said as they walked together through the kitchen towards the outside, where he said he also had some business to attend to before the day grew any older. He helped himself to a loaf of bread and jug of water on the way through, which he attacked with a ferocity that gave some insight into how much of himself he had given over to Vashon's healing.

"The poison Duvaliet used is one of the more dangerous and rare ones of which I know," Vinquist explained between huge mouthfuls of bread. "Where he came across it is anyone's guess. I thought the plant from which it is derived only grew near the mountains of the Dwarves, but it appears that he somehow got his hands on some. Normally it is fatal not long after the victim comes in contact with it, but our Alaric is no normal man. He has strength in him that most could only imagine, and he has much to live for. Geren and I have done what we can for him. Now it is a matter of his body fighting its own battle against the sickness. Sophie and Cass are sitting with him, and Geren will be leaving shortly to report to his father on what has occurred here. I can see you have much to oversee here, Lady Bette, and I want you to know how grateful I am for all you have done, but I must take my leave of you now, for one task remains unfinished for me. We will talk again soon."

With those words, he took her hand in his own and gave it a quick kiss before striding away toward the hill overlooking the sea in the back of the citadel, wrapping his black cloak tight around his body to keep the sea winds at bay.

Vinquist stood on a rocky cliff, overlooking the sea, with his cloak flapping freely in the wind. He stood as if he were cut from the rock—a mythical statue kept in place to protect their new home from the tumultuous raging of the sea below.

As he stood there, Vinquist reflected on all that had befallen him and those around him in the past months. He now had hope for the future, and his feelings reassured him that Vashon would be well again. His thoughts also flew toward the future and the part still clouded in shadow—the part that he caught only a glimpse of in the woods outside of La Croix a short while ago and a presence that he had barely felt before it had vanished with the evening wind. How long until the darkness tried once again to make its claim against them? How long until that presence he had thought lost so long ago made itself fully known? He sighed, knowing that his task would never be over and that there would always be the eternal battle of good versus evil in which he seemed destined to play a large role. But at present he had friends who needed him. More healing was needed in this place before he could move on. The only thing that brought him to this cliff was the one last task he had to complete before he could help these people with their re-building.

So he stood, a large claw held in his two hands, its twin burned many months ago in a prison cell not five miles from this spot, and he looked out over the sea and beyond.

"I thank you, my friend. You have once again done more than I could have ever imagined you would," he thought, cradling the claw in his hands.

"Vinquist, my old friend, our bond goes deep, and I do all that I can for you and always will," the Beast's rumble sounded in his mind and in the waves on the rocks below.

"You did things somewhat differently this time, I see. Left a little bit of yourself behind, did you?" Vinquist asked the waves.

"This one was different. She was special, and I think we both grew much in our time together. She taught me just as many things as I taught her," the Beast softly replied, a smile evident in its voice.

"Then shall we part ways here?" Vinquist asked.

"Yes, my dear friend, but don't let the sadness in your voice take away from your victory. You will always have a part of me in her, and when the day comes that I am needed, you have but to call and I will be at your service once again."

"Then farewell, my truest friend, farewell. I wish you freedom and joy until we meet again," Vinquist said as he tossed the claw out over the sea, watching as it blew apart into a million bits that were carried away by the howling winds.

"Farewell, Vinquist." The waves grew silent, and he heard the echo of his friend no more.

Turning his eyes reluctantly from the sea, he began the walk back to the castle to help those he loved in whatever way he could.

───────────────

As he rejoined Bette where she stood overlooking the men digging the graves for the fallen along the wild rose bushes that formed the protective border around the garrison, Vinquist smiled for the first time in days. Now that the long night was over, they could all concentrate on taking hold of their lives and rebuilding and remaking them as they saw fit.

"As things seem to be well in hand here, I think I'll go and see if that noon meal is about ready," Vinquist said to Bette before he turned to wander into the kitchen from which savory smells of fresh bread and meat provided a distraction that even he could not ignore.

"Vinquist, wait," Bette said as she grabbed his sleeve, delaying his departure a moment longer.

"What do we do now? I seem to have inherited the mantle of leader to these people, though I did not ask for it, and I don't know where to lead them from here."

"Why, go forward, dear Bette. I have all the confidence in the world that you and your people will flourish in the years to come," Vinquist said with a smile.

"But where should we go? After what everyone has been through here, I don't think anyone wants to stay here permanently. To tell the truth, I've never really thought about what would happen after we left La Croix. We can't stay here, and going back is not an option, so what should we do?"

"You know, as I came through those many months ago, I passed a large patch of land that would make a perfect town for you and your charges. The main road runs right through it, and it is near a stream so fresh water would not be a problem. All it needs is for people with vision to make it their own, maybe even set up a colony of artists and chefs. Who knows? In time, maybe it could even rival La Croix in reputation. All that limits you now is your own imagination and willpower. How far are you willing to take this?" he asked as he turned to look out over the hills toward the road leading to the garrison from the east.

"We would need supplies and more men to help us in the taking on of such a project, and unless you have another trick up your sleeve, wizard, I don't really know where we would find those things," Bette said, placing her hands on her hips in the way she did when she became irritated.

"Oh, I may have just a couple more tricks up my sleeve, dear lady," and he winked at her and pointed with one long arm at the top of the furthest hill where a wagon had just crested the horizon. Its driver gave a mighty wave in their direction as he laughed loudly and urged his horses into a faster trot. It appeared that Alain Jacoby had gotten the message Vinquist had sent by the guards in La Croix, and so he came, long mustache waxed as usual, smoking his pipe and still wearing the slouch-brimmed hat people seemed to recognize more than the man who wore it. He waved in jubilation to see his old friend again.

Behind him, stretching as far as the eye could see, snaked a caravan of wagons, all carrying food, lumber, supplies and men to aid in the building of a new town, for when Vinquist sent a request for aid, his friends sent aid in plenty.

Watching his old friend draw ever closer and lighting his own pipe, Vinquist closed his eyes and smiled as he let the sweet smoke fill his nostrils. As he turned to look back at the garrison, he saw Sophie emerge into the daylight and throw her head back in exultation, letting the sun's rays heal the night's toll on her body and spirit. When she finally brought her eyes forward again, she looked his way and smiled.

As he returned her smile with one of his own, Vinquist thought there may yet be some hope for the future and went inside to check on the man he thought of as his son, to make sure he would be there to share in it with them.

Chapter Fifty-Three

Petri, having finished his tale, sat back in his chair and took a long draught from the mug of ale that had recently been refilled by his traveling companion, who had arisen from his spot at the corner table and joined the group about halfway through the story. The collected nobles looked at one another in astonishment. Here was a tale far more intriguing than they had ever expected to find, and how it moved them. More than one eye was red from tears shed over the past hours. How long his tale had taken in its telling they did not know. For a story, once begun, has a way of changing time with it, and the minutes and hours do not pass as they normally would.

"That's it? That's the end?" one of the younger members of the party exclaimed from where he sat near the door.

"What more do you wish me to tell you?" Petri asked calmly, brows raised over his mug of ale.

"Well, what became of Vashon for one. Did he live through the poison, or didn't he? And Sophie—what became of her? And Vinquist—let's not forget his role in this—Cass, Bette, all of them. I would like very much to know what happened after that."

"The end of the tale is not fully known," Petri's companion chimed in with a voice far more sweet and melodic than they would have expected to come from a drunkard sitting in a wayward inn in an abandoned town.

"Sophie and Vashon simply disappeared after that. No one really knows if he survived his wounds or where she went. There are rumors that Cass Rochelle continues to travel abroad and sing, although the trial he went through in this place scarred him badly, and his voice never achieved its previous greatness. Vinquist's tale is the saddest of all, so I've heard. Having used a large bit of his powers in La Croix, he went from kingdom to kingdom, sometimes resorting to parlor tricks, sometimes dressing as a jester and standing on his head for the sons and daughters of noblemen like yourselves. Quite sad really … they say he was truly powerful once," he mused as he paused to take a sip from his own mug.

Petri, who had previously nodded his head in agreement, spat out his drink at the revelation of Vinquist's fate. Wiping his mouth, he shot his companion a glare and said, "Forgive me—it does make my old bones sad to hear of the lowering of Vinquist to common court jester. I have heard that those were merely rumors spread by minstrels who possessed more words than sense. In truth, the paths of those involved here are cloaked in shadow after that day. You are free to draw your own conclusions as to how they ended up. That is part of the beauty of the story and why I love to tell it when the sun is hidden safely away and the night seems to call for the past. But I fear I am not quite as young as I once was, and I must retire soon," Petri said as he drained his mug off in one mighty gulp.

"Before we all adjourn for the night, I assume you have noticed that my friend Jon here has a lute with him. Perhaps if we plead with him enough we can convince him to send us to our dreams with a song. What say you?"

"Well," Jon said cradling his lute and plucking the strings, betraying his love for the instrument in one gesture, "I admit I am no Cass Rochelle, but perhaps I do have one song that may end our evening together in a befitting manner." With that, his strumming came together into a coherent tune, which was eventually joined by a voice that surpassed any they had ever heard as he put into song the story they had just been told.

When he had finished "The Ballad of La Croix," not a single eye remained that had not shed a tear for Sophie's, Vashon's and Vinquist's struggles and the fate of this once beautiful town.

As the two began packing up the lute and putting away their used mugs, the leader of the nobles approached Petri, a black silk bag clenched tightly in his hand.

"What you have just done, this story you just told, would earn you far more than we have," he said, holding out the bag for Petri to take. "Please accept this as our meager thanks for your craft this night." Placing the bag in Petri's hands and shaking them in earnest, he added, "You have our deepest and most heartfelt thanks," gesturing with a sweep of his hands to include each member of his party, who nodded their assent. "And so we shall set sail for home on the morrow and carry the sad tale of La Croix with us and spread the word to any others who may wish to make the same journey we made."

"'Sad'? 'Sad tale,' did you say?" Petri said as he placed the silk bag of coins on the chair containing his cloak and hat. "I agree that what happened to this town is truly regrettable, but this is also a tale of love and life—the discovery of what is truly important, of dreams coming true and of finding love, even when facing down one's worst fears. I hope you do not leave here with heavy hearts, but rather with a hope that things can always be better and that each and every one of us can truly be free if only we have the foresight and conviction to make it so.

"I don't mean to lecture you before we part ways. That is certainly not the picture I would leave you of me. I only wish you to sleep on the tale tonight and decide on the morrow, as you face a new day full of new decisions to make and discoveries to unearth, what the story of this place means to each of you."

Smiling one last smile, he turned to gather his things and head for the stairs.

"Oh, I almost forgot, there is one last request I would make of you before we retire for the evening," he said, turning back to address the group.

"Anything—just ask and, if it lies within our power, I swear you shall have it," Roland replied in earnest.

"My companion and I shall depart ere the break of dawn tomorrow, and I doubt that we shall see each other again before we leave. We are simple men who do not have much use for money or material possessions, so this will benefit us little," he said as he took up the silk bag and placed it on the young nobleman's saddlebag.

"My favor is this: there is indeed a small town nearly seven leagues down the road from here. It is rumored to be a well-hidden trove of goods of fine quality, unlike any you are likely to encounter on your travels abroad. Take your coin and spend it there before you make the trip home and tell all when you return of what you find there. For in time, it may even have its own tale to tell, although I suspect it shall be a less dark story than that of La Croix. Promise me and we shall call all debts paid between us."

"We will go to this town, and you can be certain we will spread word of it upon our return home, on my honor. I thank you, gentlemen, again. You have given us more this night than we had ever hoped to find when we came here, and we are eternally in your debt. If at any time you should need aid of any kind, do not hesitate to ask, and it shall be freely given," Roland finished with a bow so low his forehead almost touched the floor, a sign of the true respect he felt for the two men who had shared their company this night.

"I shall remember your promise, young man, and do not be surprised if one day you, or one of your family, are called on for that aid. But for now, I wish you long lives, healthy and free. Until we meet again," and Petri returned the bow with one of his own, followed by his minstrel companion. They let their gazes linger a moment longer over the assembled people, knowing that each of them were busy thinking about the story they had just heard and how it would affect their lives. With a final grand smile, the two headed up the stairs for their room, followed nearly an hour later by the nobles as exhaustion finally began to take its toll and they sought sleep of their own.

More than one heard the sounds of battle and the far away roar of a beast in their dreams that night.

The next day dawned clear and crisp, with a brisk wind sweeping in off of the sea to stir the nobles' spirits as they exited the inn, blinking in the bright morning sunshine. They headed to the stables where they found their horses rested and ready to travel. Waiting at the head of their caravan, a man sat astride his horse, watching them approach and whistling as if he hadn't a care in the world.

"Hello there!" he called out with a wave of his hand. "I am Isaac, your guide. Your horses have been well cared for, and if I may offer a suggestion, perhaps we should begin our trip, if you wish to make it to La Bette before the noon meal is served at the inns. I, for one, do not intend to spend my luncheon on the dusty road when there are far better accommodations just a little further down the road." He laughed as he pulled an orange out of his saddlebag and proceeded to peel it while they simply stared at him.

"Guide? I don't really see how you could be our guide. No one knew we were going any place other than La Croix and certainly not to the next town—what did you say it was called again?" Roland asked.

"Why, La Bette, of course—named after the Lady Bette, who herself led the people of this town from their plight and on the road to freedom. She was once a simple baker's apprentice here in La Croix, you know? But now she is the matriarch of the town where we will arrive shortly, if we do not spend too much time on banter that we could just as easily carry on during our trip," he replied, his stomach growling as if on cue.

"It was she who sent me to be your guide, having received word that you and your companions were heading towards La Croix and knowing what you would find here. I'm sorry you had to weather out the storm in that drafty old inn, without the comfort of any decent food or water," he apologized.

"Drafty? No decent food? I beg your pardon, sir, but Petri and his companion made excellent hosts last night, and we benefited much from their company," Roland said.

"Did you say Petri?" Isaac asked, stopping the bite of orange halfway to his mouth.

"Yes, the older man who told us the story of this place. He had a fire going and shared his food with us. He said they were simple traveling artisans, but they seemed much more than that, especially his friend. When he sang the

'Ballad of La Croix' for us"—Roland spread his hands wide, indicating that no words would do justice to the man's skill—"it was obvious he was no ordinary minstrel."

"No ordinary minstrel, indeed. No other bard or minstrel across the lands will sing that song, as only the one who wrote it can do it justice. My friends, you have been treated to a performance by the one and only Cass Rochelle. A man without equal in his craft," Isaac said.

"Then that would make his companion ..." Roland began.

"Truly a man without equal. Wait until Lady Bette hears what those scoundrels are up to now," Isaac mused. "By the way, did you happen to offer these men anything in the way of payment for their services last night?" he asked the group.

"Well, yes. We offered them a bag of silver, but they refused, saying they had no need for such things, and now I see why," the reply came as Roland reached behind him for his sack of silver.

"That's good lad—that's very good. Now then, shall we get a move on? The glory and splendor await us." As Isaac clucked his tongue, signaling his horse to walk, the nobles mounted up and followed after.

Roland barely heard Isaac's words, so amazed was he at what he held in his hands. Instead of the simple black bag he had handed Petri hours before, he now held a finely-made bag of blue silk. Its sides bulged with far more coin than it had held last night, and as he loosened the strings to take a look inside, he found not a bag overfilled with silver, but with gold. Closing it up and preparing to return it to his saddlebag, he noticed a thin line of gold stitching on one side. In finely wrought golden thread, standing in direct contrast to the dark blue of the bag, was only one letter—and seeing that letter, he made sure his people were ready to ride. As they headed down the road towards La Bette, their leader stared at the bag even as he rode, the surprise still written plain on his face—as plain as the gold lettering, which simply read:

V.

On a hill opposite the end of town from where the party of noblemen and women mounted up for La Bette, Petri and his companion sat astride their horses, smiling to themselves as they watched the travelers depart. Once satisfied, they turned their horses in silence and headed towards their destination, one which both eagerly anticipated. They knew, however, that there was one final farewell to be made before they could be free of this town for a while longer.

"Come, Cass, let's see your father and get it over with so we can be on our way," Vinquist said as he nudged his horse into a slightly faster walk.

Cass didn't say anything but merely nodded his assent as they approached a group of trees from which they heard a man muttering to himself. As they approached, the Duke stepped out, his one hand still gripping the coin. He gave the men a slight bow before dancing a jig and saying, "Thank you so much for visiting my lovely town. I hope you return soon," without a hint of recognition crossing his eyes as he bade his son farewell. As his gaze wandered across Vinquist, his manner changed immediately, and a look of utter hate came over his face. It faded as quickly as it came, and he danced maniacally off into the trees screaming something about "town repairs" and "must get Brendan to help me" before his voice was lost to the sounds of the trees around them.

Stowing his concern for the look he had received from the Duke until some later time when he could fully dissect its meaning, Vinquist clapped his friend on the back, and they resumed their travels, eager to arrive at their next destination.

"It's been far too long since we last saw your sister, Cass; let's not make her wait any longer, shall we?"

With that, both men spurred their horses into a gallop, outpacing in moments the lingering taint of La Croix, and headed towards something far more joyous than the memories of their time in this place.

Had they listened hard enough, as they rode away, they might have heard the sound of the Duke's laughter mixed with another, much more sinister voice on the wind. It was faint for now, but in time the wind would blow it more strongly in their direction.

Epilogue

The two men rode in a companionable silence, neither one needing to tell the other in words how overjoyed he was at their imminent arrival at their destination. It felt this way each and every time they came to the crest of this last hill, where they finally got their glimpse of the little stone cottage tucked away in the greenest valley either of them had ever known. It could not be found on any map, and all involved liked it that way. Cass and Vinquist looked at each other and grinned like children at what they felt when they arrived here—they felt home.

They had been traveling together for so long now that this serene glade was the closest thing either had to an actual home. The small brook that ran the length of the valley and disappeared in the distant trees where it eventually ran into its mother river was crossed by an arched stone bridge, just wide enough for a wagon to navigate. Goats, sheep, and two small foals, their mothers keeping a watchful eye nearby, nibbled on the grass around the cottage. Each little one was marked with a white lightning bolt on its face. Sunstriker, it appeared, made an excellent father.

Behind the house, they could see a barn, nearly as large as the main home itself, which served well to hold the assorted animal life cared for in this place. Both men relaxed, the tensions of their long journey fading away, being replaced by the simple joy and feeling of life that filled this place. As they entered the yard and removed their tack from their horses, allowing them to join the other animals gazing on the sweet grass, they couldn't help but laugh as the sight they so longed for came rushing out of the cottage door at them.

"Grampen Vinquist, Uncle Cass, we didn't know you were coming. Mommy and Daddy are inside fixing dinner. What did you bring us?" Isabella was just now past her fifth birthday and assailed everything she came across with the enthusiasm and curiosity that only a five year old can muster.

"Now, Isabella, is that any kind of question for your Grampen and Uncle as soon as they get here?" said the young boy to his little sister. "But you did bring us something, didn't you, Grampen?" Duncan was seven now and quickly turning out to be a somewhat serious young man, much did he inherit his father's sense of things. However, his young face flushed bright with a smile all the way to his blue eyes which, if you looked close enough, might reveal slightly elongated pupils.

Vinquist smiled at the two young ones, and after they had finished smothering him in hugs and kisses, only to move on and attack Cass's laughing form next, he began patting his cloak as if looking for some forgotten item, though it was anyone's guess how he actually managed to carry anything at all in its dark folds. As he looked, he thought to himself that of all the titles he had taken in all of the lands over the years, none of them brought him the joy this one did. And he wore none of them better than this one, as the children loved it when he and Cass visited—which they made a point to do with some frequency. They loved his presents, as he always seemed to have something new and special to give as grandparents are wont to do, and they loved sitting around in the evenings listening to him tell his tales, followed by Cass singing his newest songs for them. While any here would have been more in place in a royal banquet hall, this was the only place in the world they wanted to be.

"Well, well, what do I have here?" Vinquist exclaimed as he finally found what he sought within his cloak. He was met with a hearty yelp of excitement from the children, who gathered around him, eager to see what wonders their Grampen's cloak would produce this time.

"You spoil them, you know that, don't you, Grampen?" Cass said in a laughing tone as he stood up, brushing the grass off of the front of his tunic.

"And you don't? Besides, that's my job, and I warned you about your insolence, boy— it's 'Vinquist the Great' to you," he retorted with mock severity, only to be met with chuckling as Cass walked over to get their bags from where they had set them under a large oak tree in the middle of the yard. Vinquist looked up and witnessed a large blue jay, in possession of impeccable timing, as it promptly relieved itself directly on Cass's shoulder.

"Much obliged, friend," Vinquist laughed as he motioned with his index finger for Isabella to come closer and receive her gift.

"This, my dear, is from the finest jeweler in the whole city of Carne. He didn't want to part with it, but when I told him that it was a gift for the most beautiful little girl in the world, he couldn't resist giving it to me." Vinquist wore a smile on his face as he produced a small necklace made up entirely of dozens of small roses, all wrought in fine silver with gold tracing on the tips of their petals, shining bright in the afternoon sun.

Isabella gave a shout of delight and "ooh'd" and "aah'd" over the necklace for just a moment before solemnly inclining her head towards him, allowing Vinquist to place the bauble, which was clearly fine enough to grace the neck of any noblewoman across the land, around her small one.

"And now for you, Sir Duncan," Vinquist said as Isabella hurried over to Cass to show off her newest treasure to her uncle, who removed the box of sweetmeats and chocolate roses from his own pack, adding to the young one's bounty of the day.

Duncan's gift was given with the same importance as Isabella's, as Vinquist leaned in close to whisper in his ear and handed him a package wrapped in blue velvet with a 'D' embroidered on it. The boy gripped it tightly to his chest, inclined his head in a half-bow to his Grampen, and yelled for Isabella to come on out back to look at his present with him. Their escape was cut short, though, as their mother appeared at the door precisely at that moment, displaying that maternal instinct for knowing exactly what her children were up to at any given time.

"Duncan, Isabella, you can play for a few more minutes, and then I want you to wash up and come inside. Dinner's almost ready. And you two," she said motioning towards Vinquist and Cass, "perfect timing as always. We were just setting the table for dinner, so I hope you're hungry." As they grabbed their saddlebags from the ground, she dropped her rag on the arm of one of the many chairs that made the front porch so cozy and ran straight to them, not stopping until she had her brother in a crushing hug, while at the front door, his massive frame filling the doorway, her husband stood waving at Vinquist, laughing at the scene playing out in front of him.

These last eight years had been kind to Sophie and Vashon. Her body was now strong and tanned from her constant work outdoors, both caring for the animals and tending to her massive flower garden. She boasted more than two dozen different varieties of roses growing in the space to the side of the cottage, and every year Vinquist or Cass would find a new kind in a city somewhere far away and bring her several flowers and seeds of the same to add to her collection. Days in the sun had brought hints of blonde to her dark mane, and her blue eyes stood out even more now that they never had to shed a tear of sadness. Both she and her husband had earned this respite from the troubles of the world, and the life they led suited them well.

Vashon came down off of the steps and embraced them both in a massive hug that nearly crushed the lute Cass was carrying. He set his brother-in-law back on his feet and gave Vinquist a hug and a smile that conveyed all the warmth the two men held for one another. Vashon's body was still lean, but not from constant running and fighting. It was no secret that he and his wife practiced the Dance every day, not from fear of becoming complacent, but rather because they both loved it so much. He no longer carried his sword, nor she hers. They hung together over the fireplace that took up half of the wall in the cottage's main room and served as a constant reminder of the past and the prices paid for them to be here. Vashon smiled and gestured for them all to follow him into the house.

"You're just in time for dinner, and tonight is special. She even let me cook today, so you're in for quite a treat, gentlemen." Vashon smiled in pride as he preceded them into the kitchen.

"Don't worry—I only let him peel the potatoes. I did the rest. Do you really think I want the children to starve? I remember that chicken he tried to fix last time you were here. His role in the kitchen since then has been minimal at best. I only let him think he helps," she winked at Vinquist as she bowed low and held the door open for him to precede her into the house.

"Oh, Alaric, I almost forgot, we picked up some of that coffee you have become so fond of on our way out of Carne," Vinquist said as he reached into his cloak and pulled out a small cask, which Vashon eagerly opened. He took a large whiff of its contents, and a smile slowly spread across his face as the pungent aroma filled his nostrils.

"I honestly don't understand how you men drink that stuff. It tastes bitter to me," Sophie groaned as she took Vashon's prize from him and placed it next to their stove where he kept his kettle and several of the earthenware mugs that had been a gift to them from the good people of La Bette.

"You just have to get used to it, that's all," Vashon retorted as he gave her backside a smack with his spoon and started setting plates and silverware on the large oak table in the middle of the room. As Vashon set the mugs down and started filling them with cold ale that he had brewed himself a week earlier, Vinquist and Cass took off their cloaks and let the warmth of the place move over them in a rush. This was home, paid for dearly by all they had gone through, but looking at things as they were now, none among them would have done anything any differently.

"It looks like Isabella and Duncan are enjoying their gifts very much," Sophie remarked from where she stood at the window overlooking the backyard.

"I'm curious. What exactly did you give Duncan, Vinquist?" Cass asked while he helped himself to a mug of ale as they all moved over to the window to watch the children.

"Oh, just something that might come in handy one day," the old wizard replied, a smile creeping its way into his beard. "Your roles in this fight are over, your dues paid in full. You have all earned this respite, and I am glad to be able to share in it with you. But I feel there is some far greater conflict looming on the horizon. I'm not quite sure what yet, or when it will sweep us up into its path, but I plan to be ready when it does."

"Whatever we can do, we will," Vashon said as he put his arm around Sophie's waist protectively, his gaze lingering on the scene outside, hoping he could protect those two from the dangers the world had to offer.

"I know you will. I know it all too well," Vinquist replied. He thought about the feeling that had come over him that night outside the mansion in La Croix those years ago—that feeling of such hate and malevolence. He also thought about his fears that a darkness grew somewhere which had not made itself known to him yet and which he couldn't pinpoint. He hoped that when the time came for him to stand, he would be ready. Looking at the two young ones in the yard, he prayed silently that they all would.

In the yard, unknowingly playing to an audience at the kitchen window, Isabella knelt on the ground, her hands clasped together, her best look of abject fright on her young face. She watched her brother using Vinquist's gifts of a small wooden crown and sword as he moved and fought with some unseen foe, seeking to protect the honor and life of the young maiden before him. Vinquist smiled as he watched the boy beat back his enemy with his weapon. Even at this young age, it was very clear: he would learn the Dance. And when he came into his own, what a sight it would be.

Turning from the window, he gestured for them to leave the darkness outside their door for the rest of the evening and enjoy their meal and fellowship together. Vinquist placed his hands on Sophie's and Vashon's shoulders.

"Train him well," he said and smiled, knowing that, whatever lay ahead for the boy, he would be well prepared for it and that maybe, just maybe, that would be the key for holding the darkness at bay yet a little while longer.

Just the beginning ...

As is with the fulfillment of any dream, this book could not have come to life without the help and support of persons too numerous to name. Thanks to Jana, Betty, and all those others who read and helped edit our early drafts. A special thanks goes out to Craig Slaven, whose touch can be seen on every page of our finished product. Thanks to Burt and Bill for their support, we hope we make you proud. Thanks to our friends and family who have contributed with both their time and patience as we worked on our dream. And thanks to my father, Dan Kingsland, the greatest storyteller I know. Without him this book doesn't exist. We would like to dedicate this book to Isabella, Sophie, and Kaleb, the next generation of dancers. May you learn how to dance, and do so well.

Jason Kingsland
November 2, 2010